Now, *that* was a move he hadn't seen coming

In fact, Harry still couldn't quite believe Pippa had shoved the envelope of money—payment he *hadn't* asked for and *wasn't* going to keep—down the waistband of his shorts.

Briefly he toyed with the idea of going after her, letting her know in no uncertain terms that he wasn't interested in her money. He imagined himself chasing her down, backing her into a corner until she was forced to take the envelope back. She'd protest, no doubt, but he'd simply look into those rich chocolate-brown eyes of hers and—

He put the cash in his pocket and turned away from the thought that had been about to insinuate itself into his head. Pippa was off-limits. She was trying to raise Alice on her own. Pippa was all about responsibility and commitment. Nothing that Harry had to offer.

Walk away, mate.

Too bad his libido wasn't getting the message.

Dear Reader,

I've written two sequels in my career so far—this one and *One Good Reason* (Harlequin Superromance, August 2011)—and both were completely unplanned. It wasn't until I started writing about a character who I assumed would be a supporting player that I realized that I wanted to tell that story, too.

Harry came to life in *All They Need* (Harlequin Superromance, November 2011), which tells the story of his sister, Mel, and Flynn, the man who teaches her that love is not about pain and shame. I loved Harry from the moment he opened his mouth. His tattoos, his attitude, his blue-collar decency. I talked about him with my editor, and she—wise, wise woman—said, "For some reason I see him with a woman who has a child." My brain lit up like a slot machine hitting jackpot. Of course Harry had to fall in love with a woman with a child! What better way to rock the world of a committed party boy?

When I started thinking about who this woman might be, it occurred to me that the lives of men like Harry revolve around their mates. They party together, they hang together, they have each other's backs. But what if one of those mates turns out to have done the wrong thing by an ex-lover who wound up pregnant? And what if Harry had always really liked this woman because she was smart and funny and sassy? Beneath his tough exterior, Harry is a huge pussycat. I figured he'd be powerless to resist the urge to step in and step up on his friend's behalf.

Those basic ideas sent my imagination off. I loved writing this book! Pippa and Harry were so much fun. I hope you enjoy reading their journey. I love hearing from readers, so please feel free to drop me a line at sarah@sarahmayberry.com.

Oh, and in case you're wondering, I've never fallen through the ceiling. But I have come very, very close!

Happy reading,

Sarah Mayberry

Suddenly You

SARAH MAYBERRY

HARLEQUIN®
entertain, enrich, inspire™

Recycling programs
for this product may
not exist in your area.

ISBN-13: 978-0-373-71812-2

SUDDENLY YOU

Copyright © 2012 by Small Cow Productions Pty Ltd.

www.Harlequin.com

Printed in U.S.A.

ABOUT THE AUTHOR

Sarah Mayberry lives in Melbourne in a house by the bay, happily sharing her days with her partner (now husband!) of twenty years and a small black, tan and white cavoodle called Max. She adores them both. When she isn't writing, she is feeling guilty about not being out in the garden more and indulging in shoe shopping and re-imagining her soon-to-be renovated home. She also loves to read, cook, go to the movies and sleep, and is fully aware that the word *exercise* should be in that list somewhere, too.

Books by Sarah Mayberry

HARLEQUIN SUPERROMANCE

1551—A NATURAL FATHER
1599—HOME FOR THE HOLIDAYS
1626—HER BEST FRIEND
1669—THE BEST LAID PLANS
1686—THE LAST GOODBYE
1724—ONE GOOD REASON
1742—ALL THEY NEED
1765—MORE THAN ONE NIGHT
1795—WITHIN REACH

HARLEQUIN BLAZE

380—BURNING UP
404—BELOW THE BELT
425—AMOROUS LIAISONS
464—SHE'S GOT IT BAD
517—HER SECRET FLING
566—HOT ISLAND NIGHTS

Other titles by this author available in ebook format.

This book was written with the undeniable distraction of a new puppy in the house. So it would be remiss of me not to thank Max for the many hours he stole from my work while simultaneously making me laugh and gnash my teeth. Bless your little furry everything.

As usual, Wanda held my hand and gave sage counsel and helped me see the wood for the trees. There would be no me without you, my dear.

And Chris. What can I say? You really are the best. The funniest. The smartest. The sweetest. (There are more -ests, but I don't want to embarrass you. You know where I'm going with this, though).

Lastly, a big thanks to the readers who take the time to put fingers to keyboard to write to me. Your letters really do make my day.

CHAPTER ONE

BEER. ICY COLD, preferably accompanied by a big, greasy burger. Oh, yeah.

Harry Porter rolled down the window of his 1972 HQ Monaro GTS and grinned into the resulting wind as he sped toward the pub. A vintage Midnight Oil song played on the radio and he tapped out the rhythm on the steering wheel, the burble of the V8 engine providing a bass beat.

It was Friday afternoon, it was summer, he'd just been paid, and half a dozen of his best mates were waiting at the Pier Hotel ten minutes up the road to kick off the weekend's adventures.

Life didn't get much better.

Whoever was in charge at the radio station seemed to agree because Midnight Oil's "Power and the Passion" was followed by Nirvana's "Smells Like Teen Spirit." He was reaching for the volume to crank it higher when he spotted the bright yellow car in the emergency stopping lane to the left of the highway, its hood pushed up in the universal signal that someone was shit out of luck.

The mechanic in him automatically diagnosed the problem—in this weather, most likely the car's cooling system—before returning his gaze to the road. Fortunately, being a mechanic wasn't like being a doctor—Harry wasn't obliged to stop for emergencies. Which was just as well, because he'd spend half his life riding to the rescue if that was the case.

Something tickled at the back of his brain as he approached the car. He realized what it was as he sped past. He knew this car—at least, he knew its owner. He hadn't seen her for nearly six months, but that was definitely her bright yellow hatchback, a fact he confirmed when he looked in his rear vision mirror and saw Pippa White standing with her hands on her hips staring into the engine bay.

He swerved into the unsealed emergency lane and glanced in the rearview mirror as Pippa turned to watch his big black car reverse toward her. She was frowning, clearly trying to work out who was coming to her rescue.

The worried expression vanished from her face when he exited his car. It was replaced with the wry, appreciative smile he'd come to associate with her during the six months she'd dated his best mate, Steve.

Pippa pushed her heavy black-framed glasses up her nose and scanned him head to toe as he approached.

"You're definitely not what I was expecting when I sent up a prayer for a guardian angel."

"Long time no see," he said easily.

Pippa's smile slipped a fraction and he knew that—like him—she was remembering the last time they'd seen each other. Driven by god-knows-what stupid impulse, he had visited her at the hospital after the birth of her daughter, Alice. The most uncomfortable fifteen minutes of his life so far, hands down. She recovered quickly, pushing her glasses up her nose again.

"How have you been, Harry? How's Hogwarts going? Cast any good spells lately?"

The Harry Potter/Porter jokes had gotten old around

the time Ms. Rowling had made her second billion, but Pippa was one of the few people he allowed to get away with them. They'd always got on well and, unlike most of Steve's girlfriends, he'd regretted it when things had gone pear-shaped and she'd disappeared off the scene. She'd always had something interesting to say, and she'd always laughed at his jokes, even when they sucked.

"Made some underwear disappear the other night, if that's what you mean."

She laughed appreciatively. "Dirty dog."

"How about you? How are things?"

"I've had better days, you know." She shrugged, her dark, wavy hair brushing her shoulders. A sparkly clip was pinned at one temple. Combined with her heavy glasses, it gave her an arty, slightly eccentric look that was reinforced by her old-fashioned floral dress and timeworn tan oxfords.

Not for the first time he wondered how she and Steve had ever hooked up. She was a million miles from the tight-T-shirted, tight-jeaned women his mate usually went for, and Harry had always figured Steve wasn't exactly Pippa's normal dating material, either. Which only made it more problematic that they'd created a little girl between them.

"How's Alice?" he asked, glancing at the backseat.

The baby seat was empty, however.

"Mum's visiting, so she's got her for the day. I was supposed to be getting a few chores sorted, but Old Yeller had other ideas." Her tone was heavy with irony as she gave her car a rueful glance.

"Let me guess—it overheated?"

"To be honest, I have no idea. One minute I was driving along, the next minute there was this bang and then steam and smoke was pouring out from under the hood…"

Harry frowned. Steam sounded right for overheating, but not smoke. He moved closer to lean over the engine bay. It took him only a moment to spot the oil dripping down the engine block and sprayed across the other engine components.

"Looks like you've blown a head gasket."

Pippa joined him, peering at the engine. "That's bad, right?"

"It's not great. It basically means the engine is no longer sealed properly, so the oil that's supposed to stop things from seizing up when they get hot leaks out."

"Does that mean the engine is seized now?" She looked alarmed.

"Not if you pulled over immediately."

"I did. Straight away."

"Then it's probably okay. But the only way to know for sure is to crack the engine block open and take a look."

"That sounds expensive. Am I right?" A worried expression filled her brown eyes.

"It can be. Depends on parts, what they find when they get in there…"

She nodded. "Right. Well, I guess me standing here swearing at it won't change any of that."

Harry pulled out his phone. Since he couldn't help her, the least he could do was organize a tow truck.

"Who normally services the car?" He knew most of the workshops in this part of the Mornington Peninsula, as well as a number of the tow truck operators.

"Oh, um, I don't know the name off the top of my head. A place down in Mornington." She waved a hand vaguely.

"Sweet Motors? Beachside Workshop?" he suggested.

Pippa shook her head, her gaze sliding from his face to the car. "I think I've got their card at home."

"Do you want to get it towed to your place, then?"

"No, then I'd have to pay twice. I'll just go home and sort it from there. But thanks for the thought."

Her words were light but the frown creasing her forehead remained. Harry hesitated, but there was something about the way she was trying to be so casual about what was clearly a major hassle that made him want to help out. Even though it wasn't his place, and they weren't really friends anymore.

"My dad owns the workshop in Mount Eliza Village. I could give him a ring. I'm sure he wouldn't mind helping out with a tow." Technically, this was true, since Mike Porter had always been a soft touch for someone in distress, but it didn't mean Harry wouldn't cop some grief for his impulsive offer. He could almost hear his dad now: *It'd be different if you actually worked for Village Motors, mate. Then you'd be within your rights to make offers on my behalf.*

The fact that Harry had chosen to work for someone else once he'd finished his apprenticeship had always been a minor bone of contention between him and his father, although lately it seemed there was more weight behind his father's comments and jokey asides.

Still, Harry was willing to wear the inevitable heat if it meant helping Pippa.

"That's really nice of you, but I don't want to put anyone out. Besides, my car club offers free roadside assistance. I can call them from home and get everything sorted."

"You won't be putting anyone out. The workshop is up the road. It's no big deal."

Pippa's expression became determined. "Thanks, but I've got it covered." She softened her rejection by touching his forearm briefly. "I appreciate you stopping, Harry. A lot of other guys would have kept going."

He frowned. The reality was, if she'd been one of Steve's other exes, he would have simply blown past without a second thought. He wasn't sure why it was different with Pippa, except he'd always liked her. And—maybe—because he felt a little sorry for her, given her situation and the way things had turned out.

"Can I give you a lift home, then?" he heard himself offer. Even though every minute that ticked past chewed up his weekend and delayed the moment when he had an ice-cold glass of beer in his hand.

"Thanks, but Mum can come get me."

Pippa tried to pull the hood stand from its notch on the side of the engine bay. Harry watched her struggle for a few seconds before leaning across her and pulling it loose. He got a whiff of hot engine oil and a rich vanilla scent—Pippa's perfume most likely—as the hood shut with a dull thud.

"Where are you living these days?" he asked.

"Frankston South. Off Karrs Road."

"Perfect. I'm driving past on the way to the pub."

She started to protest again but he walked to the driver's side of the hatchback and leaned in to grab her handbag.

"You need anything else before we lock it up?" he asked as he passed her the bag.

Her expression became rueful. "You're not going to let this drop, are you?"

"Can't be a knight in shining armor if the princess won't get up on my horse."

She scanned his face, almost as though she was looking for evidence of something. His sincerity, perhaps? Or maybe she was thinking more of his association with Steve.

"It's just a lift, Pippa."

"True. And I wouldn't want to deprive you of the chance to play Sir Galahad."

"Especially since the urge only hits once every five years or so."

She laughed, the sound loud and honest. "I bet. I've got some shopping in the back that should come home with me."

He followed her to the trunk and grabbed the bags.

"Thanks."

"All part of the service."

"There's a service? And here I was thinking I was getting special treatment."

She was so dry he couldn't help turning on the charm a little. "That's part of the service, too." He winked, deepened his voice a notch.

Pippa laughed again as they headed for his car. "My God, Harry. No wonder half the women in Frankston love to hate you."

They were on familiar ground now—Pippa giving him a hard time about the "revolving door" to his bedroom.

"You've been talking to the wrong women."

"Sure I have." She gave him a look over her shoulder before opening the passenger door.

Harry smiled. He hadn't been so sure earlier, but now he was glad he'd stopped. It was good to see her again, and even better to help her out of a jam, even in a very minor way.

Digging his keys from his pocket, he prepared himself for a challenging, entertaining five minutes.

PIPPA PRESSED A hand against her belly as Harry stowed her shopping. For some unknown reason, seeing and talking to him again had made her nervous.

A different kind of nervous, obviously, than the way she'd felt when his black car had swerved into the emergency lane so abruptly. The Nepean Highway was a public enough road that she hadn't been afraid for her personal safety, but she'd be lying if she said she hadn't been a little concerned. Then her rescuer had unfolded himself from his car and she'd known she was in good hands.

The car dipped as Harry slid into the driver's seat. Pippa eyed his worn jeans, faded black T-shirt and tattooed arms, acknowledging the irony that someone who looked so fierce could make her feel so safe.

At first glance, Harry looked exactly like the sort of man that should make a woman worry—the military-short hair, the honed power of his arms and shoulders, the sheer height and breadth of him. And, of course, there were those tribal tattoos snaking around his arms. Inky-black and impossible to miss, they marked him as an outlaw, someone who didn't color between the lines.

Not exactly your usual white-knight material, yet she knew Harry well enough to know he was a big softie underneath his fierce exterior.

"Got a big weekend planned?" she asked as he started the car.

"Always." The smile he flashed her was confident, bordering on cocky.

"Fathers of Melbourne, lock up your daughters."

"Fat lot of good that'll do."

It was true. She'd seen Harry in action enough times to know he didn't have to go hunting for women. They came to him, flicking their teased blond hair and sashaying their miniskirted hips. Watching him charm them out of their underwear had fascinated her—but then she'd long recognized that she had a self-destructive penchant for bad boys. Witness her six months with Steve, who was the blond, blue-eyed version of Harry— a teenage boy's mind in a grown man's body, all about fun and good times and no responsibility.

As always, thoughts of Steve Lawson tightened her stomach, so she pushed them away. There was no point getting herself all bunged up over a situation she could do nothing to change.

"Let me guess—you're kicking off at the Pier. Then you'll move on to the Grand or the Twenty-First Century, and you'll wind up at Macca's place playing pool in the garage till three in the morning," she said.

"Sounds pretty good, except Macca's moved in with Sherry and the pool table went west."

It wasn't hard to interpret the disapproving note in Harry's voice. He and Steve had never been shy about their disgust with their mates who'd met the right woman, married and bowed out of their boys' club.

"Oh, dear. Another one bites the dust. Next thing you know you'll be taking on a mortgage and buying golf clubs, too, Harry."

"When hell freezes over."

He sounded so grimly determined she had to laugh. "How old are you?"

"Thirty."

"Getting up there."

He shot her a look before taking a right turn off the highway. "You sound like my sister."

"Relax. I'm only yanking your chain. I honestly can't imagine you settling down. You and Steve like your lives too much the way they are to change them."

She bit her tongue, but it was too late. She'd drawn attention to the elephant in the room. A short silence followed. Harry glanced at her but she kept her gaze front and center.

"For what it's worth, for a while there I thought you had him on the ropes."

"The question is, would I have wanted him once I got him?" Again, the words were out of her mouth before she could stop them. She held up a hand immediately, signaling she knew she'd stepped over the line. "Pretend I didn't say that, okay? Strike it from the record."

Harry was the last person she wanted to vent to about Steve. The absolute last.

"So is Alice walking and talking and stuff yet?" Harry asked after a small silence.

"She's six months old, Harry." Was he really so clueless?

He raised his eyebrows, clearly wondering what he'd gotten wrong. Apparently he *was* that clueless.

"Babies don't generally start doing any of that until twelve months," she explained.

"Right. So what does she do?"

"At the moment? Eat. Sleep. Cry. Poo. She's starting to crawl, too."

"And that's all going well, then?"

She laughed. He was trying. She had to give him points for that.

"She poos like a champion. And no one can reach the high notes like Alice when she's really cranky." Her street was coming up and she gestured with her chin. "This is me."

He made a left turn.

"The one with the broken letterbox," she said, indicating the fifties brick veneer that she'd been renting since she found out she was pregnant.

Harry pulled into the driveway, eyeing the unkempt, overgrown garden and the house's faded sun awnings. Pippa felt an uncomfortable tug of shame over the shabbiness of it all. Between work and university and caring for Alice, she could barely stay on top of the inside of the house, let alone the outside. And no way could she spare any money from her already tight weekly budget to pay someone to worry about it for her.

She opened her mouth to explain, then shut it without saying a word. She didn't owe Harry an explanation. He was breezing through her life. In all likelihood, she wouldn't run into him again for another six months, probably even longer. Which was the way it should be.

"Thanks for the lift and the help with my car," she said.

"Like I did anything to help with your car."

"You destroyed my last vestiges of hope. Sometimes that's very necessary."

"Great. I'll add that to my repertoire. 'Crusher of hope.' Has a real ring to it."

"Actually, it sounds like a heavy metal band."

He laughed. She smiled and slid out of the car.

"Have a good weekend, Harry, and a great Christmas." It was only seven weeks away, after all, and it was unlikely she'd see him again before then.

"You, too, Pippa."

She turned away, then spun back. "Nearly forgot my stuff."

"Right."

Before she could protest, Harry jumped out of the car.

"Don't even think about carrying my shopping to the door for me, Harry. You've done more than enough." Plus she wasn't used to being fussed over like this.

Harry brandished the key at her. "This is an old-school car. No auto trunk release."

"Oh." She felt heat climb into her cheeks and attempted to cover her blush by pushing her glasses up the bridge of her nose.

A small smile played around Harry's mouth as he lifted out the bags and set them on the lawn.

"I'm leaving it here because I don't want you having conniptions again."

"Trust me, neither of us wants that."

"Look after yourself, okay?" His gray eyes were direct and honest.

"I will. You, too. And keep dodging those bullets. The world wouldn't be the same if you were domesticated."

"I'll do my best, don't worry."

Once inside the car, he backed onto the street. Pippa raised her hand in farewell. He waved in return, then was gone, the sound of the engine fading into the distance.

She headed for the house. Running into Harry had been the highlight of her day, which was probably a sad indictment of how pitiful her life was, but what the hell.

"Mum, I'm home," she called as she let herself into the house.

"We're in the sunroom."

Pippa dumped her things in the kitchen before following her mother's voice to the room that overlooked the rear garden. The carpet was a faded floral—probably original—the walls a grubby cream. Huge windows let in the afternoon sun. Her mother was sitting on the Art Deco couch Pippa had rescued from the side of the road and reupholstered a few years ago, a crossword puzzle book open on her knees, while Alice lay on a quilt at her feet, fascinated with one of her own small, pink toes.

"I was starting to get a little worried," her mother said as Pippa dropped a kiss onto her cheek.

"Sorry. I had car trouble."

The vague concern in her mother's eyes became real worry. "Nothing too bad, I hope?"

"Nothing I can't sort," Pippa lied, because she knew if she didn't the next words out of her mother's mouth would be an offer to help pay for the repairs.

Julie White had retired from teaching three years ago and was on a limited, fixed income. Despite her financial limitations, she'd bent over backward to help Pippa once she'd learned of her daughter's pregnancy. Pippa had been doing her damnedest to stem the tide of her mother's generosity in recent months—she point-blank refused to be the reason her mother had to cut corners in her retirement—and little white lies like this were becoming more and more commonplace in their conversations.

Still, Pippa figured it was better to tell a few porky pies now, than have her mother sell her small condo or car later on.

As she'd hoped, the fib worked. "Oh, good. Because the last thing you need right now is car trouble."

"I know. How has little miss been while I was out?"

Pippa sank to her knees to rest a hand on her daughter's warm belly. Alice gazed at her with big blue eyes, her mouth working.

"Did you miss Mummy?"

Alice beamed, both hands gripping Pippa's wrist.

"She's been a little sweetie," her mother said.

"That's because she's a shameless little con artist. Aren't you, Ali bear? Have you been charming your grandma?" Pippa kissed her daughter's cheek before rising to her feet. "Are you staying for dinner?"

"I can't. Not if I want to make it home before midnight. I promised Mrs. Young that I'd drive her to bingo tomorrow and I don't want to let her down."

Her mother lived in Bendigo, a three-hour drive north. Single since Pippa's father died when Pippa was sixteen years old, she was heavily involved in her local community, volunteering at the local retirement village and a number of charity shops.

Pippa did her best not to act relieved as she said her goodbyes. At least she didn't have to put on a brave face for the rest of the evening—the only upside she could find to her situation right now.

She waited until her mother's car had turned the corner before walking slowly into the house, Alice a heavy weight on her hip. She fed Alice, then made dinner for herself. With her daughter settled in her bassinet, happily gurgling away, Pippa fired up her laptop and logged on to her bank account to work out how on earth she would get together enough money to fix her car.

It was a depressing exercise. Despite months of scrimping and saving, she had just enough in the account to cover rent, utilities and food for the next month, but precious little contingency. Certainly nothing near the amount that Harry had implied she might need.

She stared at the figures on the screen, elbows

propped on the table, fingers digging into her temples as she racked her brain. There had to be some way to find the money.

She could ask for more shifts at the local art gallery where she worked, but that would mean bailing on classes at university and she had exams coming up... Plus she was already sailing close to the wind in the attendance department. The last thing she needed was to fail because she hadn't attended the requisite number of hours in class. The whole point of getting her Diploma of Education was to escape this cycle of hand-to-mouth, one-day-at-a-time living by landing a decent-paying job. She was halfway through her diploma, but all her hard work would be a complete write-off if she failed because of skipping class.

Of course, if she had completed her teaching degree ten years ago when she'd graduated with a Bachelor of Arts degree, none of this would be an issue. She would have a decent job, a good income, and Alice would have a stable home. But Pippa had turned her nose up at teaching then, even though her mother had encouraged her to have "something to fall back on." Pippa had been convinced that something else was out there for her, something amazing and creative and exciting. She'd spent a decade searching and had nothing to show for it except a woefully empty bank account and her beautiful, painfully precious daughter.

A headache started behind her left eye and she willed away the panic fluttering in her chest. She might not be able to see it right now, but there was a solution to her problem. She simply had to wait for it to reveal itself.

If Steve was even close to being a responsible adult, you wouldn't have to think twice about calling a mechanic.

Pippa hated the impotent, acidic burn she got in her stomach every time she thought about her ex. Hated how helpless it made her feel. How stupid.

For six incredibly foolhardy months, she'd been infatuated with a real-life version of Peter Pan. She'd laughed at his antics, been beguiled by his laid-back, take-things-as-they-come lifestyle and ignored the little voice in her head telling her nobody could live like that forever. Then she'd discovered she was pregnant, and Steve had turned from a funny, irreverent larrikin to an angry, resentful asshole. Six months of laughs, good times and fun had gone up in smoke and Pippa had been left holding the baby. Literally.

I don't want this. I didn't ask for it. I'll give you the money to make it go away. But if you decide to keep it, it's all on you. I don't want anything to do with it.

His words on that fateful day still lived large in her memory. She'd hoped his attitude would change once he'd gotten over the shock of her announcement, but he hadn't budged on his stance. She'd been forced to contact Child Support Services to pursue him for support payments. She hadn't wanted to, had tried everything in her power to work it out with him, not wishing it to become official and complicated, but Steve had point-blank refused to even come to the table. Pippa had been left with no choice but to take steps to ensure Alice had what she needed.

In theory, the law had supported her cause, but Steve had arrived with the books for his house-painting business and told the caseworker he was barely staying afloat. Alice had been awarded a paltry fifteen dollars per week based on Steve's hugely under-reported annual income. She'd listened with disbelief when her caseworker explained the outcome. She knew how Steve lived. He never denied himself anything, from holidays to Bali to a new truck to three-hundred-dollar sunglasses. But because he was self-employed, he was able to manipulate the figures to make it look as though he barely made ends meet. She'd walked away with nothing but disillusionment and the advice that she needed to file a change of assessment request to empower the agency to go after Steve through tax and bank records. She'd done so two months ago, and was still waiting to hear the result.

No surprises there. She had no doubt that Steve was doing everything to avoid, delay and prevaricate. Meanwhile, she and Alice teetered on the brink of insolvency.

Pippa rubbed her eyes. No matter how much she willed it, the figure on the screen hadn't suddenly grown an extra decimal point. She abandoned the computer and picked up Alice out of her bassinet and then lay on the floor with her baby resting on her belly. Alice pushed up on her arms and stared, eyes bright with curiosity. As usual Pippa felt the bulk of her worries slip away as she looked into her daughter's trusting face.

This is what's important. Only this.

Everything else would take care of itself. University, the car, the bills… Things would work out. She'd make them work out. She might not be loaded, but she was thirty-one years old and she was resourceful and resilient. If she had to sic yet another government agency on Steve, she would. If she had to somehow squeeze in more work shifts around her classes, she'd do that, too. Whatever it took.

She cupped her hand around her daughter's silken head and pressed a kiss to her cheek.

Whatever it took.

CHAPTER TWO

HARRY WOKE THE next morning feeling thirsty and thick in the head. No doubt the result of the many beers he'd sunk last night, along with the fact he'd crawled into bed in the early hours.

He lay in the morning sun trying to muster the energy to get out of bed and take care of both his thirst and complaining bladder.

Details from the night returned: Steve crowing as he won yet another game of pool at the pub, completely ungracious in victory. Nugga making a fool of himself chatting up a girl way too young for him. The hot brunette with the tight tank top—no bra—who had punched her number into Harry's phone and told him to call her.

Yeah, it had been a good one. Not quite up to the glory days of five years ago, when there had been more of them and fewer girlfriends and wives at home, but still a good night.

After a few minutes of drowsing, Harry threw off the covers and shuffled into the bathroom to take care of business. He hit the kitchen afterward, pouring himself a huge glass of OJ and took it to bed, which was when he noticed the sand in the sheets. He grinned, remembering the last part of the evening, when he, Steve and Bluey had played an unholy game of tag on the beach, whooping and hollering as they ran in and out of the surf and up and down the sand. They'd finally been sent home by one of the boys in blue, with a heavy-handed suggestion that they all grow up.

Harry finished the juice in one long pull. He checked his phone for the time and saw he had a text from Nugga asking if he wanted to catch a wave or two at Gunnamatta. He thought about it for a second. He didn't have any other major plans for the day beyond a vague idea that he might drop in on his sister, Mel, and her husband, Flynn. A surf was a safer bet—the moment his sister saw him she'd be sure to invent some gardening job that required muscle strain, sweat and four-letter words. Not that she wouldn't be in there right alongside him and Flynn, pulling her weight, but still.

He texted Nugga to say he was on the way, then rolled out of bed and stretched until his shoulders popped. Ten minutes later he was out the door in a pair of board shorts, a towel under his arm, a pair of thongs on his feet.

He threw his wetsuit and board into the back of his old truck and wended his way through quiet residential streets until he hit the highway.

Harry saw Pippa's car from a mile off, a bright yellow beacon on the opposite side of the road. He frowned as he sped past. He'd thought she would call her mechanic yesterday to take care of it. But maybe she'd had trouble contacting him at the end of the working week. She'd need to deal with it in short order, however, because the local council had strong feelings about abandoned cars. If Pippa wasn't careful, her car would be towed and she'd have to pay a release fee on top of everything else.

Seeing Pippa's car reminded him of something else that had happened last night. Maybe it had been stupid of him given the circumstances and how close-mouthed Steve had always been about Pippa and Alice, but when he'd hit the pub he'd taken Steve aside to let him know what had happened with Pippa. Harry had figured that if it was his ex, the mother of his child, he'd want to know. But Steve had simply nodded as though Harry was talking about someone he barely knew and changed the subject. No interest whatsoever.

Big deal. They're not together. And she sicced some government agency on to him to squeeze more money out of him. He's got every right to feel the way he does.

It wasn't as though Steve had gone looking to be a father, after all, and no one knew better than Harry how messed up and angry Steve had been when Pippa broke the news. And yet…his mate's indifference didn't sit well with Harry.

But he wasn't in the habit of sticking his nose where it didn't belong. So Pippa would have to sort her car out on her own.

Except she didn't.

When he drove to work on Monday morning the car was still there, and when he drove home at the end of the day. Tuesday, same deal. Wednesday morning he kept his eyes peeled and the moment he saw her hatchback, he pulled over. After three minutes of searching an online phone directory, he realized she must have an unlisted number. He drummed his fingers on the steering wheel for a few seconds, then waited for a break in traffic before doing a U-turn.

Five minutes later he climbed the steps to Pippa's front porch. It was only after he'd knocked that he questioned what he was doing. She was an adult, after all. She didn't need him ordering her life or breathing down her neck.

Too late. Footsteps sounded within the house, then the front door opened and a bemused Pippa stared at him.

"Harry. Hi."

Her hair was tousled, her eyes heavy. A fluffy dressing gown swamped her body, her bare feet peeking out beneath the hem.

She should have looked a mess—mumsy and suburban—but she looked good. Soft and warm and gently pretty.

"What's going on with your car?"

She blinked and it occurred to him that he may have actually dragged her out of bed.

"Sorry if I woke you, but you should know that the Peninsula council is all over abandoned cars like white on rice. If someone reports you, your car will be towed and impounded."

"Oh. Right."

Somewhere inside the house, a baby cried. Pippa glanced distractedly over her shoulder.

"I'm a bit slow this morning. I've been up since five with Alice. I only got her down again half an hour ago."

She backed up a step and gestured for him to follow her.

"Come in."

She was gone before he could explain he'd already said what he'd come to say, neatly sidestepping her way around a detached door leaning against the hall wall before disappearing from sight. He hesitated on the threshold, uneasy.

"Do you want a coffee?"

Pippa's question echoed up the hallway. He shook his head, then realized she couldn't see him.

"I'm fine, thanks."

Harry entered the house, navigating his way past the detached door. He found Pippa cradling a blond-haired, blue-eyed baby in the bright kitchen, rocking from foot to foot as she attempted to soothe her.

"Shh, sweetheart, you're all right. It's all good." Pippa's voice was soft and achingly tender. She glanced at him. "There's juice, too, if you'd prefer something cold."

He was too busy staring at Alice to respond immediately. He hadn't seen her since the day she was born. She'd been red and squashed-looking then, her eyes squeezed tightly shut, her hands clenched into tight little fists. Now, she was pink and plump, with pale, wispy hair. She looked like Steve. Almost disconcertingly so. It was weird seeing his friend's features replicated on a tiny baby girl.

"She looks like Steve," he said.

"Yes."

The way she said the single word made him remember he had no business being here. Steve was his mate, after all. Harry owed his first loyalty to him.

He cleared his throat. "Anyway. The car. You should chase up your mechanic because the council are real sticklers about towing anything that looks like it's been abandoned."

"I didn't realize. I thought I'd have a few weeks…"

A few weeks? To do what?

Then it hit him—her worry at the roadside, the slightly shabby house, the fact that she was a single mother.

She couldn't afford to get her car fixed.

Hence her delaying tactics when he'd mentioned having her car towed, and hence her need to wait *a few weeks* before she had the funds to repair it.

He glanced around the room, racking his brain for

a way to offer help without stepping on her toes—because he might not know Pippa that well, but he knew she had way too much pride to ask for help.

"Listen, Pippa, why don't I get my dad to tow the car to your place? At least you won't have to worry about it being impounded."

She was shaking her head before he'd even finished speaking. "It's great of you to offer again, Harry, but I'll sort it. Thanks, though. And thanks for the heads up. I appreciate it." She glanced at the wall clock. "I don't want to hold you up."

She was fobbing him off. Getting ready to send him on his way.

"How are you going to sort it?" he asked bluntly.

"Sorry?"

"How are you going to sort the car when you can't afford to get it fixed?"

Her chin jerked with surprise. "That's not what this is about."

She was a terrible liar, her eyes blinking rapidly behind her glasses.

"So I should call A1 Towing and get them to take the car to my work and ask my boss to quote on it for you, then?"

She stared at him, her expression half frustrated, half chagrined. After a second she shook her head. "You don't beat around the bush, do you?"

"I'm hoping I might have a chance of getting to work on time if we cut some of the back and forth out of the way."

She gave a short, sharp laugh. "You always were honest to a fault. Okay, you're right, Harry. I can't afford to fix the car right now. I'm scraping some money together but the gas bill came in and I figure we need hot water more than we need a car. So maybe the council will impound my car and I'll have to live with that until I can figure something out."

Pippa shrugged as though she didn't give a damn but her cheeks were pink and her shoulders tense.

He ran a hand over the top of his head, unsure where to go now that he'd gotten her to admit the truth. If it was one of his mates, he'd simply open his wallet and offer a loan on the spot. But as much as he liked her, Pippa wasn't really his friend and he had no idea how she'd react if he offered her money.

"What about Steve?" Because it seemed to him that was the next natural step, no matter the tensions between them.

"No."

One word, very firm.

"I know you guys have some issues, but he'd help out if he knew you needed it."

"I appreciate that you're trying to help. You're very sweet. But I can handle this."

"I'll ask him. If it'd make it easier for you to swallow."

He didn't know why he was making a federal case out of it. It was her car, her life. She was free to do whatever she liked. Certainly none of it was his responsibility. So why was he offering to be her mouthpiece with his best mate?

Pippa sighed. "It's incredibly generous of you to offer, but you don't want to do that."

"I wouldn't offer if I didn't mean it."

"I know. But it won't make any difference. Steve won't want to help me."

"Look, even if Steve's pissed with you, he'll step up."

"It's nice you believe that, but since he's gone to the

trouble of falsifying the books for his business to avoid paying child support, you'll understand if I don't hold my breath on that one."

He was ready to jump to his mate's defense. No way would Steve turn his back on his responsibilities. Alice was his kid, after all. His daughter.

Something stopped him before the denial left his mouth, however.

Maybe it was the world-weary note to Pippa's voice and the steadiness of her gaze.

Or maybe it was the memory of the utterly blank, disinterested expression on Steve's face Friday night.

"Like I said, I appreciate the heads up, Harry."

A phone rang in the next room.

"I need to get that. It's probably my boss…."

She slipped into the adjacent room. A few seconds later he heard her take the call. Harry glanced around the kitchen again, his gaze landing on a stack of textbooks on the table. He read the title of the top book— *Teaching Studies of Society & Environment in the Primary School*—before his attention was drawn to the large bowl in the center of the table. Filled with odds and ends, it clearly functioned as a tabletop junk drawer—and right on top was a key ring with two car keys.

In the next room, Pippa told someone she was ready and willing to do any and all extra shifts that were on offer. He could hear the strain in her voice. The fear.

He didn't stop to consider it, simply pocketed the keys. When Pippa returned, he said goodbye and bowed out. Once he got to his car, he tossed her keys onto the passenger seat then drove to work.

He'd taken them on impulse, because the idea of walking away from her when she was clearly in need stuck in his craw, and because he couldn't see any other way of convincing her to accept his help. Maybe it had been a mistake. Maybe he'd overstepped the mark, big time. After all, he had no vested interest in her or Alice or any of it.

But he couldn't stop thinking about what she'd said about Steve, about him having engineered his finances to minimize his child support commitments. Harry couldn't conceive of a circumstance where the mate he knew would do that. Steve was always first to buy a round of drinks or help out a friend moving furniture or some other favor. No way could all that generosity dry up when it came to his own flesh and blood.

Pippa must be exaggerating. It wasn't as though things had ended well between her and Steve. She was probably bitter and angry with him. Disappointed, too.

Except she hadn't exactly volunteered the information. Harry had had to push a few times before she'd spelled it out for him.

Deeply uneasy, he grabbed his phone and dialed his father at the workshop.

"It's me. I need a favor. There's an acid-yellow hatchback on the Nepean near the turnoff for the winery. Can you tow it to the workshop and I'll come by to take care of it after work?"

"You think I've got nothing better to do than run around doing favors for your mates?" His father's words were tough, but there was no rancor behind them.

"No. Can you do it?"

Harry half expected his father to have another go at him, but he didn't.

"What's the problem?"

"Head gasket, I think. I'll do the work if you don't mind me using the garage tonight."

"I'll make sure you've got the parts on hand. Who am I doing this for, by the way? Steve? That red-headed idiot?"

"Her name's Pippa. She's a single mum. I'm helping her out."

A profound silence ensued on the other end of the line and Harry could practically hear his father's brain grinding away.

"She's Steve's ex," Harry added.

Just in case his father started getting crazy ideas.

"Fair enough. I guess I'll see you tonight, then."

"Thanks, Dad."

"Don't thank me yet. You haven't seen my bill."

There would be no bill. Mike Porter might look like a hard-ass, but he was the softest touch in town.

As Harry turned in to the parking lot at work, it occurred to him that instead of pulling out all the stops for Pippa himself, he could have simply called Steve and filled him in and let him take care of things. Proving to himself—and Pippa—that she was wrong.

If it hadn't been for the blank look on Steve's face the other night, Harry might have, too. But that look… that look combined with Pippa's comments had sprouted some ugly ideas in his head, and the fact was, he wasn't ready to have them confirmed.

He and Steve had grown up together. Played footy together. Had their first beers, their first fights, their first girlfriends together. He didn't want to think that his mate was capable of letting down people he should care about so profoundly.

So Harry would help Pippa. And he would hold off talking to Steve until he'd had a day or two to digest. And he'd hope that someone, somewhere, had got it wrong.

TWO DAYS LATER, Pippa eased back onto the couch and propped her aching feet on a cushion. Alice lay on her play mat, batting at the Fisher Price mobile Pippa had bought from the local charity shop. It was Friday night and she was exhausted.

It wasn't ordinary, run-of-the-mill exhaustion, either. Having no car meant everything had to be started early and finished late, which meant she was waking earlier, going to bed later. Alice's day care might be around the corner and the gallery only a little farther than that, but when she threw in grocery shopping and other errands, plus getting to the university and back, Pippa figured she was walking more than ten kilometers a day. Great for her thighs and ass, not so great for her feet or her schedule.

In short, it sucked, hard. And she still had no idea how she would get her car repaired. She'd managed to scrape together nearly five hundred dollars, but the two mechanics she'd called had quoted a minimum of one thousand to fix a head gasket.

Pippa pressed her lips together, staring at her much-abused feet. There was no getting around it—she'd have to ask her mum for the money. She would pay her back, of course—but it would take time. And it was humiliating.

Thirty-one and running to Mummy. Well done, Phillipa. Way to be an adult.

To think that not so long ago she'd prided herself on being unconventional and marching to the beat of her own drum. Whenever one of her more conservative friends had asked if she ever worried about the future, about owning a house or being able to afford to retire or having a career, Pippa had laughed and assured them she didn't lose sleep over that stuff because she was too busy enjoying the journey.

What a load of old bullocks.

She'd been off with the fairies, tripping around in a fantasy world. Alice had been a cosmic wake-up call that it was time to stop playing around and grow up—there was nothing like being responsible for a tiny, helpless human being to sort a person's priorities out, quick smart.

Pippa propped an ankle on the opposite knee and massaged the arch of her foot, digging in her thumbs until it hurt. Her thoughts drifted to Harry's visit the other morning. He'd been the last person she'd expected to find on her doorstep at 7:30 a.m. Definitely he was one of the last people she would have chosen to catch her in her fluffy robe, complete with tangled bed hair and smudgy glasses. There was something very unsettling about being caught unprepared for the day by someone as dynamic and charismatic as Harry.

Still, it had been nice of him to drop in and warn her about the council's policy on towing abandoned cars. The bit where he'd forced her to confess that she couldn't afford to have her car fixed hadn't been so great, but since he'd followed it with yet another offer of help, she figured his heart was in the right place. Fortunately, she wasn't that desperate a case yet—stress on the *yet*.

That's right. You're only at the mooching-off-your-retired-mother stage. Mooching-off-strangers is a highlight for coming months, yet to be enjoyed.

A knock echoed through the house. She almost welcomed the interruption, even though it meant she had to get to her feet. Anything was better than lying around brooding.

"Ow," she said as she started up the hallway. "Ow. Ow. Ow. Ow."

Funny how shoes that she'd thought were perfectly comfortable had turned on her after a few days of hard labor. Once she'd dealt with whoever was at the door, she would run herself a bath and soak her feet.

She pushed Alice's stroller out of the way so she could reach the door. Because it was clearly her lucky day, the lock stuck and she swore under her breath.

Like the broken bedroom door, the dodgy lock had been reported to the landlord, but Pippa figured both would be repaired around the same time that Dairy Queen opened a concession in hell. The pitfalls of paying low rent in a working-class suburb.

She shouldered the door, pushing the lock up before twisting it. It gave grudgingly and she—finally—opened it to find Harry filling the frame for the second time in as many days.

"Harry," she said, blinking up at six foot two of solid male dressed in an old gray surf T-shirt, faded jeans and steel-toed boots.

Why did she keep forgetting how *big* he was? And why did he keep turning up on her doorstep?

"These are yours." He caught her hand and dropped a set of keys into it. "Before you say anything, it was my pleasure. Consider it an early birthday present for Alice."

It took her brain a full ten seconds to process his words and understand their meaning.

"You fixed my car," she said stupidly.

Sure enough, Old Yeller was in the driveway, brighter and larger than life.

"It was no big deal. Like I said the other day, it was the gasket. A few hours and the problem was solved."

"But…how did you get my keys?"

Then she remembered she'd left him alone in the kitchen while she took the phone call from her boss.

The first emotion to hit her was shame. She'd thought she'd been doing a decent job of covering how damned desperate she was, but clearly Harry had seen straight through her. That he understood exactly how powerless she'd been to change her situation and had been moved to act was galling and humiliating in the extreme.

Hard on the heels of shame came anger, a knee-jerk, defensive, irrational response to feeling so vulnerable and exposed. Who was he to take so much upon himself? To force his charity on her—stealing her car keys, no less—without asking if she wanted his help?

Finally, relief hit, so profound, so all-encompassing there was no room for anything else and she clenched her jaw to stop an instinctive, deeply pathetic sob from escaping. She curled her fingers around the keys, squeezing them tight, trying very, very hard not to cry with gratitude and relief. She blinked repeatedly but wasn't entirely successful in vanquishing the tears.

"I don't know what to say. You shouldn't have. It's too much. It's amazing…. But it's too much, Harry."

"It was a couple of hours' work, and Dad let me use his shop. Like I said, not a big deal."

Pippa took in his tired eyes, five-o'clock shadow and fingernails still dark with grease. She knew from her inquiries that replacing a head gasket in a standard, four-cylinder car was an eight-hour job, minimum. He must have worked around the clock after hours to do this for her.

A thousand thoughts battled for supremacy, but there was only one thing she could say.

"Thank you. This means so much to me and Alice. You've literally saved my bacon."

She held Harry's gaze as she said it, wanting him to see how sincere she was, how grateful. It might embarrass her to have to be the recipient of his charity, but no way was she rewarding his generosity with anything other than sincere appreciation. The shame was her problem, not his.

He stuck his hands into his back pockets, stretching his T-shirt across his broad chest. "It wasn't anywhere near as bad as it could have been. A clean replacement, no complications."

He was clearly uncomfortable, which, oddly, made it easier to swallow her own discomfort. She felt a rush of fondness for her ex's best friend. Harry had always been her favorite of Steve's mates. No competition.

"You're a good man, Harry."

He frowned.

"If I can be a gracious receiver, the least you can do is accept my thanks," she said.

"Thanks are fine. But we both know I'm no saint."

"Did I call you a saint? I said you were a good man." She stepped to one side. "Come in so I can make you even more uncomfortable with my gratitude."

He glanced over his shoulder as though looking for an escape route.

"Come on. A little slavish gratitude won't hurt you," she teased.

His gray eyes creased at the corners as his mouth curled into a reluctant smile. He stepped over the threshold, brushing past her, and she caught the scent of clean sweat and spicy deodorant. Her gaze scanned his broad back before dropping to his butt.

She stopped the moment she realized what she was

doing. Harry was Steve's best friend. In every way that counted, he was completely and utterly off-limits. She didn't need or want to register him as a man. She definitely didn't want to notice he had a nice ass.

Even if he did.

Pippa shut the door, being careful to shoulder it so the lock slipped into place. She was aware of Harry watching her and she shrugged philosophically.

"This place is a bit of a work in progress," she said and headed down the hall.

She heard Harry follow, his tread steady and sure. When they entered the kitchen she threw him a quick smile.

"One sec while I check on Alice."

She ducked her head into the sunroom. Her daughter was chewing on the sleeve of her Onesie, a sure sign she was hungry. Pippa scooped her into her arms.

"We've got a visitor. You want to come and say hello?"

Harry stood in front of the photographic montage she'd made of the first few months of Alice's life, his expression unreadable.

"Sorry about that," she said. "Now, can I offer you a coffee or a tea? I think I may even have a stray beer in the fridge. And have you had dinner?"

"Coffee's great, thanks." He turned from the photographs, and his expression softened when he saw who she was holding. "Hello, little lady."

Alice blew a bubble and gurgled in the back of her throat.

"That's hello in baby-speak, in case you were wondering."

Pippa settled Alice on her hip and crossed to the kettle to set it boiling. Acting on a hunch, she pulled out the leftover roast potatoes and chicken schnitzel from dinner and ferried them toward the microwave.

"If that's for me, please don't bother," he said.

She slid the plate into the microwave before facing him.

"Tell me what you had for dinner and I'll put it in the fridge." She was aware of Alice latching on to one of the buttons on her bodice and she ran a finger distractedly over her daughter's head.

He eyed her for a beat before responding. "Okay. I haven't eaten yet, but I've got food at home."

"If I can accept you repairing my car for me, you can accept a meal." She hit the button to start the microwave and waved him toward one of the two stools tucked beneath the kitchen counter. "Especially when the reason you went hungry is because you were doing me a favor. Grab a seat."

"I don't remember you being this bossy."

"Maybe you don't know me as well as you think you do."

"Maybe."

He sat as she collected coffee-making paraphernalia from the cupboard.

She laid out a knife and fork for him, grabbed a glass of juice, too, then folded a paper napkin and placed it beside the cutlery.

"Don't go to any trouble." He seemed awkward as hell sitting there, waiting for her to feed him.

"Relax. It's a paper napkin." She went very still when his gaze dropped to her breasts.

In all the time she'd dated Steve, she'd never—not once—gotten the vibe that Harry was interested in her as a woman. His attitude toward her had always been strictly friendly—no eye drops, no ass checks, no speculative looks. If she'd been asked by someone to describe the way he treated her, she'd have said his attitude was fraternal. Big brotherly.

Yet right now, right this second, he was staring at her chest with a single-minded intensity that made her belly tighten with nervous self-consciousness.

The moment seemed to stretch. Then Harry lifted his gaze to hers and realized he'd been busted. Dull color stained his cheeks.

"Sorry. It's just…your dress…" He gestured toward her chest, his gaze trained resolutely over her shoulder now.

She glanced down and discovered that the top two buttons of her bodice were undone, offering him an untrammeled view of her deep red bra and a whole lot of cleavage.

CHAPTER THREE

SHE GATHERED THE sides of her dress together in her free hand, heat burning its way into her face. "Sorry. Alice must have— She's never done that before...."

It was true. Alice was always fiddling—with Pippa's necklace, her earring, the collar of her shirt or the buttons on her coat—but she'd never unbuttoned anything before.

Pippa tucked her chin and tried to rebutton her bodice one-handed, very aware of the warmth in her cheeks. Unlike many of the women in her mothers' group, she had been unsuccessful at breast-feeding. A series of infections and an inadequate milk supply led her pediatrician to recommend bottle-feeding Alice when her daughter was barely a month old. Consequently, Pippa wasn't nearly as casual about flinging her breasts around as some of her friends. To her, they were about sex and intimacy, not sustenance.

And Harry had copped a very decent eyeful.

"Here, I'll take her." Harry held out his hands, ready to accept the baby so she could secure her dress.

"You're sure?" she asked, surprised. He didn't exactly seem the baby type.

"She hasn't just eaten, right?"

"She won't throw up on you, if that's what you're worried about."

"Then we're cool."

She had to release her dress to pass Alice to him, and Harry kept his eyes averted during the exchange. She quickly refastened her dress, fingers racing to push the buttons home.

"Sorry about that," she said once she was decent. "Bit more than you bargained for."

She couldn't quite make herself meet his eye.

"Should I slip the kid a tip or would that be overkill?"

He surprised a laugh out of her. "I don't think she needs the encouragement."

"Guess it depends on where you're sitting."

She risked a glance at his face. He was smiling, a devilish glint in his eyes. She grinned.

"You're hopeless."

"Because I've got eyes in my head?"

"Something like that." She glanced at Alice, who was happily balanced on his knee, her back supported by one of Harry's big hands.

"Are you okay with holding her for a few more minutes or are you going to break out in hives from all the responsibility?"

"I can handle it."

"Brave man."

"Weren't you making me dinner?"

She rolled her eyes comically before checking on the microwave. The timer was almost done and she opened the door to test the temperature of the potatoes. She was aware of Harry watching her as she worked and an odd little frisson ran up her spine. A couple of minutes later, she slid the plate in front of him, complete with gravy and a slice of fresh bread.

"Looks good," he said.

"Well, it's food, anyway," she said modestly.

She enjoyed cooking, but she wasn't about to volunteer for *Masterchef* or anything. Definitely her efforts veered more toward the everyday and practical than haute cuisine.

She reached for Alice, sliding her daughter off his thigh so he could eat his meal unhindered. At the last minute, Alice caught a fistful of Harry's T-shirt in her small hand, clinging to it as though her life depended on it.

"Alice. Sorry, Harry. She's not used to men, so you're a bit of a novelty item."

"It's all part of being a babe magnet."

She winced to let him know his joke was really bad before prying Alice's fingers loose. Her daughter had a fierce grip, however, and it took Pippa a few seconds to convince her to let Harry go. She was very aware of the firm warmth of his chest beneath the fabric and how close she stood to him. It hit her that this was the most intimate she'd been with a member of the opposite sex since she'd gotten pregnant. A less than impressive reflection of her social life, but also a solid explanation for the way her heart suddenly pounded in her chest.

"You live to fight another day," she said as Alice finally relinquished her prize.

"Phew," Harry said. "Thought it was all over for a moment there."

Pippa moved to a safe distance and gestured for him to eat. "Dig in. Don't let it get cold."

He dutifully picked up his cutlery and started eating. She took a deep breath and let it out slowly, trying to regain her equilibrium. From the moment he'd dropped her car keys into her hand she'd been off balance. Exposing herself and then prying her daughter off him hadn't helped matters.

Funny, but she'd never thought of Harry as someone she could ever be nervous around. But then she'd never been alone with him at nine o'clock on a Friday night before, either.

Right, because so *much is going to happen. He's probably just waiting for his moment to pounce, single mothers being a huge turn-on for him and all. Add to that the fact you're his best mate's ex and you're practically irresistible. It's a wonder he's still got his pants on.*

The thought calmed her. The very idea of Harry being interested in her or her being interested in Harry was absurd. Beyond absurd, really, moving into insane territory.

Common sense restored, Pippa crossed to the sideboard to find her handbag. She grabbed her checkbook from the side pocket and found a pen.

Behind her, Harry made an appreciative noise. "This is really good. I love schnitzel."

"It's my Aunt Bev's recipe. She married an Austrian."

"Go Aunty Bev."

She opened the checkbook to a fresh page.

Harry's eyebrows rose as he registered what she was doing. "That had better not be what I think it is."

"You have to at least let me pay for parts. I've gotten some money together, so I'm not a total charity case."

"It was a gasket and some oil. A few bucks. Like I said, consider it Alice's birthday present."

"Except it's going to be another seventeen-odd years before she actually needs her own car." She fixed Harry with a level look. "I appreciate your generosity, and I know I can't fully repay you for your time, but please let me make sure you're not out of pocket."

He gestured toward his plate. "You cooked me dinner. We're square."

She made a frustrated noise. Harry cut another slice of schnitzel and popped it into his mouth. He chewed slowly, purposefully, a steady, confident expression in his eyes that as good as said, "I just had the final word and you can't do anything about it."

He really was a cheeky bastard. Too cocky and smug and charming for his own good.

"I'll find a way to pay you back, Porter."

"You can try. But I don't like your chances."

She harrumphed to let him know she didn't agree, then crossed to the fridge and refilled his juice glass. Alice started fiddling with her buttons again and Pippa switched her to the opposite hip in the hope that it might distract her.

"I have to ask—what's with all the books on teaching?" Harry asked.

"I'm studying to get my Dip. Ed."

"You're going to be a teacher?"

"No need to sound so surprised. It's not *that* shocking."

"You've never mentioned it before, that's all."

She pulled a strand of her hair free from Alice's grasping fingers. "I need a job. A real job, not a joke job that I can pick up and put down whenever I feel like it."

Harry's gaze went to Alice and she knew he understood.

"Do you like it?"

"Sometimes. I've had two class placements so far and they both went pretty well. No one died on my watch, at least."

"Setting the bar pretty low there."

"These days I find it's best to have low expectations."

They talked about her studies as he finished his meal, leaving nothing but a thin trail of gravy. Testament, she hoped, to how much he'd enjoyed it. Afterward, he set his knife and fork neatly side by side on the plate and carried it to the sink. She watched as he glanced around for the dishwasher—there wasn't one—then proceeded to wash his plate.

"Wow. You're actually house-trained. Who knew?"

There was a reluctant grin on his lips as he glanced over his shoulder at her. "Jesus, you're a smart-ass. To think I used to miss you hanging around."

If the look on his face was anything to go by, he'd surprised himself as well as her with his inadvertent admission. She smiled, oddly touched, as he focused on rinsing his plate. She'd missed him, too, when things had gone south with Steve. Harry's irreverence and easygoing charm had always appealed to her. In another time and place, perhaps, they might have been friends. In this lifetime, however, it was never going to happen. Too many old loyalties on his side and too many bad associations on hers.

"I should get going," Harry said as he set the plate on the drainer.

"Okay."

She led him to the hallway, edging past the broken door. "Sorry about the obstacle course. The landlord assures me he's going to fix this thing before the turn of the next century."

This time, thankfully, the lock opened easily and she watched Harry step onto the porch.

"Thanks for dinner. And the show," he said.

Trust him to bring up the moment with her bra again.

"And I'm the smart-ass?"

"Maybe it takes one to know one."

"Maybe." The smile faded from her lips as she held his eyes. "Harry, what you did tonight… I will never be able to tell you how much your generosity means. I feel as though I've had a visit from my fairy godmother or something."

He shrugged modestly. "Honestly, I could do it in my sleep. It's really not a big deal."

"It is to me and Alice. A very big deal."

On impulse, she stepped forward, stood on tiptoes and flung her free arm around his shoulders.

"Thank you for being so damn kind," she said fiercely, pressing a kiss to the angle of his jaw. His shoulders were warm and firm beneath her arm and his five-o'clock shadow tickled her cheek. She inhaled the good, honest smell of him, touched all over again by what he'd done.

Before she could withdraw, his arms came around her, returning her embrace, and for a split second she and Alice were pressed firmly against his chest and side. Then he let go and she sank onto her heels. When she went to step away, however, she discovered Alice had once again grabbed Harry's T-shirt and was not about to let go.

"Maybe you really are a babe magnet."

Harry eyed Alice indulgently. "Nah. She's just got good taste."

He brushed his forefinger across the back of Alice's knuckles. Alice lifted her face to his, eyes wide, her mouth open in an almost-smile. Full of curiosity and wonder.

"Come on, cutie," he said gently, smiling in return.

He brushed her hand again and Alice let go, transferring her grip to his finger. Pippa stepped back, and after a long second Alice let Harry's finger slip from her grasp.

"Should have known you'd be an expert at the cut and run," she said.

"Lots of practice."

For a moment they simply smiled at each other.

"I'll see you around."

"Yeah. Look after yourself, okay?" she said, a little alarmed to feel her throat closing over with unexpected emotion.

Although maybe it wasn't that unexpected—he'd saved her ass tonight, after all.

"Sure thing."

He raised his hand in farewell and headed for his car. She watched him, only belatedly realizing it must have been quite an operation to get both her car and his here. She wondered how many favors he'd called in and knew she'd never know. Just as she'd never know how much she really owed him for parts and labor.

Grateful tears stung the back of her eyes as she waved him off. Pippa wasn't one of those people who had random good things fall in her lap every day, and she'd never considered herself particularly lucky, but there was no doubt the universe had been smiling on her when Harry drove past on the highway last week.

Suddenly she wished she'd said more to him, even if it would almost certainly have made him deeply uncomfortable. They'd been so busy giving each other a hard time, playing up their old dynamic, that she didn't feel as though she'd properly expressed her feelings.

Right now, Harry was her hero. Pure and simple.

She felt a tug, and when she looked down she discovered Alice was once again undressing her. Clearly, she needed to either invest in some safety pins or a pair of mittens for her daughter. Or, alternatively, some truly excellent underwear if she was destined to be flashing all and sundry on a regular basis.

For a split second—the most fleeting of moments— she allowed herself to wonder what Harry had thought of the "show" she'd put on tonight. Then she as quickly pushed the thought from her mind.

After all, it was absurd to even think—

Shaking her head, Pippa went to put her daughter to bed.

HARRY DIDN'T CONSIDER himself a saint. Not by a long shot. He had his faults and flaws, and some of them were worse than others, but one thing he'd never done was look twice at a mate's girlfriend or wife.

It simply wasn't in his makeup. As far as he was concerned, there were more than enough single, ready and willing women in the world without him even considering a woman who was taken.

So why in the name of all that was good couldn't he get the memory of Pippa's creamy, curvy breasts out of his head?

It wasn't just that she'd been wearing a cherry-red bra—not what he would have guessed was under her old-fashioned dress, that was for sure—although the way the bright lace had cupped her pale skin had been pretty damn memorable.

It was everything. The sway of her body as she'd moved around the kitchen, the way she'd tilted her head when she sent smart-mouthed zingers his way, the way she'd turned pink when she'd realized what her enterprising daughter had done.

Pippa White, it turned out, was sexy. In a quiet, subversive, get-under-a-man's-skin kind of way. She might not put it all out there like the brunette who'd punched her number into his phone last week, but there was something about Pippa that made a man think about things he shouldn't be thinking about when she was his best friend's ex-girlfriend—or, better yet, the mother of his best friend's child.

The worst thing was, Harry suspected he'd always been aware of her in that way on some level. When she'd been going out with Steve, Harry had always been able to pick her voice out in a crowd. Same with her laugh. And he'd whiled away more than one night lounging around a pool table with her, shooting the shit, laughing at her jokes and enjoying her sharp take on the world. Enjoying her.

Not gonna happen. Ever. So get that dirty little thought out of your head right now.

Harry pulled into his driveway and braked with more force than necessary, slamming the car door hard as he exited and headed for the house.

It was just as well he wouldn't be running into Pippa again in the near future, because he wasn't interested in being either the nobly-tortured, self-restrained chump or the dick-driven moron who threw away years of friendship for a roll in the hay. He liked things nice and easy. No complications. Lots of fun. Pippa didn't fall under any of those headings.

He strode into the living room, automatically reaching for the remote to flick on the TV. He wasn't really hungry, but he went into the kitchen and made himself a big bowl of ice cream. He sat on the couch and dug in, kidding himself that he was watching the cricket report when really he was thinking about the way Pippa had hugged and kissed him on her doorstep.

She'd called him kind, which was a pretty big joke given all he'd been able to think about was her breast pressed against his biceps. And when he'd returned her embrace—an impulse he hadn't been able to control—he'd sucked in a lungful of her perfume and the warm, milky smell of her daughter.

Who—yeah—had totally been in Pippa's arms while he was thinking about how soft her breast felt against his arm.

He was *so* kind. Practically a saint.

Disgusted with himself, he pushed his half-full bowl onto the coffee table and dropped his head against the cushion, trying to find some clarity. Or at the very least a little peace of mind.

He'd left as soon as he'd registered his own interest—he figured that counted in his favor. And he'd held her for only a second. And even though he wouldn't swear on it, he was pretty sure he'd helped out with the car with absolutely no expectations. Just as, even now, a part of him itched to grab his toolbox and go over to her place to fix that ridiculous abandoned door leaning against the wall, as well as that stupid, half-assed lock she had to wrestle with.

So what? She's Steve's ex. Doesn't matter what good deeds you want to perform, Boy Scout. She's out-of-bounds.

She was. Even if she and Steve had ended things amicably, the same would be true.

Which meant it really was time to stop thinking about her.

Harry reached for the remote, cranked up the volume and pretended that that was what he was doing.

PIPPA PRACTICALLY LEAPED down the steps the next morning, eager to get into the day. She had a car again! She felt as though she was rejoining the modern world after a week in the Stone Age.

Alice talked to herself in the backseat as Pippa drove to the village, her head full of plans. Once she had restocked the pantry, she might make a run to the library to check if the textbooks she'd ordered for her classes had arrived. Then she should probably get a head start on the five-thousand-word assignment that was due before the end of the month.

But first there was something she wanted to do. She parked in front of the liquor store and strapped Alice into her stroller, then went inside and bought some beer. The salesman helped her stow it on the rack at the back of the stroller before she exited and crossed the road. A bell rang as she entered the cement-floored reception area of Village Motors and a young girl looked up from behind the counter.

"Hi. How can I help you?"

Pippa offered up her best smile. "Would it be possible to speak to Mr. Porter?"

The girl's gaze flicked between Pippa, Alice and the beer. Lord only knew what she was thinking.

"I'll see if he's busy," she said primly.

Pippa pushed the stroller back and forth while she waited, hoping to keep Alice distracted. When Alice started vocalizing, she squatted to play peek-a-boo, making her daughter smile.

"I'm Mike Porter. How can I help you?" a deep voice asked.

She glanced up to find a powerfully built older man with a graying horseshoe mustache and Harry's eyes and nose towering over her. Like Harry, he was tall and broad. She would have recognized him as Harry's father anywhere.

She stood. "My name is Pippa White. I own a bright yellow hatchback. Your son Harry repaired it for me…."

"Right. The head gasket."

"That's me. I wanted to drop by and say thank you for your help, and to offer you a small token of my appreciation."

She collected the carton of beer from the luggage rack, offering it to him. His forehead pleated into a perplexed frown.

"You didn't have to do that," he said gruffly.

"I wanted to. I really appreciate what you and Harry did for us. I can't tell you what a relief it is to have a car again." Her arms were starting to get tired and she adjusted her grip a fraction. "Unless you like your beer frothy, you might want to grab this. I'm afraid my upper-body strength isn't what it should be."

"Sorry." Mike took the carton, placing it on the counter. He looked uncomfortable and a little uncertain as he faced her. Pippa stifled a smile. Like Harry, he didn't know what to do with her gratitude.

"Please take it. It's a tiny fraction of what the repairs would have cost, and I really want to acknowledge your generosity."

"Harry won't like this. He was pretty keen to help you out."

For some reason, his words sent a wash of warmth up her chest and into her face.

"I know. But he needs to accept that I'm pretty keen to thank you for that help, too."

Mike's gaze moved to Alice, his mustache twitching around his smile as he studied her round face. "This your daughter?"

"Yes. Alice."

"How old is she?"

"A little over six months."

His gaze returned to her and she could tell he'd made a decision. "Thanks for the beer, Pippa. It won't go to waste. And I'll be sure to direct Harry's comments your way when he hears about it."

She smiled. "You do that. I can handle it." She slid her hand into her handbag and grasped her checkbook. "Now, I don't suppose you could tell me what I owe for parts?"

Mike's eyebrows shot toward his hairline. "You don't need to worry about all that. Harry covered everything."

"I know. That's why I want to make sure he isn't out of pocket. It's one thing to give up his time, but I can't let him pay for parts, as well."

Mike shook his head. "Sorry, but that's something you'll have to take up with Harry."

"Mr. Porter—"

"Mike."

"Mike. Harry is a great guy, but I don't feel comfortable having him pay out money on my behalf. I know I didn't ask and he offered, but I can afford to cover the parts, and I really want to. It's important to me. I've got Alice to look after now and standing on my own two feet means a lot." She could hear the emotion vibrating in her voice and she swallowed. For a woman who had spent much of her adult life merely getting by, being responsible for another person was a profound shift. More than anything, she wanted to be up to the challenge, to be worthy of Alice. That meant not relying on her mother or anyone else. Definitely it meant not taking handouts if she didn't have to.

"I understand where you're coming from," Mike said after a short silence. "Things were tough when we first had Justine, our eldest, but I still had my fair share of pride. I get it."

"So you'll let me reimburse you?" she asked hopefully.

He allowed himself a small smile at her persistence, but he shook his head. "I'll tell you what the parts are worth. You can take repayment up with Harry."

Which meant she had yet another battle on her hands, but so be it.

Mike pulled open the top drawer of a beaten-up filing cabinet. After a few seconds he extracted a folder and opened it.

"Okay. The gasket itself was fifty, but you've got an aluminum head, which had to be resurfaced before the gasket was replaced, so that was three hundred. Then there was five liters of oil at thirty, a new oil filter at twenty-five for a grand total of four-oh-five." He glanced at her. "Which Harry can well afford, by the way."

Pippa pulled out her phone and made a note of the figure on the notepad app. "So can I. Thanks for this, Mike. I appreciate it."

"My pleasure. I appreciate you taking the time to drop in. Not sure I'll feel the same once Harry hears what went down, but I'm still bigger than he is so he can suck it up."

Pippa wasn't too sure about him being bigger than Harry—it looked like a pretty close call to her—but she offered Mike her hand, said thanks once again, then pushed a dozing Alice outside. She paused, thinking about how Harry had shouldered four hundred and five dollars on her behalf without so much as batting an eyelid, yet his best friend wouldn't even pick up the phone to discuss his daughter's welfare.

Someone sure picked the wrong hell-raiser to fall into bed with.

It was a dumb thought and she pushed it away the moment it occurred to her. It wasn't as though she'd ever had a choice between Steve and Harry—Harry hadn't even been around when she'd started going out with Steve. He'd been on holiday, touring the U.S., and she and Steve had been seeing each other for nearly a month by the time he returned home.

She could still remember the day she'd first set eyes on him. He'd walked in the door of Steve's place, two small silver rings shining in his right earlobe, tattoos black against tanned arms, and more than a little intimidating in a plain black T-shirt, worn jeans and steel-toed boots. *Here comes trouble* had been her first thought. Then he'd smiled and she'd seen the mischief, curiosity and intelligence in his eyes and she'd realized he *was* trouble—just not the kind she'd first anticipated.

Alice shifted, making the stroller rock, and Pippa snapped to. She had things to do. She didn't have time to stand around lollygagging. Especially not over Harry.

Her step brisk, she headed for the supermarket.

CHAPTER FOUR

THE REST OF the day sped by. She left Alice with a fellow student she traded babysitting duties with while she went to the university to get a head start on her assignment, a dry-as-dust examination of "the effect of government policy on the new national curriculum." She collected Alice midafternoon and swung by the gallery to check her roster for the next week. She'd requested extra shifts when she'd still been flailing around, trying to work out how to pay for car repairs, and she saw that her boss, Gaylene, had come to the party. The two extra shifts would mean some juggling of Pippa's schedule, but the extra money would give her the opportunity to build a little nest egg so that the next time life threw her a curve ball, she wouldn't feel quite so desperate.

In theory.

She thanked Gaylene, then checked the time. It was a little after five. She chewed her lip, then decided that this was as good a time as any to swing by Harry's place to see if he was around. It was tempting to simply leave the money in an envelope under his door when she knew he'd be at work, but leaving it without talking to him smacked of cowardice, and she wasn't afraid of him or the argument they were bound to have over her insistence on repayment. Far from it.

Pippa had only been to his place once when Steve had parked in the drive and honked the horn to let Harry know they were there to pick him up. Consequently, she knew the street but not the house number, but the big black muscle car in the driveway put paid to any doubts she might have had that she had the right place. The house itself was nondescript, a seventies brown brick with a neatly manicured lawn and a garage to the rear.

She pulled into the driveway, aware that her pulse had sped up and butterflies were doing a lap of her stomach in anticipation of the battle to come. She checked on Alice and discovered she was fast asleep. Well, Pippa was only going to be a minute, so there was no point disturbing her. She cracked the window to ensure there was a breeze and got out of the car.

The Red Hot Chili Peppers' "Under the Bridge" filtered through the warm afternoon air as she made her way to the front door. She knocked and waited. Seconds ticked past and she grew more and more tense. Which was ridiculous. This was Harry, and she'd already established she wasn't even remotely scared of locking horns with him.

When he didn't appear, she knocked again and tapped her foot impatiently. When he still didn't answer, she stepped back and regarded the house. The music told her that someone was home, and it belatedly occurred to her that he might not be able to hear her over the racket. She walked to the side of the house and peered up the driveway. The side door of the garage was open, and the music seemed to be emanating from there. Maybe he was working on a car or something.

She checked on Alice, then made her way past the house. The music switched to Pearl Jam as she neared the garage and she took a deep breath.

"Knock knock," she said as she stepped into the doorway.

And promptly lost the power of speech.

Harry was lying on his back on an incline bench, part of what was clearly an elaborate home gym. His chest was bare, sweat glistening on the muscles, his legs bent at the knee, his feet planted wide. A pair of faded tracksuit pants cut off raggedly at the knee rode low on his hips, and his stomach muscles rippled with effort as he pumped a loaded barbell above his head.

He looked…amazing. Huge. Sweaty. Ridiculously masculine. For the first time she saw that the tribal tattoos that snaked around his arms also flowed onto the left side of his chest, licking up his side like sinuous black flames. His pecs were powerfully defined, his nipples flat brown circles. A dark trail of hair bisected his belly, traveling down from his navel and disappearing beneath his low waistband.

She swallowed and became aware that she was clutching the envelope in her fist and staring like a nun at a strip show. She blinked, cleared her throat.

She'd seen near-naked men before, after all. So what if none of them had looked like Conan the Barbarian? It was no big deal. She wasn't even that into muscle-bound men anyway.

She cleared her throat a second time and knocked on the open door.

"Hey. Harry, you got a minute?" she called over the music.

The barbell crashed onto the uprights on either side of the bench as Harry registered her presence.

"Pippa." He looked surprised—and, unless she was wildly mistaken, pleased. As though he was happy to see her.

He sat up, an action which caused his abdominal

muscles to do amazing things, then leaned over to turn down the volume on the stereo. "What's up?"

"I came by to drop this off." She waved the envelope.

His gaze went from it to her, then he snagged a hand towel from the adjacent bench and wiped first his face then his chest.

"If that's money, I don't want it."

"It's four hundred and five dollars. Fifty for the gasket. Three hundred for resurfacing the head. Twenty-five for the oil filter and thirty for the oil."

"You spoke to Dad."

"I did. I took him some beer to say thank you."

"You didn't have to do that."

"Yeah, I did. Just like I have to do this."

She took a few steps into the room and slid the envelope onto the workbench that ran along the rear wall.

"Pippa…"

She held up a hand. "Harry, you need to let me do this. I am incredibly grateful for what you did, but it's enough that you gave me eight-plus hours of your time. I can't let you cover the parts, as well."

He scowled and pushed himself to his feet, setting off another chain reaction of rippling muscles. She fought the need to take a step backward as he advanced on her, reaching to grab the envelope.

"I'm not taking this," he said, thrusting it into her hand.

"Well, that makes two of us," she said, pulling her hand away before he could release the money.

His scowl deepened. This close she could see that his skin was still damp. She could smell his deodorant, too, and see the veins in his arms where his muscles were pumped from his workout.

"I can't take money from you. Put it toward something else," he said.

"*You* put it toward something else."

Like maybe a pair of workout pants that didn't seem as though they were in imminent danger of falling off his narrow hips.

"You mentioned being a graceful receiver the other night. Here's a newsflash for you—you could do with some lessons," he said.

"I *am* grateful. But I'm not a charity case. I don't need you paying my way."

"Who said anything about you being a charity case?"

An inch of what looked like black boxer-briefs showed at his waist. She felt a little dizzy, a little overwhelmed by all the raw masculinity on display.

"If you don't think I'm a charity case, let me pay for the parts," she said, trying to stop her gaze from sliding down his body.

"No. I wanted to help you and Alice. I did. End of story. I'm not taking your money." He grabbed her hand, slapping the envelope into it. "Save it for when the car breaks down next time, which it will, because it's a piece of yellow crap."

He was probably right, but her back went up anyway.

"Just because it's not some big macho muscle car from the days when dinosaurs roamed the planet doesn't mean it's a piece of crap."

"For the record, there weren't many dinosaurs roaming Australia in the seventies. And that hatchback is a piece of crap, and we both know it."

"Fine. Whatever. The point is, it's my piece of crap, and it's my responsibility. What you did was fantastically generous, but you need to let me cover the parts, Harry."

"Not gonna happen."

"Harry."

He shook his head slowly, his jaw set. She glared at him.

"I'm not letting this drop," she warned.

"Then I guess you've got a problem, because I'm not taking your money."

For a split second Pippa almost caved. Almost. But then she thought about how desperate she'd felt this week, and how relieved and pathetic she'd felt when Harry had shown up last night. She didn't want to be a damsel in distress. She needed to be strong, for both her and Alice's sake. That was what getting her Diploma of Education was all about. That was why it was so important that Harry let her pay her way.

"You know what Mick Jagger says. You can't always get what you want," she said.

Then she stuffed the envelope down the front of his shorts and swiveled on her heel, but not before she saw the shock on his face. She raced out the door. She figured she had the shortest of leads before he came after her. Sure enough, she was nearing the car when she heard him calling her name.

She scrambled into the driver's seat, jammed the keys into the ignition and hit the locks. Harry strode toward her, looking for all the world like an escapee from *Gladiator*.

"Sorry," she mouthed as she reversed out of the driveway.

HARRY STOPPED IN his tracks, hands on his hips, a pissed/resigned expression on his face. She hoped the resigned part signaled he would accept her money.

She glanced in the rearview mirror to find that Alice

was awake again, her blue eyes taking in the world. A smile crept onto Pippa's face, quickly turning into a grin.

She'd stuck a wad of cash down Harry's pants. She probably needed to get out more, but it was the most outrageous thing she'd done in months. Possibly even years. And it felt good.

You do *need to get out more.*

She was still buzzing with triumph when she turned onto her own street. Then she realized that the butterflies-doing-a-lap feeling was still there and in a flash of insight understood it wasn't nervousness. Not by a long shot.

It was excitement—because she'd seen Harry.

That quickly her goofy smile was gone, as was the feeling of triumph.

Harry was Steve's best friend. Furthermore, he was as feckless, as childish, as immature as her ex. Another overgrown teenager who viewed life as a big amusement park.

She didn't want to be excited about seeing him. God, no.

She parked and got Alice out of the car. As it had the other night, holding her daughter's warm, soft body grounded her. Alice was the ultimate invitation to live in the now, to experience only this present moment. Rubbing her cheek against her daughter's, Pippa let whatever silliness had gripped her this afternoon slide away.

Harry was not someone to get excited about. Lovely and funny and generous as he was.

It's hardly going to be a problem. There's no reason on earth for you to see him again now your car is fixed and the money sorted.

She should have felt relieved, but she didn't. She felt disappointed, which went to show that she really was an idiot.

HARRY RETURNED TO the garage. The envelope with Pippa's money lay on the floor where he'd dropped it—after he'd pulled it out of his pants.

Now, *that* was a move he hadn't seen coming. In fact, he still couldn't quite believe she'd done it.

Briefly he toyed with the idea of going after her, letting her know in no uncertain terms that he wasn't interested in her money. He imagined himself chasing her down, backing her into a corner until she was forced to take the envelope back. She'd protest, no doubt, but he'd look into those rich chocolate-brown eyes of hers and—

He bent and collected the money, pushing it into his pocket and turning away from the thought that had been about to insinuate itself into his head.

It wasn't quite so easy to ignore he had the beginnings of a hard-on, however. All because of a schoolboy fantasy that involved Pippa and a hard wall.

What is going on with you?

It was a good question. He wasn't sure what the answer was. Pippa wasn't the sort of woman he usually went for. She was older, for starters. Smarter, too. Then there was the not-insignificant fact she was a mother.

He gave himself a mental shake. It didn't matter why he liked Pippa or how different she was from his usual type. The important thing was that she was Steve's ex, and therefore officially off-limits.

As if his thoughts had conjured him, he heard the distinctive, low rumble of Steve's new truck pull into the drive. Guilt stabbed at him, but he rejected it instinctively. He hadn't done anything wrong.

Yet.

And it was going to stay that way, because Steve was one of his oldest friends.

He reached for his T-shirt and pulled it on as he exited the garage. Steve was sliding from the cab of his shiny red truck, a six-pack under his arm.

"Yo. What's up?" he called out. He was dressed in board shorts and a loose tank, his hair held back by a pair of sunglasses pushed high on his forehead.

"You been out today?"

"Hell, yeah. Suicide was going off," Steve said, naming a brutal surf beach farther south on the peninsula. "You should have come, man."

Harry shrugged. He'd been through this with Steve during that morning's phone call. "Mel needed my help with installing the rose arbors."

Steve tugged a can free from the plastic ring holding it to the six-pack, passing it to Harry. "Don't know why Mr. Richy-Rich doesn't hire a bunch of muscle to do it all for him. Not like he can't afford it."

"Flynn likes getting his hands dirty," Harry said, shrugging to let Steve know that he didn't want to get into yet another conversation about what Steve would do if he had the Randall millions at his disposal. The truth was, Harry's brother-in-law never flaunted his wealth and Harry had long ago stopped thinking of him as anything other than a good friend and the man who'd made his sister smile again.

"Yeah, yeah, whatever. So, what are we up to tonight? The Pier? Or do you want to hit the Portsea pub for a change, crash at Nugga's place?"

Harry led the way inside. "Not fussed. Whatever tickles your fancy."

Steve sat on the couch and propped his legs on the table, crossing them at the ankles. "You think that little blonde chick will be working at the Pier tonight? The new girl?"

"Who knows?"

"If I had to give her ass a score out of ten, it'd be eleven." Steve laughed and took a pull from his beer.

Harry drank a mouthful of his own can, his head full of everything that had happened with Pippa. He wasn't used to feeling guilty, and he didn't like it.

"So, did you call that girl from last week yet?" Steve asked.

It took Harry a beat to drag his head out of his own thoughts. "Didn't get around to it."

Steve made a disgusted sound. "Dude. What's wrong with you?"

"You want her number, it's yours."

Steve paused with his beer halfway to his mouth. "Seriously? You're not going to call her?"

Harry shook his head.

"Bloody hell. Never thought I'd live to see the day. You losing it in your old age, mate? Having trouble getting it up?"

"Thanks for the touching concern, asshole, but everything is in perfect working order."

Steve laughed and reached for the remote, flicking on the TV. "Did you catch any of the cricket today?"

Harry paused before answering, unable to shake the sense of unease dogging him. He felt like he was holding back. And it was because of Pippa. Because of how she made him feel, and—more importantly—because of what she'd said about Steve.

He grabbed the remote from Steve's hand and killed the TV.

"Hey. I was watching that."

"We need to talk. About Pippa."

The look of comic outrage on Steve's face disappeared as he put on his poker face. "What about her?"

"I told you about her car breaking down last week.

Well, I wound up helping her out. Had her car towed to Dad's and fixed the gasket head for her after hours."

Steve's eyes narrowed. "Why'd you do that?"

"Because she couldn't afford to have her car fixed, and she needed to get around."

"Pity you're not in the Scouts still. That'd earn you a merit badge for sure." Steve lifted his beer in a mock-toast. "Here's to Mr. Good Deeds."

"I told Pippa that if she wanted, I'd let you know what had happened on her behalf. See if you couldn't help her out, since she's struggling at the moment."

Steve leaned back in the chair and rested his right ankle across his left knee. "I bet she loved that."

There was no mistaking the resentment in his tone.

"She told me not to. And when I kept pushing she told me you'd dodged paying child support for Alice, so she doubted you'd be helping with the car." Harry didn't say anything more, simply waited for Steve to set him straight.

His friend gave him a derisive look. "What? Is this the bit where I'm supposed to step in and defend myself? Sorry, mate, but I'm not playing that game."

"That's all you have to say?"

"Yeah, it is. I don't even know why we're having this conversation, to be honest." Steve's gaze was hard with anger and suspicion.

Harry could only think of one reason why his friend would come out swinging so hard: because it was true. Because he really was ignoring his obligation to help support his daughter.

"She's your kid, man," he said quietly, hoping to cut through the bull. "Pippa's doing it tough and Alice is your kid. You should be helping them out."

"Should I?" Steve's tone was deceptively mild.

"You know you should."

"I'll tell you what I know. I told Pippa at the time that I wasn't up for a kid. Even gave her the money to get rid of it. She knew that, and she decided to keep it anyway. Her decision, right? That's what all the women's libbers tell us. So she made her decision, and I made mine. And I'm not changing it."

Harry blinked at the unvarnished fury in his friend's voice.

"Mate, it wasn't like she got pregnant on purpose."

"Yeah? How do you know that? How do you know she didn't see me as the perfect meal ticket?"

"Pippa wouldn't do that. She's not like that." He knew that in his gut. Pippa had far too much integrity to trap a man like that.

"So you're an expert on her now, are you?" There was an ugly suggestion behind Steve's words.

Harry gave his friend a look. "Pull your head in. As if."

"So why am I getting the public service message, then?"

"Because she needs help. And whether you like it or not, Alice is your kid."

"Like I said, Pippa wanted to keep the baby. I'm not wearing the consequences."

"*The consequences* is six months old, man. She looks like you. She's your kid."

Steve stood. "This is getting old, fast."

"So, what? You're going to pretend she doesn't exist? That your kid isn't walking around out there in the world without your protection?"

"Man, she really did a number on you, didn't she? What'd she do? Turn on the waterworks?" Steve's posture was tense, his expression ugly.

Harry pushed to his feet, not liking feeling at a disadvantage. "She didn't say a word about you that I didn't push out of her. She knows we're mates. She respects that."

"So why are we even having this conversation?"

Steve seemed genuinely puzzled, as though it was beyond him why Harry would take up the cudgels on behalf of Pippa and Alice without someone holding a gun to his head.

"Because she needs your help," Harry repeated.

"Not gonna happen." Steve headed for the door. "And you might want to think about whose side you're on in this, *mate*."

The door slammed as Steve exited the house. Harry stared after his oldest friend, trying to reconcile the man he knew—the guy who could make him laugh till his sides ached, who he trusted to have his back through thick and thin—with what he'd just heard.

And couldn't.

Not a single excuse sprang to mind for Steve's refusal to step up and take responsibility for his own child. Being angry wasn't enough. Feeling trapped also didn't cut it. No doubt Pippa must have felt all those things when she first found out she was pregnant, yet she had taken on motherhood with an open heart and mind.

Harry walked to the kitchen and dumped what was left of his beer down the sink. He watched the amber fluid circle the drain, going over Steve's words, wondering if there was anything he could have said that might have made a difference. It was so obvious to him that Steve was in the wrong, however, that he simply couldn't conceive of the mind-set that allowed Steve to carry on with his life as though things hadn't changed six months ago when Alice was born. Harry might prefer to live his life a certain way—no strings, no heavy responsibilities or burdens to get in the way of having a good time—but if he'd found himself in Steve's shoes he would do the right thing, no questions asked.

And not only because it was the right thing, either. If he'd helped make a new life, he'd want to get to know him or her, to pass on what skills or knowledge or advice he might have. He'd want to be a part of his child's life.

Steve clearly didn't feel the same compulsion or curiosity, however. Again, a mind-set that was so far beyond Harry's comprehension it baffled him.

He tossed the empty can in the trash and walked to the bathroom. He left his sweaty workout gear on the floor and stepped beneath the shower spray. Steve's angry departure had left him with an evening to fill. Which was just as well. He didn't particularly want to spend time with Steve right now.

An uncomfortable thought. When they were younger, he and Steve had fought over stupid stuff all the time. Once, Steve had even broken Harry's nose with a badly aimed punch. As adults, however, they pretty much saw eye to eye on everything.

Until now.

Harry scrubbed his face with his hands and dropped his head forward, letting the water pour down his back and shoulders.

He wasn't a grudge keeper, and he didn't consider himself any more or less stubborn than the next guy, but there was a heavy feeling in his gut that told him he would have a hard time forgetting what had gone down with Steve today. Which would be a problem, because he knew that Steve sure as hell wasn't going to be changing his position anytime soon. Harry knew his friend too well to even pretend that that would happen.

Now he was in the unenviable position of having a bone-deep moral objection to his best mate's actions.

The thought was so foreign to him he made a spluttering sound, half appalled, half bemused by the workings of his own mind. As his sisters were only too keen to point out, he wasn't exactly a choirboy. He'd never set himself up to judge anyone in his life. And yet here he was.

He dressed in jeans and a fresh T-shirt before returning to the living room. Habit told him to call Bluey or Macca, but the thought of spending the night at the pub had lost its appeal. Plus the odds were good Steve had called them as his backup plan once he'd blown Harry off.

Sitting on the edge of the couch, Harry stared down the barrel of a Saturday night home alone. Not something he'd done for a long time.

He turned on the TV and flipped through the stations, searching for something—anything—to grab his attention. If he found something decent to watch, he could grab a pizza and chill for the evening. Might even be good for a change.

He scrolled through all the likely channels without finding anything that hooked him and started all over again. When the second trawl still didn't produce fruit, he went in search of his car keys. Maybe he'd go over to Mel and Flynn's place, see what they were up to.

He found his keys in the pocket of his workout shorts—along with Pippa's wad of cash.

He stared at the creased and battered envelope, key scenes from this afternoon playing in his head. Pippa standing tall and proud, telling him she wasn't a charity case, that she could pay her own way. Steve, denying he had a duty to support his own flesh and blood.

The memory alone was enough to make Harry burn with shame for his friend. He felt an absurd, ridiculous urge to pick up the phone and apologize to Pippa on Steve's behalf.

He wanted to tell her that Steve was a good guy, even if he was acting like an asshole right now. He wanted to somehow impart to her all the positive things he knew about Steve, all the memories and goodwill they'd built between them over the years.

Not a call she'd be likely to take well. And not one he would ever make, either. He wasn't stupid. He wasn't about to get involved in Steve and Pippa's very private business.

He opened the envelope, eyeing the crisp fifties inside. Money that Pippa had had to scramble to find. Because Steve had his head up his own ass.

His jaw set, Harry tossed the money onto the couch and headed for the door.

He couldn't fix Steve, but there were other things he could do. And it wasn't like he had anything better to do tonight.

CHAPTER FIVE

PIPPA CLOSED HER eyes and breathed deeply, willing her body to relax into the warm water. Alice was asleep—bless her little cotton socks—the world was quiet, and the bathwater was scented with jasmine. Not a bad combination.

And yet her mind still refused to let go of the usual fistful of worries that were on high rotation in her mind. Money—naturally—study, Alice, the situation with Steve and Child Support Services…

Stop thinking. Breathe and relax and enjoy this little slice of paradise.

She made a conscious effort to relax the muscles of her neck and shoulders. She was floating with her eyes closed, contemplating running the hot tap to heat the water a little when a loud knock echoed through the house. Her eyes popped open and she scowled at the ceiling.

Who on earth would come calling unannounced on a Saturday night? And why had they come when she was finally giving herself over to the whole sinking-into-relaxation thing?

Muttering beneath her breath, she stood and grabbed a towel. Water splashed onto the floor as she climbed from the tub. She blotted the towel against her heat-flushed skin as she made her way to her bedroom. She put on her robe and headed for the front door. Whoever was there knocked for a second time as she paused to cinch her belt. She checked the spyhole.

A muscular male back filled the lens, along with a strong neck and a well-shaped skull covered with close-cropped dark hair.

What on earth was Harry doing on her doorstep again? This was seriously becoming a habit.

If he was here to make her take her money back, he was wasting his time. Something she was more than happy to tell him to his face.

She did the usual shoulder-against-the-door routine to unstick the lock, then pulled the door open. Harry had been contemplating her overgrown lawn but he turned to face her.

A jolt of awareness zinged through her as she met his gaze. Man-woman awareness—the kind she had no business feeling around Steve's best friend.

She was so thrown she launched straight into speech, sidestepping niceties like saying hello and asking after his health. "Before you start, there is no way in the world I'm taking that money back. So forget about trying to browbeat me into accepting. It's not going to happen."

"I'm not here about the money."

"Oh." She blinked, nonplussed.

"I came to fix your bedroom door. And the lock." For the first time she noticed the honking great tool-box at his feet.

"Why on earth would you want to do that?"

"Because it needs doing. The hall's a fire hazard the way it is. And that lock is a disaster waiting to happen. I figure it will take me an hour, two at the most, then I'll be out of your hair."

He stooped to pick up his toolbox and stepped forward. She held up a hand to halt his advance.

"Whoa, whoa, whoa. Hold your horses a second." She shook her head, trying to get her brain working. "I still don't understand."

It was Saturday night, after all. Prime partying time. What on earth was he doing on her doorstep, preparing to DIY?

"What's to understand?" He shifted impatiently, clearly ready to jump in.

She stared at him, perplexed, even as a little voice in her head told her to simply thank him profusely and take him up on his offer. After all, she'd been sidestepping that stupid door for months now, and the lock had never worked properly. If she waited around for the landlord to take action, she'd be pushing daisies before it was done. And having both issues fixed would make her life infinitely more pleasant.

But there was no reason for Harry to be volunteering to help her out like this. No reason that she could think of, anyway. Harry wasn't her friend, he was Steve's friend. But clearly *something* was motivating him.

"At the risk of sounding like an ungrateful cow, I really don't get why you would want to do this for me. Don't get me wrong, it's awesome, but until you saw me on the side of the road last week we hadn't seen each other for months."

Harry's dark brows creased into a frown. After a long beat he set his toolbox down and met her eyes. "I talked to Steve today. Told him what had happened with your car."

She crossed her arms over her chest. She could imagine exactly how that conversation had gone, how completely disinterested Steve would have been. "Right."

"I'll be honest, when you said that stuff about him not paying any child support, I didn't believe you. Not that I thought you were lying, but I thought there must have been more to it."

She didn't like the idea that Harry—or anyone, for that matter—might see her as a bitter, resentful ex, ready to tarnish her former lover at the drop of a hat. This was why she didn't talk about Steve to anyone other than her mother, as a general rule.

"And what did Steve say?" she asked carefully.

"He told me that you'd made your decision, and he'd made his."

She gave a tight nod. "That's about it, yes."

If she ignored the part where he'd lied to the government to avoid paying for his daughter.

"I didn't know any of this stuff. He never talks about you or Alice. I figured things were just ticking over...."

Harry looked acutely uncomfortable. She felt a stab of sympathy for him. She knew how much history he and Steve shared. Discovering that someone you respected and admired had feet of clay was never a pleasant experience.

"He thinks I tricked him into becoming a father because I didn't have a termination."

Harry winced. She tilted her head, trying to work him out. "So you talked to Steve, and your first thought was to grab your toolbox and come over to fix my door?"

"I figured that if he wasn't going to step up, the least I could do was make sure things are okay for you. It's not much, but it's something."

She stared at him as the meaning behind his words hit her.

He felt sorry for her.

He pitied her because her no-good ex wouldn't cough up child support and she'd been left to manage on her own. He thought she was barely keeping her head above water, that she needed all the help she could get, and he'd come rushing to her rescue.

It felt like a slap in the face, like a huge, unequivocal vote of no confidence. It felt as though he'd judged her and found her wanting and was now stepping in to sweep up the broken pieces and glue them back together for poor, struggling Pippa.

Suddenly she felt acutely, inordinately foolish for that small zing of pleasure she'd gotten when she'd opened the door. For a few silly, pointless seconds, she'd allowed herself to believe that he had come calling again *for her*. Because of the way he'd looked at her breasts the other night and teased her and returned her impulsive hug. She'd been flattered, excited and energized by the notion that sexy, bad-boy Harry might find her attractive. She hadn't planned to do anything about it— dear God, there were so many reasons *that* was a bad idea she couldn't even begin listing them—but there was no denying that her feminine ego had stretched and purred a little at the notion that he might be interested.

And he'd come calling because he felt sorry for her.

Yeah.

She took a deep breath, conscious of the embarrassed heat that was rising in a slow wave from her chest, up her neck and into her face. "I appreciate the thought, Harry," she said tightly, "but I'm not quite at the begging bowl, prostrate on the sidewalk stage just yet."

His scowl deepened. "What's that supposed to mean?"

"What it sounds like. I don't need you playing knight

errant for me. The car was one thing, but this… No. Alice and I are getting by just fine."

"Did I say anything about how you and Alice are getting by?" Harry sounded aggrieved and baffled in equal measure.

"Yeah, you did, when you came thundering over here full of good intentions. It would be different if we were friends, Harry, because then I would know that I could return the favor for you some time in the future. We'd have a history of give and take. But we're not friends, are we? And you're doing this because you think I've gotten a raw deal and you feel sorry for me. Right? I'm the human equivalent of one of those plastic seeing-eye dogs that you slip a coin into at the supermarket."

"Does it matter? Isn't the important thing that the door is fixed and the lock works properly?"

It was such a rational, calm, measured response that a red haze came over her vision.

"What, just because I'm a single mother, I don't get to have any dignity, is that it? Just because I've hit a temporary rough patch, I get to be painted as a victim who needs to be rescued? Well, guess what, Harry, I don't need your help. I can get my own damn door fixed. And I definitely don't need you feeling sorry for me."

He held up his hands, palms out, as though he was warding off a madwoman. "Okay. Calm down. I was only trying to help."

"Well, *don't*. I'm not your responsibility. I'm *my* responsibility, and so is Alice, and everything here is fine, thank you."

"Fine. Whatever. *Jesus.*"

She grabbed the door. "Boy, am I glad I got out of a nice warm bath for *this*."

She swung the door shut, remembering the temperamental lock at the last second. Before she could catch it, the door hit the striking plate and bounced open. The door was open for only a split second, but it was more than long enough for her to see the I-told-you-so expression on Harry's face. She pushed the door shut again and woman-handled it into position, swearing under her breath. Finally the latch clicked closed and she exhaled in an angry, impatient rush.

She heard Harry's heavy tread on the steps, then, a few seconds later, the sound of an engine starting. She swiveled on her heel and made her way up the hall to the bathroom.

How dare he come over here to shove his good intentions down her throat like that? How dare he take her up as his own personal charity?

She wrenched the tie on her robe free and tossed it into the corner. Every muscle tense, she stepped into the bath and sat in the water.

The whole thing was made even worse by the fact that for a few crazy seconds she'd thought he was here because he'd been thinking about her as much as she'd been thinking about him. So much worse. While she'd been battling an unwanted attraction, he'd been giving his pity gland a good workout.

She rested against the end of the tub, flinching at its coldness. The water was tepid, too, and instead of being a comforting haven, the bath suddenly felt wrong and awful and irritating.

Another thing to thank Harry for: ruining her first moment of decent alone time in months.

Oh, yeah, what an evil despot he is. The way he came over wanting to help you out because he'd learned that his friend is a jerk. Lock the man up and throw away the key for his crimes against humanity. What a scumbag.

She closed her eyes, but it didn't stop reality from sinking in.

The way she'd responded to Harry...

The things she'd said...

The way she'd said them...

She'd overreacted. Big-time. Her pride had been stung, and she'd lashed out like a sulky kid. Yes, Harry could have been more diplomatic with his offer, but it had been made with the best of intentions—and she'd shoved it down his throat because she'd been embarrassed and angry. Embarrassed because she'd imagined the glint in his eye had been about her and not just because he was an inveterate ladies' man, and angry with both herself and Steve that she was in need of help in the first place.

She was the one who had frittered away her twenties working in bars and tourist hot spots in far-flung destinations, instead of planning for the future. *She* was the one who had chosen to give six months of her life to a man who had proven as deep as the nearest puddle and as reliable as a house of cards. Harry had nothing to do with any of that. He'd been kind and generous and noble—and she'd been a shrew. A crazy, irrational shrew.

She got out of the bath and reached for her towel. It was damp from the first time she'd used it, but she managed to blot up the bulk of the water before slipping into her robe.

She owed Harry an apology. Actually, she owed him a major grovel. On her knees, beseeching hands, the works. The sooner the better.

If Alice weren't sound asleep, Pippa would go to his place right now, before the memory of her behavior had a chance to solidify in his mind.

She sat on the end of her bed, regret making her toes curl into the carpet. She didn't consider herself a rash person, but every now and then she did something really stupid. Like take antibiotics then forget to use backup contraception, or blow up at a nice guy like Harry because he was being a decent human being.

She fell back onto the mattress, staring at the ceiling. She'd learned a lot about herself since having Alice. She'd learned that she was more resilient than she'd ever imagined she could be. She'd learned that if push came to shove, she could bear almost anything as long as her daughter was safe and well. She'd learned that she was stubborn—sometimes unattractively so—and more independent than she'd ever given herself credit for. And, apparently, she also had her fair share of pride.

She pressed her hands to her face, thinking about what she would say to Harry when she went to see him tomorrow. She hoped he'd at least hear her out. If he didn't… Well, she'd have to find some other way to make it up to him.

HARRY SLAMMED HIS way into the house, tossing his car keys onto the coffee table with so much force they skidded off the other side.

Perfect. Another thing gone wrong in what was shaping up to be an incredibly shitty day. Next time he felt the urge to get involved in someone else's life he was going to bite his tongue off and swallow it.

He went to the kitchen and grabbed a beer from the fridge, then crossed to the back door and let himself out into the yard. There wasn't much to look at out here, despite his sister's constant nagging for him to "do something" with the patch of lawn and jumble of trees, but he felt like he needed a bit of fresh air after his encounter with Pippa.

She'd been so angry. She was always so good-natured, such a good sport, he'd been taken aback by her fiery response to his offer. For the life of him, he couldn't understand where all that anger had come from. It wasn't as though he'd insulted her or gone out of his way to make her feel small. He'd simply wanted to help, to right one small wrong in her life because he couldn't fix the greater wrong.

I've gotten a raw deal and you feel sorry for me. Right? I'm the human equivalent of one of those plastic seeing-eye dogs that you slip a coin into at the supermarket.

He took a big swallow from his beer, shaking his head. He didn't see her as a walking-talking charity appeal. Far from it. He felt bad for her—and for Steve, for that matter. In a few years' time, he couldn't help but think that Steve would look back on how he was behaving now and feel about three inches tall. For sure that was how Harry saw him—as a man who didn't have the cojones to step up when it counted and own his responsibilities.

As for Pippa… Well, he'd tried. If she didn't want his help, if she was too proud to let an old friend lend a hand, that was her call.

It was probably just as well. The whole time they'd been talking—even when she'd been yelling at him—he'd been painfully aware that she was fresh from the bath or shower and almost certainly naked beneath her thin robe. The outline of her nipples had been visible beneath the fabric, her arms and legs pink and bare, her hair damp and clinging to her neck and shoulders… Every time she'd gestured or shifted her weight he'd caught a waft of something heady and floral that made him think of warm summer nights.

Stop thinking about her, man. This is not helping anyone or anything.

He took a pull from his beer, then paused with the can midair as it occurred to him that tonight was the first time he'd seen Pippa without her heavy-framed glasses. He'd always wondered how she'd look without them, and now he knew: too damned attractive for his peace of mind. Without them, the curve of her cheek had been revealed and there'd been nothing to distract him from the plushness of her mouth or the upward tilt of her small nose.

Which bought him full circle to tonight's argument being a good thing. The best thing, really.

He swallowed the last of his beer, then crushed the can and tossed it into the bin. He still didn't feel like watching TV, so he decided to drive to his parents' place. There was a fifty-fifty chance they wouldn't be home, given his mother's love of socializing, but the lights were on when he arrived.

He made his way up the path and gave a perfunctory knock before letting himself into the house.

"It's just me," he called as he shut the door behind him.

"In the kitchen." His mother's voice echoed down the hallway.

He found his parents seated around the table, the plates from their evening meal stacked neatly together, a half-empty bottle of wine and a handful of travel brochures on the table between them.

"Hey. What's up?" He pulled out a chair and dropped into it.

His mother looked at him for a long beat, her gaze unnerving in its intensity.

"What?" Harry said.

"I'm trying to work out why you're here."

"What do you think I'm doing? I'm visiting." He crossed his arms over his chest and stretched his legs out.

"It's Saturday night," his mother said.

"So?"

"When was the last time you stayed in on a Saturday night?"

"I have no idea. And I'm not in. I'm here."

"Which is even more strange." His mother stood. "Is everything all right?"

"Everything's fine. Why wouldn't it be?"

His mother carried the plates to the dishwasher. As usual, she wore a pair of jeans that most of the world would consider too tight for a woman pushing sixty. Her red tank top was equally tight, and the nails on her bare, tanned feet were painted a matching scarlet.

"Are you feeling sick or something?" she asked, concern wrinkling her forehead.

Harry resisted the urge to roll his eyes. "Mum, I'm fine. Change the record. How have you two been?"

"Same as we always are," she said.

His father shuffled the travel brochures together, crossing to the sideboard.

"What are you doing?" his mother said, a sharp note in her voice.

"Putting these away," his father said.

"But we haven't finished talking yet."

"Nothing's going to change, Val, no matter how many times we talk it over." He dropped the brochures into the drawer and pushed it shut.

Harry watched as his mother's mouth got thin, a sure sign she wasn't happy. "Maybe you can talk some sense into your father, Harry. He seems to think we should wait until we're completely fossilized before we start having fun."

"I have fun with you every day," his father said, sounding aggrieved.

His mother made a rude noise, clearly unmoved by the blatant flattery.

"What's the problem?" Harry asked, since it appeared to be expected of him.

"I want to go on a cruise. Libby and Dave up the road went on one and haven't stopped raving. But your father keeps coming up with excuses why we can't go."

Harry looked at his father, who shrugged eloquently. "I can't leave the business. You know what it's like."

Harry frowned. "What about Ben? Can't you leave him in charge for a few weeks?"

"Your mother wants to go for six weeks."

"Why fly all that way if you're not going to make the most of it?" his mother said.

Ben was his father's most senior mechanic, but there was no getting away from the fact he wasn't the most social bloke in the world. Great with an internal combustion engine, not so great with people. While the business might survive a week or two with him at the helm, six weeks was asking for trouble.

"What about Julian?" He was less senior than Ben, but more personable and sharp.

"He's too unreliable, especially now he's broken up with his girlfriend."

"What the business needs is a good senior mechanic with a smart head on his shoulders and a vested interest in the business," his mother said pointedly.

His father shot her a look. "Val."

"I'm just making an observation."

Harry contemplated the toes of his boots, aware that his mother's comment was a dig at him. When he didn't rise to the bait, she shut the dishwasher door so hard the plates rattled.

"Sometimes, Harry Neville, you really try my patience."

Harry sighed. It seemed his day was destined to suck no matter where he went. "Dad would be better off hiring a manager. I'm not cut out to run a small business."

It was the same argument he'd put forward the last time they'd had this discussion.

"Bullshit, Harry. God, it drives me crazy when you say that."

"It's true. I'm hopeless at admin stuff. I wouldn't have a clue how to hire and fire staff. Just because I'm family doesn't mean I'd be any good."

"You could do anything you put your mind to, and you know it. Don't think I've forgotten those straight A's you got in high school. The truth is you don't want to do it. That's all it is."

Harry met his mum's gaze. He was sick of pussyfooting around this issue. Maybe it was time to put it to bed once and for all.

"Okay. You want the truth? You're right, I don't want it. Dad's the one who had the burning desire to be his own boss, but that was never my dream. I like being a soldier ant. I like doing my hours and taking my wages and living my life without all the stress and crap I see Dad go through, worrying about taxes and superannuation and workers' compensation and whatever." Harry cut his gaze to his father. "No offense, Dad, but I don't want to be a slave to anyone or anything."

"Why do you think your father started the business? For exactly that reason. How are you not a slave when you're marching to the beat of someone else's drum, jumping when he says to?" his mother demanded. "Honestly, Harry, I don't understand how you can have this so backward."

Harry rose. If he stayed any longer, he would say something he'd regret.

"I'm going. Sorry for upsetting you." He glanced at his mother first, then his father. Then he headed for the door, shoulders tight.

He was descending the steps when he heard the screen door swing shut behind him.

"Wait up a minute."

He paused, giving his father a chance to catch up. He eyed him warily when his father joined him.

"I'm sorry, Dad, but I don't want to get into this now. I've had a crappy day, and this is pretty much the cherry on top."

His father's hand landed on his shoulder, heavy and warm. He squeezed once, firmly, before letting go and walking toward Harry's car.

"How's the Monaro running? You ever get around to switching out the fuel pump?"

It took Harry a moment to understand his father hadn't followed him to keep prosecuting his case.

"Haven't got around to it yet, but she's been running sweet lately so I might hold fire for a bit."

"Still thinking of replacing the shockers?"

"Yeah. Next month, maybe."

"Let me know and I'll help you out."

"Thanks."

They stopped beside the car. Even though it was his mother who had pursued the why-won't-you-come-work-with-your-father line this time around, Harry knew it was something his dad wanted. It was impossible to tell what his father was thinking or feeling, however. He'd always had a good poker face and tonight it was utterly inscrutable as they both pretended to inspect the Monaro.

"There must be some way you and Mum can take that cruise," Harry said after a short silence.

"We'll work it out. Don't worry about it." His father offered him a small, distracted smile and took a step backward. "Everything turn out okay with your friend?"

It took Harry a moment to understand his father meant Pippa.

"You could say that."

His father smiled properly this time. "Give you a hard time, did she?"

"Something like that."

His father turned toward the house, still smiling. "Thought she might."

He lifted a hand in farewell. Harry watched him walk away, noting the gray in his father's hair. There had been a time when his father's hair had been more pepper than salt, but the ratio had reversed in recent years. His father's shoulders were still strong and broad, though, his arms still thick with muscle. To Harry, he seemed as powerful and vital a presence as he'd ever been.

Unsettled, he got in the car. As much as his mother's emotional appeal had made him uncomfortable, he disliked his father's quiet acceptance even more because he knew it hid a wealth of disappointment.

Harry thumped the heel of his hand against the steering wheel, feeling cornered and small and immeasurably shitty as a result. Not once had he ever indicated by word or deed that he was interested in taking over the garage. In fact, he'd done the exact opposite, leaving his father's employ the moment his apprenticeship was finalized to avoid setting up expectations that would never be fulfilled.

He didn't want the responsibility, and he didn't want the worry. He wasn't the kind of man who craved big houses and expensive cars. He valued his freedom more than any material thing money could buy, and the thought of taking on the burden of the business, of being responsible for eight employees and his father's legacy... It made him feel like he was choking. As though the walls were closing in.

The Monaro started with a dull roar and he headed for home, where he probably should have stayed in the first place.

CHAPTER SIX

PIPPA WOKE TO Alice crying at five in the morning. She prepared a bottle and sat in the old armchair in Alice's room, watching her guzzle half a bottle before falling into a milky drowse. Smiling, Pippa put Alice to bed and went into the kitchen to make her own breakfast. It was still dark outside and she sat on the arm of the sofa in the sunroom, eating her toast and watching the dark sky turn gray and then pink with dawn.

Because Pippa didn't want to put off making her apology any longer than she had to, the moment Alice woke again at nine she dressed her and packed her into the car. Pippa swung by the bakery on the way to Harry's place, picking up a bag of doughnuts to sweeten her apology. When in doubt, bribe with food. It was a strategy that usually worked with Alice, and Pippa figured Harry probably wasn't that different.

She had an apology worked out. She'd started formulating it last night and perfected it this morning while she cleaned the house and waited for Alice to wake. She would tell Harry he was generous and kind and that she had spoken too hastily last night, letting her pride do the talking. She would tell him she appreciated everything he'd done and that she hoped he might one day forget she had been such a prickly, ungrateful cow. Then she would offer him the doughnuts and hopefully a miracle would occur and he'd smile and tell her it was okay, he didn't think she was a complete psycho-hose-beast.

The last bit was wishful thinking, but she figured she was in with a mild chance that he'd forgive her. Maybe.

She chewed her bottom lip as she parked in front of his house. Both his car and the old truck were in the driveway, a good sign he was home. This time she took Alice with her as she approached the front door. After knocking three times, she was forced to conclude that either Harry wasn't home, or he was so deeply asleep he was in a coma. She suspected it was option A, which meant she would have to delay her apology. Damn it.

She could leave the doughnuts on his doorstep, but they were covered with sugar and redolent of jam and the odds were good that the ants would find them before Harry did.

She drove home, set the doughnuts on the kitchen counter and told herself she would try again in the afternoon. Then she dragged out her textbooks to look for quotes to support the central argument in her essay.

She studied all morning and into the afternoon. At three o'clock she drove to Harry's place again, only to discover that his car was gone this time, a sure sign he was out.

She stared at his house, frustration welling inside her. She wanted this done, wanted to right her wrong, if that was possible, and get on with her life.

Fate had other ideas, because Harry still wasn't home when she tried again in the early evening, and he wasn't there the next day, either, when she'd be certain she would catch him after work. By that time the doughnuts were past their best—certainly they were past being used as a shameless suck-up. She ate three, then gave the remainder to the family next door in deference to the size of her backside.

Tuesday dawned gray and overcast, a perfect reflection of her mood. She worked a long shift at the gallery, picking up Alice from day care as the heavens opened and it began to pour. Pippa swung past Harry's place, feeling like a stalker, she'd been up and down his street so many times. Surely he must be home. Who went out in weather like this?

She swore under her breath when she saw that, once again, the black muscle car was missing.

What is wrong with you, Harry? Don't you like your home or something?

Where on earth could he be? Not surfing, which had been her explanation of choice on Sunday. Not in this weather. And even Harry couldn't hang out with the boys this much.

She frowned as it occurred to her that it was possible he was with a woman. As in a girlfriend. He hadn't mentioned that he was seeing anyone, but that didn't mean anything. It wasn't as though he'd ever been short of female companionship in the time she'd known him. Women responded like catnip to his hard body and the cheeky, knowing glint in his eye.

She was feeling more than a little disgruntled when she turned Old Yeller for home. She told herself she was frustrated because her attempt to do the right thing had been stymied. Definitely it had nothing to do with the idea that Harry might have a girlfriend. His love life had nothing to do with her. At all.

Perhaps it was time to give up on the notion of a face-to-face apology and move to Plan B. Not that she had a Plan B, but she could formulate one.

For instance, when she got home, she could compose

a written apology. She could then leave it on Harry's doorstep with a nice bottle of Scotch, ready for him to discover when he returned home. She had no idea if he drank Scotch, having only ever seen him drink beer, but she hoped that, like the doughnuts, it would be interpreted as a gesture of goodwill.

She liked the idea so much she drove home via the liquor store, purchasing a single malt Scotch with an appropriately Scottish name with lots of badges and coats of arms on the label and a hefty price tag. Between the beer she'd bought for Harry's dad and the bottle of Scotch, she'd pretty much annihilated her budget for the next couple of weeks, but it couldn't be helped. She needed to make amends.

She kissed her daughter's warm cheek as she left the shop. "We're in business, Alice. Once the letter is delivered, we—by which I really mean me—are home free. Sort of."

And hopefully the next time she ran into Harry in six months' time they would both be able to smile at one another the way they had last week.

The house was gloomy when she got home and she flicked on lights and even considered turning on the central heating. She made do with a shawl for herself and a blanket for Alice and sat with her laptop on her knees.

It took her an hour to compose a suitably friendly, regretful apology—not too formal, not too casual, not too sucky, not too flippant. She'd walked a fine line, but she was pretty sure she'd gotten there. Or thereabouts. She printed it, sealed it in an envelope and wrote Harry's name on the front with a sense of relief.

There. Almost done. Once it stopped raining, she'd deliver it and the Scotch. Problem solved.

Dusting her hands together, she stowed away her laptop, then registered the steady drip-drip-drip of water. She went into the hall, looking toward the bathroom. But the sound was coming from somewhere much closer. She frowned at the closed doorway to Alice's bedroom, then pushed it open. She flicked on the light. The room was illuminated for half a second before the bulb blew, but it was long enough for her to see a growing wet patch on the carpet.

The roof was leaking. Just what she needed.

She grabbed the flashlight from the kitchen cupboard and returned to Alice's room, aiming it at the ceiling. A dark stain marred the plaster, and water dripped down the wiring for the pendant lamp.

She didn't know much about electricity, but it struck her she had been extremely lucky she hadn't been electrocuted when she flicked on the light.

Thank God Alice hadn't been in her room during any of this.

She grabbed her phone and called the landlord, Peter. He was a master of excuses, but he had to do something about a leaky roof. If for no other reason than that it could cause permanent and expensive damage to his property.

The phone rang and rang before going to voice mail and she listened with growing outrage as her landlord explained he was on holiday and wouldn't be back for another two weeks.

Two weeks!

She was so busy reacting to the news she forgot to leave a message and had to call back to ask Peter to please phone her as she had an urgent repair that needed attention. Surely he must have organized for someone to keep an eye on things while he was away?

She aimed the flashlight at the ceiling again, studying the growing damp patch. The way things were going, the plaster would come down in a sodden mess unless someone took care of the leaky roof pronto. Pippa made a rude noise as she imagined how long it would take for Peter to get on to *that* repair. Judging by his track record so far, a year or two. In the meantime, she would have the privilege of living in a house with a hole in the ceiling.

"Damn it."

Mouth pressed into a grim line, she changed into yoga pants and a long-sleeved top, then tied her hair back with a scarf. She made her way to the laundry where the access hatch to the roof space was located.

She'd spent the week lamenting being a victim of circumstances. She wasn't going to wait around for someone to rescue her this time—she would take action herself.

The access hatch was above her washing machine. Even standing on the machine she had no chance of reaching it. She glanced around the room, her gaze falling on the storage unit she'd bought to hold her towels and linen.

Perfect.

A bit of grunting and groaning saw the unit moved into position next to the washing machine. She went into the kitchen and gathered the stack of old ice-cream containers from under the sink. Alice was playing with her Fisher Price toys again, but to be safe Pippa put her in her playpen. Then, armed with the flashlight and her stack of containers, she prepared to do battle with the roof.

It took her a full minute to clamber onto the washing

machine, then onto the storage unit and finally through the access hatch.

It was very dark in the roof cavity, despite the flashlight beam. Unease trickled down her spine as she balanced on a rough wooden rafter on her knees. What were the odds that there were rats and mice up here? She shone the torch around the roof cavity, noting the thin layer of fiberglass fluff masquerading as insulation. No wonder the house was so hot in summer and cold in winter. She aimed the light toward the front of the house. Something glinted in the far distance. It took her a moment to realize it was the flashlight beam reflecting off the stream of water coming in from the roof.

Well, at least she knew which way to crawl.

She made her way slowly forward, shifting from rafter to rafter on her hands and knees, the flashlight clenched between her teeth. Every few feet or so she tossed the ice-cream containers ahead of herself to keep her hands free. She was well aware that any slips would see her crashing through a thin layer of plaster into the room below, and she concentrated fiercely on where she put her knees and hands.

Every now and then she looked up to gauge how much farther she had to go. By the time she'd entered the space above Alice's bedroom, her knees were aching and her nose was itching from all the dust and fiberglass. She sat back on her heels and located the leak with the flashlight beam. Fortunately there was a rafter directly underneath and she was able to place the largest of the containers on a stable footing.

"Thank. God."

She was desperate to make her way back to the access hole, but she forced herself to inspect the surrounding space while she was there. She groaned with dismay when she saw another flash of light on water. Another leak. Above her bedroom, if she hazarded a guess.

"This is ridiculous."

She sighed heavily and clenched the flashlight between her teeth again and crawled, slow painful inch by slow painful inch, toward the second leak. It was close to the front wall where the roof sloped and she had to crouch low and slide the container into position.

"I am so asking for a discount on my bloody rent for this," she muttered as she swiveled on one knee to face the way she'd come.

This time she didn't scan for more leaks, even though she had one remaining container. She was over the dank darkness, her hands and chest felt itchy, her knees ached. She figured she'd done her bit, the rest was up to her landlord.

She was starting the homeward journey when the flashlight beam flickered dramatically.

"No. Don't even think about it." She froze, waiting for the beam to steady again.

When it kept flickering, she tapped it against her thigh.

"Come on. I only need a couple more minutes. Five, tops."

As if in response to her request, the flashlight flickered one last time before it steadied. She let out a grateful sigh.

Then the world went black.

"No. No way. Please don't do this to me," she pleaded as she fumbled in the dark, trying to find the switch on the side of the flashlight.

She flicked the flashlight on and off, then unscrewed the battery cap and jiggled the batteries around a little before screwing it back on.

No dice. The flashlight had deserted her. Leaving her stranded miles from the access hole in a very dark, potentially rat-infested attic.

Pippa swore vehemently, the worst four-letter words she knew. This was what she got for taking action and rescuing herself. Next time she was letting the stupid ceiling cave in.

Her knees screamed for her to move. Her heart in her mouth, she shuffled forward a couple of inches. The distant access hole was the only source of light. She could barely see her own hand in front of her face, let alone the detail of the rafters ahead of her.

Swearing repeatedly under her breath, she crawled forward another few feet. It wasn't as though she had a choice—it was shuffle forward into the unknown, or remain stuck in the dark with no hope of rescue. Especially since she hadn't been smart enough to bring her phone with her.

Her groping hands told her she'd reached a complicated part of the roof where the rafters changed direction, a mess that had been a whole lot easier to navigate with the help of the flashlight. Now, she groped and frowned and inched forward cautiously, flinching every time a splinter dug into her knees or hands but persevering because the only hope of relief was to reach that distant square of light.

A rustling on her left had her head whipping around. She froze, staring into the darkness, one knee balanced precariously on a rafter, the other midair.

Please let that not be a rat. Please.

She couldn't see or hear anything. Maybe it had just been wind. Maybe the noise had even come from *outside* the roof.

Her arms were starting to shake from supporting

the bulk of her weight. She put her knee down. She was lifting her leg to resume her journey when something skittered across her hand. Something sinuous and furry with a long tail and eyes that glinted in the dark.

Pippa didn't think. She simply reacted, screaming and rising up on her knees and flailing with her hands to beat off whatever rodent was in the vicinity.

Everything happened in a blur after that. Her head connected painfully with one of the rafters overhead, her knee slipped, and the next thing she knew she was off balance and toppling to her right. She hit the plaster sheeting with a resonant thunk. It gave instantly, cracking beneath her like too-thin ice and she shrieked as she plunged toward the floor and almost certain injury—only to land on something resilient and forgiving and springy.

It took her a few seconds to understand she was lying on her bed, fragments of plaster beneath and around her. She hadn't broken her leg or fractured her skull. She was alive and relatively well and incredibly, ridiculously lucky.

Her first impulse was to laugh, a great guffaw that spoke more of shock and relief than mirth. Then she rose onto her knees and did a quick body pat to confirm she really was in one piece.

She was. A minor miracle. Heart still hammering against her breastbone, she stood on distinctly shaky legs. Only then did she look up.

She silently mouthed yet another swear word as she took in the woman-sized hole in her bedroom ceiling. Bits of ragged plaster dangled from the hole, and insulation fluff and plaster dotted the bed and floor. She was covered in dust, plaster and cobwebs, with yet more insulation clinging to her clothes.

For a moment she was so overwhelmed she couldn't think. It was such a big hole. Then she remembered Alice and went to check on her daughter.

Alice was sobbing quietly to herself and Pippa guessed she'd probably been crying while Pippa had been stuck in the attic. She didn't dare touch her baby while covered in fiberglass, however, so she made reassuring noises before heading into the bathroom to shower. Barely two minutes later and wrapped in a towel, she lifted Alice into her arms.

"It's okay, sweetheart, Mummy's here. It's all right."

Holding her daughter against her chest and crooning reassurances, she returned to her bedroom doorway.

The hole in the ceiling seemed to have grown since she'd last seen it. She stared into it, cold water dripping down her back from her wet hair.

She needed to have it fixed, of course. She was no expert on home renovation, but she was pretty sure that would run into the hundreds, maybe even the thousands to repair.

For the second time in as many weeks she felt the bite of despair. She'd survived one financial crisis, only to find herself in the middle of another. All because she was an idiot. She should have let the stupid leaky roof destroy the ceiling. At least the repairs would have been the landlord's problem. Now, they were hers.

Even if she couldn't afford to replaster a matchbox, let alone a whole bedroom ceiling.

Pathetic, self-pitying tears pricked the back of her eyes. It was all very well to keep telling herself that things would be better in a year's time when she was qualified and teaching and earning a decent wage but right now, right this minute, she felt helpless and hopeless. It was the car all over again—she didn't have the skill to fix it on her own, and she didn't have the money to pay someone to do it. Not right away, anyway.

Alice stirred in her arms, hands grasping the edge of Pippa's towel. Pippa rocked her automatically, trying to push the horrible overwhelmed feeling to one side so she could think.

She didn't have to repair the ceiling immediately. She could simply sit tight and wait till she had the money to pay for the repairs, as she'd planned to do with her car before Harry had come riding to her rescue. Obviously, she wouldn't be able to use her room, since the thought of sleeping with a gaping hole above her head made her shiver. But there was a perfectly good couch in the sunroom. She could sleep out there until she'd saved the funds.

Even as the thought crossed her mind her mood dropped another notch. She didn't want to camp out in her own home. There must be some other way. Maybe she could patch the ceiling herself somehow or come up with some other kind of temporary measure?

She dismissed the notion after barely a moment's thought. She was about as handy as Ivana Trump—i.e. not very. Pippa had wreaked enough havoc without attempting to do some sort of half-assed, half-baked repair job.

She would simply have to suck it up, the way she'd sucked up everything else life had thrown at her in the past couple of years. Living with a dirty great hole in the ceiling wouldn't kill her.

Turning her back on the mess she'd made, she returned to the kitchen, telling herself that within a day tonight's events would be miraculously transformed into a hilarious dinner party anecdote thanks to a good night's sleep and a little perspective.

Here's hoping.

She was rounding the counter to turn on the kettle when her gaze landed on the bottle of whiskey she'd bought for Harry. She stopped dead in her tracks as a single, incredibly inappropriate thought hit her.

Harry would know what to do.

Hell, Harry could probably fix her ceiling with one well-muscled arm behind his back.

She shook her head. It was a dumb thought. She couldn't ask him to come running to her aid again. Not after the way she'd gotten all over him when he'd offered to fix her door. Any goodwill he might have had toward her had been well and truly worn out by her own stubborn, prideful behavior.

You are such an idiot.

She didn't flinch from her own self-assessment because she knew she deserved it. Not simply because of the way she'd reacted when Harry had so good-naturedly offered to help her out, but because even now when she had the opportunity to ask for help from someone who had always been kind to her, her pride demanded that she find some other way to handle the situation rather than throw herself at Harry's mercy. Even if that meant sleeping on the couch for weeks, and even if she knew in her bones that he wouldn't hesitate to help her, no questions asked.

The other night she'd asked Harry if her being a single parent meant that she wasn't allowed to retain any dignity. Standing in her self-sabotaged house, she couldn't help thinking that maybe she'd valued dignity a lot higher than perhaps she should have.

Maybe survival was more important. Maybe gracious acceptance of the fact that, at this particular moment in her life, she needed help held more weight.

Maybe she couldn't afford to be proud right now. Maybe that was what being a good mother and growing up was all about.

She stared at the bottle. Then, before she could talk herself out of it, she reached for the phone.

HARRY SPENT THE ten-minute drive from his place to Pippa's trying to understand why she'd phoned him. After the way they'd parted, he'd figured he'd be at the very bottom of her SOS list. Yet something bad had happened, and he was the person she'd turned to.

Even more confusing and mysterious to him was his reaction. He'd felt a definite thud of satisfaction when he'd heard her voice, a feeling that had only intensified when she'd confessed why she was calling. He'd been on the way out to play basketball with some friends, but he'd bailed on his mates rather than disappoint her. Because she needed him.

Crazy, confusing, messed-up stuff.

The porch light was on when he pulled into the driveway. He ran through the rain, his toolbox a heavy weight against his leg. She opened the door wearing a pair of old jeans and a sweatshirt, her wet hair in a messy ponytail, her glasses balanced near the end of her nose.

"You didn't have to come straight over, you know. It's not that kind of an emergency." She looked guilty, uncomfortable and sheepish.

He tightened his grip on the handle of his toolbox. It was either that or give in to the sudden urge to grab her by the shoulders and shake her till her teeth rattled.

She'd fallen through the ceiling. She could have broken her neck, her back, an arm, a leg…. She could be lying unconscious right now.

"Are you okay?" he asked.

"I'm fine. As I said on the phone, the bed broke my fall."

"You didn't knock your head or twist anything?" He didn't know why he couldn't take her at her word.

"I'm fine. Honestly. Apart from feeling like the biggest dick under the sun."

"Yeah, well. If the shoe fits…"

"Thanks."

He shrugged. She could have killed herself. He wasn't about to let her off the hook.

"If the flashlight hadn't gone out, I would have been fine."

"If the bed hadn't been there, you'd be in hospital."

"You sound like a parent."

He felt like one, too. Not a sensation he was particularly familiar with.

"Maybe you should show me the damage."

"There's something I need to give you first." She started down the hallway.

It took him a moment to follow her. He was too busy watching her ass as she walked toward the kitchen. He'd never seen her in jeans before. It was a revelation—and not a welcome one.

The soft denim hugged her full, rounded bottom. Her hips swayed from side to side. He found himself wondering if her panties were as colorful as the cherry-red bra she'd been wearing the other day and if she was a matching set kind of girl, or more the mix and match type. Then she stepped around the door she'd refused to let him fix and suddenly it was a whole lot easier to remember why he was here and why it was a bad idea for him to be staring at her butt.

His mind firmly on the matter at hand, he followed

her into the kitchen. She picked up a bottle of whiskey and offered it to him.

"This is for you. To apologize for the other night." She pushed her glasses to the bridge of her nose, a sure-fire giveaway she was nervous. "And this, too."

She offered him a crisp white envelope bearing his name in neat black handwriting.

He frowned. "You don't need to apologize."

"Harry, come on. We both know I do. I behaved like a petulant, spoiled schoolgirl."

He opened his mouth to deny it but she simply thrust the letter into his hand.

"Read it. Put me out of my misery."

"I don't need to read it. Apology accepted."

She gave him a pained look. "You can't just let me off the hook like that."

"Why not?"

"Because I deserve to squirm."

"Pippa, we're cool. Relax."

"Okay, if you won't read it, I'll say it. I was horrible the other night. I took all my frustration with Steve and my life in general out on you, all because you had the gall to offer to help me out. God forbid. Which was incredibly kind and generous and noble of you, by the way. In short, Harry, I'm unreservedly sorry for everything I said, and I hope you can forgive me."

"There's nothing to forgive."

She made a frustrated noise. "Sometimes you're too nice for your own good, do you know that?"

"I'm not nice." If she knew he'd been staring at her ass thirty seconds ago, wondering what color panties she was wearing, she wouldn't think he was nice. If she knew that he'd been thinking about the creamy fullness of her breasts for the past few days, and how good she'd felt when she'd embraced him, baby and all, she'd know exactly how down and dirty he could be.

"Well, I've yet to see any evidence of that, so we'll have to agree to disagree on that one."

She smiled at him, a cheeky, challenging smile that reminded him of all the smart-ass wisecracks she'd thrown his way. He felt a sudden, almost overwhelming surge of affection for her. He liked this woman. He liked her honesty. He liked her attitude and her smarts—hell, he even liked her feistiness, though it meant he'd been on the wrong end of her tongue more than a few times.

If it hadn't been for Steve, if they'd met anywhere else, under any other circumstances...

"So where's this hole?" he said.

Because there was no point thinking about what might have been. Nothing would change who she was or who he was.

Anyway, she'd probably laugh in his face if she knew what he was thinking. She'd never said it, but she'd been slumming it when she went out with Steve. She was educated and smart and arty—he and Steve were blue-collar guys who worked with their hands for a living and only opened a newspaper to find the cartoons and the sports section.

"It's in my room."

He kept his gaze strictly on the back of her head as she led him to her bedroom. She gestured for him to precede her into the room. His gaze swept briefly over the bed and tallboy, and a pile of debris that had been pushed into the corner, before rising to the ceiling. He whistled when he saw the mighty hole she'd punched in the plaster and she gave him a nervous look.

"So, what do you think? Is it fixable? Or do I need to

call in a builder?" She pushed her glasses up her nose again, then crossed her arms over her chest.

"You ever thought about getting a pair of glasses that stay up on their own?"

"Sorry?"

"Your glasses. They're always falling off."

"Oh. Right. That's because they're vintage. Technically, they're probably too big for my face. But I love them." She shrugged, her eyes lifting to the ceiling, worry once again filling their depths as she waited for his assessment.

"Relax. It's fixable."

"Really? Honestly?"

"Yeah. It'll take a bit of patching and some paint, but it's not a big job."

"Really?" She sounded hugely relieved. As though he'd taken a massive weight off her shoulders. "I thought it would cost a fortune to fix. But if it's not that big a deal, maybe I should talk to a plasterer or a builder or whoever fixes these kinds of things."

"Save your money." He walked to the kitchen to collect his toolbox.

When he returned, Pippa moved to one side as he stood on her bed and reached up to assess the plaster more closely. Using the claw on his hammer, he dragged the dangling chunks of board free and tossed them to the floor.

"You've punched through two sheets of plaster. The easiest thing to do is to rip them out completely and replace them. Once the joins are patched and plastered and the whole lot painted, no one will ever know anything happened."

"Apart from the fact that it will be the nicest, newest, cleanest part of the house," Pippa said.

"If you say so." He glanced around her room, noting the embroidered cuff on the snowy-white sheets on her bed, the silky-looking robe hanging on the hook near the door, the many-hued floral patchwork quilt folded across the foot of the bed. Pairs of well-worn shoes sat along one wall, lined up like good little soldiers, and a chair in the corner was draped with colorful scarves and discarded pieces of clothing.

It was a feminine room, but not in a bad way. It was soft, comfortable and welcoming. The kind of room it would be easy to while away a lot of hours in. Unlike his own bedroom, which boasted a bed, one bedside table and precious little else.

"It'll take a day to get the supplies, then I'll start."

"It's not urgent. I can sleep on the couch for a few weeks," Pippa said quickly.

He glanced at the hole again. "Afraid there are rats up there, huh?"

"I *know* there are. Why do you think I fell through the ceiling?"

"Then I'll pick up some bait stations, too, while I'm at it. And I'll be here after work tomorrow. That okay with you?"

Pippa's warm brown eyes softened with gratitude. "Harry… Thank you. For coming so quickly. For being so bloody generous—"

"About that. I have a couple of conditions." Might as well get a few things straight up front.

"Conditions?"

"If I fix the roof, I also fix the door and the lock. It's a package deal."

She blinked, then a slow, grudging smile curved her mouth. "You've got a real thing about that door, haven't you?"

"It's a fire hazard."

She gave him an assessing look. "Okay. You can fix the door and the lock—on the proviso that I cover any and all expenses, and that you accept dinner from me every night you work here." She raised her eyebrows expectantly as she waited for his response.

"I don't eat salad," he said, tossing his hammer into his toolbox. "And I hate pumpkin."

"Then I definitely won't make you my roast pumpkin and feta salad." She was grinning, pleased with herself.

For some reason, he thought of Steve. His friend had had this woman with her infectious smiles and wit and creamy skin and colorful underwear in his life, and he'd let her go. Worse, he'd abandoned her when she needed him the most.

"I should go." He hefted his toolbox and headed for the door. He could feel her following him.

"Sure. I'll see you out," she said, brushing past him.

It was tempting, but he didn't say a word as she wrestled the door open. Her expression was wry as she stood to one side to let him pass.

"Very big of you."

"No point being a sore winner."

She laughed, low and throaty. He'd always liked her laugh.

"I'll see you tomorrow night," he said.

"Bring your appetite."

Like that was going to be a problem.

He stepped out into the rainy night. When he got to his car, he glanced over his shoulder. Pippa was silhouetted in the doorway, the hall light a golden nimbus around her head.

He had a sudden, stupid urge to climb the steps and ask her if she felt it, too—the sharp, insistent pull of desire and need and attraction whenever he was with her. Did she look at him and wonder what his mouth would feel like on hers? Did she think about his body, about how his skin would feel against hers? Did she wonder what it would be like to be naked, to have him slide inside her...?

He got in his car, started the engine and reversed into the street, not allowing himself another glance at the house. There was no way he was having that conversation with her. Steve might be behaving like an asshole of the highest order right now, but it didn't change the fact that he was Harry's oldest friend.

Pippa was taboo. End of story, nothing to see here, please move on.

Any second now he figured the raging hard-on in his jeans would get the memo. Any second.

CHAPTER SEVEN

SHE HAD OVER-PREPARED. She knew she had, yet it didn't stop her from peeling another potato and placing it on the baking tray.

Pippa couldn't afford to pay Harry in any conventional sense, but one thing she could do was ensure he never went home hungry while he helped her out. Tonight she was offering him roast beef, roast potatoes, fresh green beans and peas, homemade gravy and apple pie for dessert. She had beer in the fridge, and the moment she'd arrived home from university she'd showered and changed into her jeans and a T-shirt so that she'd be ready to act as his right-hand woman, should he need her.

A little voice pointed out that the shower part hadn't been strictly necessary, nor had the bit where she'd smoothed on lipstick and spritzed on perfume. She chose not to examine her motive for either too closely. Mostly because she was already more than aware she'd developed what could only be described as a crush on her ex-boyfriend's best friend.

She wasn't sure when she'd stopped kidding herself. Maybe it was the moment when she'd opened the door last night to Harry on her porch, rain glinting in his short dark hair, toolbox by his side, looking lean and mean and powerful in a black T-shirt and dark denim jeans less than fifteen minutes after she'd asked for his help.

Or maybe it was the moment in her bedroom when he'd insisted on striking a deal with her before he consented to helping out with the ceiling repair.

Maybe it was a combination of all of the above, along with the fact that when he was in the vicinity she was achingly aware of where his body was in relation to hers, of how wide his shoulders were, how deep his chest, how powerful his thighs. If she closed her eyes, she could summon the smell of him—warm skin and clean soap—and she could remember exactly how hot and hard his body had felt when she'd given him that impulsive, impromptu hug.

Your basic, garden-variety crush, really, complete with inappropriate sexual fantasies and sweaty palms and racing heart rate because he was due any second and she'd been both anticipating and dreading seeing him again all day.

The anticipation was for obvious reasons, the dread because she was terrified she would embarrass herself by doing or saying something over the next few nights to clue Harry in to her developing obsession. She was smart enough to know that nothing would ever happen between them. Not only was she the absolute antithesis of the bar bunnies he usually hooked up with, she was also Steve's ex-girlfriend. Harry might look like an outlaw, with his tattoos and his piercings and his burly build, but at heart he was a deeply honorable man with a very strict personal code. In his head, she was Steve's, even though the relationship had ended more than a year ago and they were about as estranged as two people could get.

Satisfied that dinner was more or less ready to roll,

she went to check on Alice. Sure enough, there had been action down south and she gave her daughter a quick bath after wiping up the mess. Dressing her daughter, Pippa reminded herself there were other reasons why her crush on Harry should remain only her private, dirty little secret.

Like Steve, Harry was a player. A sexy boy-man who treated life as though it was an extended long weekend. He lived for his mates, saw women as playthings and avoided responsibility as though it was contagious.

A woman would have to be crazy in the coconut to even consider going there.

Okay. We done with the protesting-too-much? Because it's getting wayyy *old and it's pointless. Nothing will happen with Harry for the very simple fact that you have learned your lesson where guys like him are concerned. Right? Right?*

Pippa's hands stilled on the snap fasteners on Alice's Onesie.

She didn't like thinking about the dark days immediately following her discovery that she was pregnant, but perhaps now was a good time for a reminder of how grim it had been. She had been alone and scared, and she had been bitter, angry and hurt after Steve's rejection. Most of that bitterness and anger had been directed at herself. She was the one who had chosen Steve, after all. She was the one who'd entrusted him with her body. It had been her decision to spend six months of her life with him. Her poor judgment. And the knowledge that her unborn child would be the one to bear the consequences of her choices had sent Pippa spiraling into despair.

Her mother's warm, practical support and her own innate fighting spirit had saved the day. She'd pulled herself together, gotten her life on track. Enrolled for her diploma, started saving in earnest for the hard months after the birth when she wouldn't be able to work. And she hadn't looked back.

Pippa closed the last snap, smiling as Alice gurgled her approval. The anxiety and excitement had all but faded in the face of her self-enforced reality check.

Harry might be roguish and hot, but he was not for her. Not in a million years.

The doorbell rang, and she hoisted Alice into her arms and went to answer the door.

"I do like a man who's prompt," she said as she swung it wide.

Harry's gaze swept over her before returning to her face. "Is that dinner I can smell?"

"Why, yes, honey, it is. Can I take your tool belt for you before I fetch your pipe and slippers?"

He didn't say a word, simply gave her a look before carrying his toolbox into the house. The moment he'd dumped it in the hall, he headed back out to his car. She tucked Alice into her crib for safety before joining him to help bring in the remainder of his gear and supplies. After several trips there were two sheets of plaster leaning against the hall wall, a ladder, a can of ceiling paint and a bunch of painting gear. Harry dropped a power saw beside it all and dusted his hands together, eyeing her expectantly.

She laughed. "All right, I'll feed you."

She waved him into a chair at the dining table, which she'd set for two, then crossed to the fridge for a beer for him.

When he saw it in her hand he shook his head.

"Not for me, thanks. Not while I'm working."

"Oh. Okay."

Nonplussed, she put the beer back. Steve had never said no to a drink. In fact, he'd never said no to anything that involved pleasure or excess.

She felt oddly domestic as she carved the roast beef and served the vegetables, very aware of Harry at the table, waiting for his meal.

She tried to think of something to say, but her mind steadfastly refused to come to the party. In the end, she fell back on convention.

"So, um, how was your day?"

"Busy. But it always is at this time of year."

She looked at him blankly.

"Summer, the lead-up to Christmas holidays," he elaborated. "Everyone suddenly remembers they should get their car serviced before they take off on the family holiday."

"Right. Of course."

She poured gravy onto both plates, then ferried them to the table.

"This looks great."

She gave him a quick smile to acknowledge his compliment. For some reason she was having trouble meeting his eyes. "Let me know if you want more gravy."

Right on cue, Alice's cry cut through the house. Pippa stood.

"Don't even think about stopping eating. I'll be back in a tick."

She returned with Alice in her arms, then sat and balanced Alice on her knee with well-practiced expertise.

"One-handed eating," Harry said. "Haven't seen that since Justine's kids were little."

"It's a life skill, that's for sure."

Silence fell as they both concentrated on their meals. Pippa tried to work out why everything felt so strained all of a sudden. She and Harry had never had trouble finding something to talk about before.

"How are your studies going?" Harry asked after a few uncomfortable minutes.

"I'm getting there. I have a killer assignment due before the end of the year, but then I'm free until March. Which will be a relief, because homework sucks as much as an adult as it did when I was in high school."

"I've been thinking about it, and I can't imagine you as a teacher."

"Why not?"

"I don't know. You don't look like any of the teachers I had when I was at school."

"I'm not sure if that's an insult or not," she said.

"It's a compliment. Trust me. I don't think we had a female teacher under fifty at our school."

"Poor you. Guess you had no distractions in class, then."

He grinned suddenly. "Oh, no. There were always plenty of distractions. Shannon Lewis, Carolyn Crosby, Nicole Townsend…"

"Even you didn't have that many girlfriends in high school," she scoffed.

"Define *girlfriend*."

She held up a hand. "You know what? I don't want to know."

He laughed. "Relax. I wasn't that much of a player."

She gave him a skeptical look. "When did you have your first kiss? Eleven? Twelve."

"How precocious do you think I was?"

"Very."

He shrugged a shoulder. "I was thirteen."

She pointed a thumb at her chest. "Sixteen."

"Late starter, huh?"

"Just picky."

"You think I'm not picky?"

She took a moment before responding, spearing peas with her fork. "Actually, I think you're very picky. Why else would you still be single?"

He sat back in his chair and frowned at her. She had surprised him.

"I'm single because I've tried it the other way and it didn't work for me."

Honestly, she couldn't imagine him all settled down and domesticated.

"What?" he asked.

"I'm trying to imagine you buying tampons and milk."

"I did it. Mowed the lawn and opened up a joint bank account, too."

"When was this?" Not in the past few years or she would know about it already.

"When I was twenty-three."

"Pretty young to settle down."

"Yeah."

"Do you still see her?"

"Deb? No. She wound up hating me." His gaze was distant for a moment.

Not a happy time, clearly. She felt bad for bringing it up. "Sorry."

He shrugged. "Why? It wasn't your fault. If it was anyone's, it was mine. I'm not cut out for that kind of life."

"So, what? You're just going to play the field for the rest of your life? A different woman every week?"

He looked amused. "I don't have a different woman every week."

She made a disbelieving noise. She'd seen the way women eyed him off at the pub.

Harry took a long swallow from his water. "I don't get around as much as you seem to think I do. And I'm always up front with women. Always."

She propped an elbow on the table and rested her chin on her hand, genuinely fascinated now. "*Up front.* Tell me what that means." She made a "gimme more" motion with her fingers.

"It means what it says. I tell them I'm looking for a bit of fun and that I'm no good at relationships. If they want to leave it at that, they can. But if anything happens afterward, they know the score."

Poor, poor women. The man should come with a health warning tattooed on his forehead.

"You realize that's like catnip for some women, right? The whole 'I'm no good at relationships' thing. Some women hear that and automatically add 'because I haven't met the right woman yet' in their heads. Which makes you a challenge, and them the transforming magical woman who convinces you love and marriage isn't so bad after all."

"I think you're making it far too complicated."

"I'm a woman. Being complicated is part of my stock in trade."

"At least you admit it."

She cocked her head to one side. "Why do men always think that being simple is a virtue?"

"Because it is?"

She pretended to think about it. "No. That's not it."

He grinned.

She leaned across and collected his empty plate. "Hold that thought."

She dumped the plates in the sink, feeling unaccountably buoyant. She got a kick out of sparring with Harry. She always had.

Good for you—as long as you keep in mind what he just told you while you're getting your kicks.

It was a timely warning, but it was hardly needed. She knew the score with Harry. She always had. He was fun. Cocky and cheeky and sexy—and a terrible, terrible bet for any woman who was looking for more. As he'd admitted.

Only an idiot with strong self-destructive impulses would sashay into that particular dead-end alley, and she might be many things, but she wasn't *that* stupid.

She was simply enjoying herself. Enjoying a bit of harmless banter with a hot member of the opposite sex. For Harry this kind of thing was like breathing and sneezing—utterly instinctive. It meant less than nothing and was going nowhere—hence the reason it was so enjoyable.

They kept up the banter through dessert, then Harry took their plates to the sink and rinsed them.

"Time for me to meet my end of the bargain, I think," he said as he turned away from the sink.

"I'll try to settle Alice, then I'll be in to help."

She carried her daughter into the sunroom and set her in the bassinet. Harry entered as she was tucking the blanket in around Alice's feet.

"I put her in here so she won't wake up if we make noise," she explained, glancing over her shoulder.

He looked at Alice with an unreadable expression on his face. "I didn't notice before, but she's got your nose and jaw."

Pippa considered her daughter's face. "It's funny, but all I can see is Steve. She has his hair and hairline. And his eyes."

"She looks like you, too." He crouched beside Alice and ran a finger lightly over her downy hair.

Pippa wasn't sure what it was, but there was something about his large, work-toughened hand touching her daughter so gently, so tenderly… All of a sudden a lump formed in her throat and she blinked rapidly to dispel totally inappropriate tears.

As if he could sense her inner turmoil, Harry glanced at her. She pulled a face, trying to make light of her stupid emotionalism.

"Sorry. Mummy hormones. Steve has only seen her one time, the day she was born…." She sniffed mightily, willing her stupid tear ducts to dry up.

Harry's mouth settled into a tight line as he returned his gaze to Alice. They both watched her daughter in silence.

"He'll come round, you know," Harry said. "I know him pretty well, and he'll come round."

"It says a lot of good things about you that you believe that, Harry, but I can't live my life banking on that. It's not fair to Alice. And it's not fair to me, either."

He didn't argue with her. What was there to say, after all?

She slapped her palms against her thighs and forced a smile. "So. This hole we're supposed to be repairing…"

Harry led the way to the bedroom, surveying the area briefly before turning to her. "It's going to get messy. I've got some drop sheets, but I think we should put your bed in the hall, since you're sleeping on the couch anyway."

"Okay, sure. I'll get rid of the bedding…."

She'd done a cursory cleanup last night, removing the worst of the debris and vacuuming up the insulation. Now, she tugged the quilt and sheets free and dumped them in Alice's room. When she returned, Harry already had her mattress off the bed and was manhandling it through the door. She helped him lean it against the wall, then returned to the bedroom to move the box spring. Lifting it revealed the many small odds and ends she stored beneath the bed—a pretty keepsake box, stacks of books, a few pairs of old shoes, her radio—as well as dust bunnies the size of small ponies.

"What can I say? Vacuuming is not my forte," she said when Harry nudged one with the toe of his boot.

"Better be careful one of them doesn't crawl up and eat you in your sleep."

"Idiot. Everyone knows dust bunnies are vegetarians. As if."

They were both smiling as they shuffled the box spring into the hallway and leaned it against the mattress. When they returned to the bedroom she knelt on the floor and began collecting the books. Harry leaned down to unplug the radio. Out of the corner of her eye she saw him reach for the keepsake box and an alarm sounded deep in her brain, sending a spurt of adrenaline rocketing through her body.

If anyone should be moving that box, it was her. In fact, if she'd been thinking with even a single brain cell, she would have anticipated this scenario and hidden it deep in the closet hours before he was due.

Acting on instinct, she shot out a hand to intercept him, hoping to beat him to the box. "I've got it," she blurted.

Not her smartest move ever.

Her hand collided with the side of the box as Harry grasped it, knocking it from his hand. She watched with dawning horror as it tumbled to the floor. The lid popped off, and the contents fell out and rolled across the floor.

Shit.

For a moment they were both very still as they stared at her hot-pink silicone vibrator, complete with spare batteries—just in case—and a small tube of personal lubricant.

Heat roared into her face. For a moment she could do nothing but breathe. She didn't dare think of making eye contact with Harry. Instead, she reached out and ever-so-calmly popped the vibrator into the box, along with her other goodies. Standing, she crossed to the tallboy, opened the top drawer and stuffed the whole thing in amongst her underwear.

She pushed the drawer closed, her hand clenched around the knob, painfully aware that she needed to face Harry.

Pippa didn't move. She felt as though every muscle in her body was stiff with embarrassment. God only knew what he was thinking of her.

That she was a horny single mum.

That she lay in her bed at night thinking about sex and men. That she was gagging for it.

You've got to admit, some of those things are true.

Not all of them, and not all of the time. For example, she didn't lie in bed *every* night thinking about sex and men. And she wouldn't describe her desire for sex as *gagging,* exactly. But she did miss sex. She did miss the hard strength of a man's body. She missed the sweaty earthiness, the needfulness of the sex act. She missed the intimacy and simplicity and the rawness and the release of it.

She missed feeling desired, and the warm, languorous few seconds afterward when her body was loose and satisfied and her brain ceased to function and simply *was*.

She missed feeling like more than a mother, missed feeling like a woman.

It won't get any easier. Turn around, say something clever, move on.

She unclenched her hand, took a deep breath and turned around.

Harry was winding the cord around the body of the radio, his movements very neat and precise. He didn't look up, and he didn't say anything. She tried to think of something witty to say, but her brain was still ringing with humiliation. Instead, she resumed collecting the books. She transferred them to the hall. Harry followed, placing her radio alongside them. They returned to her bedroom together and stared at the empty space they'd created.

"Lots of women have one," she said suddenly. "Women have needs, too, even if we don't run around advertising them on billboards. I refuse to feel embarrassed about a perfectly natural act."

"Then don't." He sounded pretty matter-of-fact.

She looked at him out of the corner of her eyes. He appeared pretty matter-of-fact, too. He caught her looking and shrugged.

"In case you haven't worked it out, I'm the last person who will ever judge a woman for seeking a little pleasure."

Huh.

She thought about it for a second and decided she believed him. Some of the tension left her shoulders. So he knew that she occasionally got off in the privacy of her bedroom with the aid of a battery-operated device. Big deal. They were both grown-ups. He probably did…things in the privacy of his own bedroom, too.

She cleared her throat. "I guess you'll want to set up the ladder now, yeah?"

He did, putting down drop cloths first before positioning the ladder to one side of the hole. She stood clear as he donned a face mask, grabbed his hammer, climbed the ladder and started pulling down the remainder of the two sheets of plaster. Dust filled the air and she retreated into the hallway. Five minutes later, that job was done, the room was filled with what looked like mist and Harry was standing in the middle of it, his hair and face and body covered with plaster dust.

Any other man would look stupid, like a man-sized sugar-doughnut. Harry looked like a Greek statue come to life, hard and tough and perfectly proportioned.

She crossed to the window and opened it, then they put the debris into garbage bags. It wasn't comfortable—she was still way too self-conscious over the *reveal* to feel comfortable—but it was bearable, and the next hour flew by as Harry hauled the new plaster sheets up the ladder and screwed them in place. She helped by holding each sheet up with the aid of a broom to extend the reach of her arms, bracing her body beneath the handle and gritting her teeth until her arms and legs trembled with the effort. By the time he'd installed both sheets she was dripping with sweat and wrung out.

"Enough for tonight," Harry said, tossing his hammer into his toolbox.

"If you're stopping because of me, I can keep going."

"Sure you can, slugger."

She decided not to argue with him, since she really

didn't have the energy. She helped him pack his gear for the night then offered him a coffee.

He hesitated a moment before shaking his head. "Thanks, but I'd better make tracks."

She saw him to the door and waved him off, just as she had last night. The second she closed the door, the moment with her vibrator sprung out from the vault she'd confined it to in her mind. She'd managed to keep it at bay while they worked, but now there was nothing stopping her from reliving the whole debacle in vivid Technicolor.

She closed her eyes and moaned pitifully as the image of her hot-pink vibrator tumbling at his feet played over and over in her mind. Talk about humiliating. No, it was beyond humiliating. Someone needed to invent a new word to cover the level of embarrassment she was currently experiencing.

She didn't want Harry knowing such a personal, private thing about her. It was way too intimate. And they weren't intimates. At best, they were sort-of friends— *sort-of* because there were a bunch of things standing in the way of them ever being true friends, Steve being the major impediment.

Despite that, Harry now knew that sometimes, when the need took her, she spent some up-close and personal time with her hot-pink battery-operated boyfriend.

She moaned again and clenched her teeth. If she could, she would erase those few seconds from the history of the world.

But she couldn't. Harry knew what he knew, and she knew that he knew, and nothing would ever change that. And tomorrow night he would arrive at her house promptly at six o'clock and she would have to look him in the eye and pretend it was business as usual, as she had tonight.

This would be a really good time to run off and join the circus, in case you were wondering.

The phone rang, the sound startlingly loud in the quiet of the house. Pippa raced to get it before Alice woke.

"Pippa. Sorry it's a little late, but I've been meaning to call all day and check how you are," her mother said. "Did the money come through all right?"

Pippa had called her mum last night to explain about the ceiling and ask for a small loan to cover the building supplies for the repair. True to form, her mother had agreed immediately and the money had landed in her bank account this morning.

"It did. Thank you. You're a life saver."

"You sound a little rushed. Is this a bad time?"

"No, Harry was here but he's gone now. I ran to get the phone so Alice wouldn't wake up."

"Harry?"

"He's the friend I mentioned who was helping with the repair."

"Oh, that's right. He's clearly a good friend to have. Would I have met him?"

"No." Pippa could hear the stiffness in her own voice. She wasn't sure why, but she felt uncomfortable talking about Harry.

"Sorry. Am I being nosy?" her mother asked in her blunt, no-nonsense way.

"There's nothing to be nosy about." More stiffness, with a side order of defensiveness. What on earth was wrong with her?

"Okay," her mother said diplomatically. "How's my favorite granddaughter?"

They talked about Alice for a few minutes before her mother wound up the call.

"Speak soon, okay?" she said.

"Okay. Love you."

Pippa was about to put the phone down when her mother spoke up.

"Pippa…if you ever wanted to go out to dinner or a movie, I'd be more than happy to come down and baby-sit. You only have to ask."

Pippa was so surprised she took a moment to respond. "Um, sure. Thanks."

"I want you to know the option is there, if you need it."

"I appreciate it, but don't hold your breath." It wasn't as though her social life was exactly jumping these days.

"Being a mother doesn't mean you're not a person still. You know that, right?"

Where was all this coming from? "I know that."

"I hope so."

They said their goodbyes then and ended the call. Pippa tried to understand why her mother had suddenly decided to give her a pep talk on getting a life. Was she really that sad?

She thought about the vibrator incident and groaned. Certainly, Harry thought she was that sad.

Because it didn't bear thinking about—any of it— she went to bed. Tomorrow was another day, after all, full of fresh opportunities to humiliate herself.

PIPPA HAD A vibrator. Not just any vibrator, either. A hot-pink, generously proportioned device that would give plenty of guys a permanent case of performance anxiety.

She had spare batteries at the ready, too, as well as a

tube of lubricant. She kept it all in a neat little box beneath her bed, within easy reach should the mood take her. Any time she got the urge, she had only to reach her hand down to find instant satisfaction....

Harry pulled over to the side of the road with a screech of tires. He gripped the steering wheel, shut his eyes and tried to banish the images filling his head—Pippa, flushed and breathless, pleasuring herself with Mr. Pink a dozen different ways. In the bath, in the shower, on her bed...

"Stop it."

He was out of control. At least, his libido was. The rest of him was fighting a valiant rearguard action, but he wasn't sure how much longer he could hold out.

It had been bad enough that she'd been wearing those jeans again. He'd been half expecting it, since she'd made it clear she planned to help him, but he'd still had trouble keeping his eyes off her ass as she moved around the kitchen.

Then there'd been their conversation over dinner. With any other woman, he'd have called their light, teasing conversation flirting. With Pippa... He didn't know what it was. They'd always teased each other, going out of their way to coax a smile or a laugh. They'd always bounced ideas and insults around. Before, though, she'd been Steve's, and it had seemed harmless to enjoy that kind of verbal play with her. Now, it felt different. He'd never let himself see her as a desirable woman before, but after tonight and the incident with her bra he had all these pictures in his head and it was getting harder and harder to stop himself from doing something stupid.

Something that would probably get his face slapped and make it impossible for him to help her in the future. The thought sobered him, not so much because he was worried about getting his face slapped, but because he hated the idea of Pippa needing help and not being able to ask for it.

A car sped past, rattling the truck windows. He unclenched his hands from the steering wheel.

He wouldn't make a move on Pippa. She wasn't some girl at the bar looking for fun times. She was serious. She had a daughter she was raising on her own. She was studying and working part-time. Her life was complicated and intense and full of compromises and responsibilities.

He wasn't up for any of that, and she wasn't the kind of woman who would be interested in a no-strings roll in the hay. It was never going to happen.

Harry felt a little calmer, a little more in control as he signaled and pulled out into the road. All he had to do was survive a couple more nights of close contact, then he could bow out of her life and go back to being a distant friendly face she saw in passing every now and then. A friendly face who kept his thoughts above her neckline.

A familiar truck was parked out front of his house when he turned onto his street. His foot stilled on the accelerator for a split second before he got a grip on himself. He pulled into his driveway and watched in the rearview mirror as Steve stepped out of his truck and made his way up the drive.

In all of Harry's justifications and excuses and rationalizations over the past few minutes, not once had Steve figured in his thinking—yet his friendship with Steve should have been the primary reason preventing anything from happening between him and Pippa. It should have been the first thing that came to mind, not the last.

It didn't matter that they'd parted badly the other night. It didn't matter that they hadn't spoken since. He and Steve had a shared history that stretched back more than fifteen years—not something a man threw away because he had an itch to scratch. Even if that itch was approaching unbearable.

Steve's expression was masked by darkness as Harry joined him in the driveway.

"You been waiting long?"

"Long enough." Steve ground the words out, low and angry.

"What's going on?"

"I saw your truck at Pippa's."

There was an unspoken accusation in his friend's tone. Harry went still. "And?"

"I want to know what you're playing at." Steve shifted, his booted feet scuffing the cement.

Harry might not be able to see Steve's face clearly but he could read his body language just fine. He was squaring up. Spoiling for a fight.

"I'm not playing at anything. I'm helping her out."

"You think I'm an idiot? You think I didn't notice the way you used to look at her when we were going out?"

Harry's temper rose. He'd never so much as looked sideways at Pippa when she and Steve were an item.

"Think really carefully about what you're about to say, because I've had a long freakin' day."

"Are you, then? Are you screwing her?"

"You're an idiot." Harry brushed past him, heading for the porch.

"What's wrong? Can't look me in the eye and admit it?"

"Go home, mate," Harry said without turning around.

"If you're not doing her, then why were you over there at ten at night?"

Harry unlocked the door and swung it open, reaching inside to flick on the porch light. Only then did he turn toward Steve, taking in his friend's strained, unhappy face and tense posture.

"I told you, I was helping her out. She had some things that needed fixing around the place and she can't afford to pay for it."

"So she called you? Out of all the people in the known freakin' universe?"

"Yeah, she did. Because I offered to help. Because I could see she was doing it tough and I knew you weren't going to step up."

Steve's eyes narrowed. "What I do or don't do is none of your business. Just like Pippa and Alice are none of your business. Stay away from both of them."

Harry couldn't believe what he was hearing. Steve had burned Pippa when she'd gotten pregnant with his child, essentially abandoning her, and now he wanted to dictate who she had in her life? He never would have thought his friend was capable of being such an asshole.

"What's your problem? You don't want her but no one else can have her? Do you have any idea how big a dick that makes you?"

"So you do want her." Steve sounded triumphant.

Harry stared at his friend. Out of everything he'd said, *that* was the bit that stood out to Steve?

"What's going on with you, man? How can you not see that what you're doing is wrong? You have a daughter. A gorgeous little kid. Doesn't that mean anything to you?"

Steve laughed, the sound bitter and hard. "As if this is about the kid. You want in her pants, that's all this is. You always have, and all this bullshit is your way of justifying it to yourself." Steve threw a hand in the air, as though he was throwing something away. "Go ahead, screw her if it's that important to you. Do her every which way from here till Sunday."

He headed for his truck. Harry watched him, frustration and anger warring inside his brain. Part of him wanted to tackle Steve to the ground and pound some sense into him the way he would have when they were both fourteen, but he knew it wouldn't change anything.

He didn't understand where his friend's head was at. The way Steve had treated Pippa, the way he was denying Alice... It was messed up, and Harry couldn't reconcile it with the guy he thought he knew. Better yet, he didn't want to.

If someone had asked him a month ago to come up with a scenario that would threaten his friendship with Steve, he would have drawn an absolute blank. He hadn't thought it was possible—maybe because he simply didn't have the imagination required or perhaps because he was too freakin' naive for his own good. Certainly he never would have imagined that Steve could be such a jerk.

The way his mate was behaving was deal-breaker stuff. The kind of stuff that made a person reevaluate everything.

Harry stepped backward.

He didn't want to go there, even in his thoughts. In his heart, he still believed Steve would come around. Maybe not as unequivocally as he had earlier... But the hope was still there.

Harry went inside, but instead of stripping for the shower he'd been looking forward to, he headed out to the garage. He pulled on his boxing gloves then he zeroed in on the long bag, pounding the padded vinyl with everything he had.

He rained blows on the bag until he was breathless and shaky and covered with sweat. Gripping the bag with both arms, he leaned his head against it, sucking air into his lungs.

Everything was messed up—and for the life of him he didn't know how to fix it.

CHAPTER EIGHT

THE NEXT DAY, Pippa woke at five o'clock to a crying child, worked on her assignment till eight, dropped Alice at day care, went to university till lunchtime, then raced to the gallery for an afternoon shift.

It was delivery day, when all the artists delivered their latest works. As well as dealing with any customers, Pippa's job was to unpack and catalog the new pieces and enter them into the computer system. The gallery dealt with in excess of fifty local painters, sculptors, jewelry makers and other artists, many of whom weren't naturals at organization or administration. By the time she'd put out a few spot fires, soothed some ruffled feathers and listened to several life stories there was precious little time left to get the actual cataloging done and she wound up doing nearly an hour of unpaid overtime.

She didn't begrudge it, because Gaylene had always been so supportive of her, but she was aware of time ticking away as her fingers flew over the keyboard. The moment she was done she locked up and sped to day care, apologizing profusely for being so close to the final pickup time. Alice was pleased to see her, all bright-eyed and smiley, and Pippa spent more time than necessary strapping her into the baby seat, kissing her cheeks and tickling her belly.

As she let herself into the house, she was very aware

that Harry was due in under half an hour. Feeling more than a little frazzled and stressed, she warmed up a bottle for Alice and started the sauce for spaghetti bolognese. She was mixing garlic butter for garlic bread when the doorbell sounded.

She glanced at the clock. Harry was early. Just her luck.

Pippa sucked a smear of garlic butter off her thumb as she walked to the front door, trying to think of something suitably light and smart-arsey to say to him to smooth over the hump of what had happened last night.

She swung open the door, witty quip ready to roll—and stilled.

It wasn't Harry filling the doorway, it was Steve.

For a moment she was so gobsmacked words deserted her, witty or otherwise. She hadn't seen him, even in passing, since the day she'd given birth to Alice. Her stomach dipped unpleasantly. Her hand tightened on the door.

"Hi," she finally managed to say.

His face was expressionless as he flicked a glance up and down her body. "We need to talk."

Just as he was the last person she'd expected to find on her doorstep, those were the last words she'd expected him to say. She'd been trying to get him to talk to her—for Alice's sake—for more than a year.

Yet the thought of him being in her home made her deeply uncomfortable. She was so angry with him, so disillusioned. She didn't want to sit at her dining table and talk as though he hadn't tried to will their daughter out of existence for the past six months. If she was free to obey the dictates of her gut and her emotions, she'd screech at him like a fish wife and order him off her front porch.

She compromised by nodding and gesturing for him to fall back. "Okay. But out here, not inside."

He retreated to the top of the steps and she joined him on the porch. Even though she knew it would appear defensive, she crossed her arms over her chest. She couldn't help herself—she *was* defensive. This man had set himself up as her enemy, and now he was here, out of the blue. She didn't trust him and she had no idea what he was about to say to her... She'd be out of her gourd not to be defensive.

"So, what's going on, Steve?"

He looked exactly the same as he had when she'd first met him—slightly scruffy sun-bleached hair, deeply tanned skin, bright blue eyes, well-muscled body— but his undeniable good looks left her completely cold today. Knowing that beneath his happy-go-lucky, laugh-a-minute facade there was a scared, angry little boy who didn't have the backbone to shoulder his responsibilities killed any lingering appeal he might have had for her.

"I wanted to give you this," he said, pulling something from his pocket.

It took her a moment to register that it was a wad of cash, held together with a grubby rubber band.

"I figure the baby must have expenses. Things she needs."

Pippa blinked. "I beg your pardon?"

He gestured with his outstretched hand. "It's a couple of thousand. To help you out."

Her gaze dropped to the money almost against her will. Two thousand dollars would be a wonderful, luxurious safety net to have in her bank account right now. She wouldn't have to juggle her school fees with her medical insurance payments. She wouldn't have to take every shift that came her way. She could let down her guard enough so that her shoulders didn't feel as though they were permanently up around her ears with stress...

"I don't understand," she said.

Because it wasn't as easy as simply accepting his money. Child Support Services were investigating him. He'd lied and falsified his business books to ensure he didn't have to provide her with adequate child maintenance payments. It didn't make sense that he was suddenly on her doorstep, keen to help out with "the baby's" expenses.

Steve sighed and let his hand drop to his side. "I heard you'd had some car trouble and that things were tight. I figured this would help."

"It would."

"So?" He held out the money again.

The practical part of her brain screamed at her to take the cash and worry about the whys and wherefores later, but everything else in her baulked. Legally and morally, he owed her a great deal more than two thousand dollars. If she took his money now, she would be signaling to him that she was prepared to forgive almost anything as long as the price was right.

She wasn't. She couldn't. This wasn't the kind of relationship she wanted with Alice's father.

"Why now?"

"I told you, I heard you'd had car trouble."

"You didn't think we might have needed some help before now? Why do you think I went through the nightmare of dealing with Child Services, Steve?"

His face fell into the impatient, frustrated lines she'd become so familiar with after their breakup. "Look, either you want the money or you don't. I just figured you'd like to be in a position where you didn't have to accept favors to get stuff done. But what do I know?"

"Is this because Harry's been helping me out?"

It was a stab in the dark but the way his expression instantly shuttered told her she'd guessed correctly.

She stared at him, even more confused. Harry was Steve's friend. Why on earth would Steve be over here offering her money so she wouldn't have to *accept favors to get stuff done* from *Harry,* of all people?

Steve jammed the money into his pocket. "It's none of my business, but you know what Harry's like. He's a dog. If he hasn't tried to throw the leg over yet, it's only because he hasn't got around to it. This way, you can pay someone to help you out."

Steve watched her closely as he spoke and it struck her that he was trying to gauge her reaction.

He wants to know if I've slept with Harry.

The realization hit like a lightning strike. Suddenly it all made sense: the impromptu visit, the unexpected money offer, the sudden interest in Alice's expenses. All of it driven by jealousy. Or, more accurately, a proprietal, dog-in-manger sense of territory. After all, Steve had had her first. God forbid that anyone else want her now that he'd discarded her, especially someone he considered a friend.

A friend who'd called Steve on his poor behavior and made him feel small—Harry had all but admitted as much the night he'd shown up on her doorstep, determined to ride to her rescue.

For a second anger was a physical burn in her belly.

This man was the father of her child, and the only thing that had prompted him to make contact with her was pride. Big, fat, wounded male pride.

"Wow. That is— Wow." She gestured forcefully, unable to articulate her outrage. "You have got balls of steel, you know that? Big, dumb balls of steel."

As if he sensed the Vesuvius of fury welling inside her, Steve took a step backward.

"How *dare* you come over here pretending you give a shit about me and your daughter when all you want to know is if Harry's been in my pants. I have *begged* you to take some interest in Alice. I've offered you access despite the fact that you lied your ass off so you wouldn't have to support her. I pleaded with you to at least talk to me so we wouldn't have to go to Child Services, and you wouldn't even give me the time of day. But the thought that Harry might be sleeping with me brings you running with a big wad of cash in hand—"

She ran out of words, made speechless by the sheer, unmitigated gall of the man with his dumb surfer-boy hair and his thigh-hugging jeans and his striking aqua-blue eyes.

How could so much asshole be contained in one person? He was the worst mistake of her life, a catastrophic walking-talking failure of judgment. The thought that she'd once let him inside her body, that she'd slept beside him and showered with him and shared meals with him literally made her stomach turn.

And yet he'd given her Alice, and her daughter was the best thing that had ever happened to her. The jury was still out, but Pippa was almost convinced Alice had even been the making of her.

The thought punctured her anger and suddenly she simply felt tired and sad. "You know what? Just go. I don't have the time or the energy to deal with your bullshit."

She turned to re-enter the house but Steve stopped her with a hand on her arm.

"You think you're special? You think you're any different from all the other girls he's screwed and left behind?"

It was too much. She'd tried to take the higher ground, she'd tried to walk away, but Steve clearly couldn't let it go and she was only human.

Her chin rose. She looked him dead in the eye. "Oh, I know I'm different. Last night, Harry told me I'd ruined him for all other women—this is while we were still lying in the hall because we didn't make it to the bedroom. Most of the time we don't, actually. Not that it matters. Harry's pretty creative, if you know what I mean." She glanced at the hand that still held her forearm.

He released her, his mouth an angry line. She had no idea if he believed a word she'd said, but she didn't really give a damn. She just wanted him gone, out of her life.

Pippa stepped into the hall and shut the door firmly behind her. She held her breath, waiting for the sound of his boots on the steps. Only when she was sure he was gone did she lean against the door and take a deep, shuddering breath.

What a jerk. What a gold-plated, shameless, egotistical jerk.

She couldn't believe he'd come over here and gone through the charade of pretending he gave a fat rat's caboose about his daughter in order to safeguard the sanctity of his ex's vagina. That was what it came down to, after all. He wasn't interested in any other part of her. He certainly wasn't interested in Alice or whether Pippa had enough money to care for her adequately. He simply wanted to ensure that Harry didn't have what he'd once had.

Pathetic, ridiculous caveman stuff. And it made her

want to weep for her daughter. The other night she'd told Harry that she couldn't afford to hope that Steve might one day come around. It was a lie. In her heart of hearts, buried deep, was a foolish, naive dream that one day Steve would get past whatever was stopping him from having a relationship with his child and come looking for Alice.

It's never going to happen. Face it and accept it and let it go.

She returned to the kitchen and resumed mixing the garlic butter. It came as no great surprise that her hands were shaking. She concentrated with all her might on slicing the bread and slowly the shaky feeling subsided. It wasn't until she slid the foil-wrapped roll into the oven that it occurred to her that Harry must have really struck a nerve with Steve for him to be so bent of shape and angry about Harry possibly being involved with her.

She stilled as the implications of her realization hit home.

Harry and Steve had known each other for years. She didn't even know how long, although the stories and anecdotes they'd recounted to her had gone back into their early teens. They surfed together, they hung out together, they had each other's backs... And now they were at odds because Harry had been kind and foolish enough to pull over when he saw her stranded on the side of the road.

It didn't sit well with her, even though she knew that she had done nothing to create a wedge between the two men.

Apart from telling Steve that you and Harry were doing each other, you mean.

She winced. She'd been so busy spitting in Steve's eye she hadn't stopped to consider the repercussions of her hasty words. Whatever was going on between Harry and Steve would only be exacerbated by what she'd implied—okay, by what she'd blatantly rubbed in Steve's face.

Sometimes she wished she could uninstall her stupid temper like an underperforming phone app and get on with her life. This was the second time in as many weeks it had gotten her into hot water. And both times she'd ended up owing Harry an apology.

Right on cue—because apparently her life had become a French farce—the doorbell rang. She smoothed a hand over her hair, then made an impatient noise. Not only did she know, without a doubt, that she looked worn out and pale and definitely not at her best after a long day and a wrangle with her ex, she also knew it wouldn't make any difference to Harry. Especially once he'd heard what she had to confess.

Bracing herself, she went to answer the door.

"HEY. RIGHT ON TIME. Sadly, dinner is not, but it won't be long," Pippa said as she opened the door.

The moment Harry laid eyes on her he knew something was wrong. He didn't know how he knew, he just did.

Maybe it was the way she was smiling with only her mouth. Or maybe it was the way she held herself, as though expecting something bad or painful to happen in the next few seconds or minutes.

"What's wrong?"

She blinked. Then quickly shook her head. "Nothing. Why?"

"Bullshit. What's going on?"

She eyed him for a beat, and he guessed she was trying to work out how much effort it would take to convince him to believe her lie.

"Steve was just here."

Damn.

Last night, after Steve had taken off and Harry had finished pummeling his punching bag, he'd debated with himself over whether he should tell Pippa what had happened. His conclusion, after more than an hour staring at his bedroom ceiling, was that what she didn't know wouldn't hurt her. Whatever was going on, it felt like it was between him and Steve. He'd figured it would stay that way.

He'd figured wrong. Obviously.

He'd been silent too long and Pippa tilted her head to one side as she studied him.

"Why don't you look surprised?"

"He was on my doorstep when I got home last night. Saw my truck in your driveway, wanted to know why I was spending time with his ex-girlfriend."

She blinked again, but this time it read more like amazement at Steve's gall than surprise.

"He came right out and asked you that?" Her voice was a little on the high side, her eyes wide.

"Not in those exact words." He wouldn't repeat what Steve had said. It wouldn't do anyone any favors.

Pippa's chin lifted and he had a feeling she didn't have many illusions about the flavor of the conversation they'd shared.

"I'm sorry you had to go through that, and I'm sorry that helping me has made trouble between you and Steve."

"You've got nothing to apologize for. It's not your fault Steve's acting like a dick."

"But it's because of me. Because of our history."

"It's because of Alice and because Steve has got some shit he needs to deal with. Neither of which places you in the firing line."

Her expression softened. "You're a nice guy, Harry. Sometimes too nice."

"I wish you'd stop saying that."

"Tough luck." She smiled. Then she lifted a hand and pushed her glasses up her nose and he knew there was more.

"What else do you need to tell me?"

This time her look was incredulous. "Have you been taking mind-reading pills or something?"

He gestured with his index finger around his own eyes to indicate her glasses.

"You muck around with your glasses when you're nervous."

"I do not." Her hand lifted to adjust her frames again. She caught the action midair and returned her hand to her side, but her expression was rueful.

"There goes my career as a covert double agent," she said.

Harry crossed his arms over his chest and propped a shoulder against the door, letting her know that they weren't going anywhere until she came clean.

She sighed, tweaked her glasses again, then shook her head in frustration at the gesture.

"Okay. Fine. The truth, the whole truth and nothing but the truth. But you won't like it. And this is definitely my fault."

He made a winding motion with his finger, encouraging her to stop tap-dancing and start talking.

"Okay. I'm getting there. In case you haven't noticed, I have this ridiculous temper. Sometimes it takes the wheel and dumb-ass things come out of my mouth.

Like the other week when I gave you a hard time for offering to help out when it was really myself and my stupid feckless life I was angry with."

He raised his eyebrows, waiting.

"Steve pretty much wanted to know the same thing—what you were doing over here last night—but he offered me money for Alice before going there. When I told him I didn't want his money under those circumstances, he warned me off you, told me I was stupid to think I was special and you would treat me exactly the same as all your other women."

Her face and chest were pink but she didn't look away. Harry had to school his own features to keep a lid on the anger growing inside him. Last night Steve had been an asshole, but tonight he'd stepped over the line. Big-time.

"He made me so angry, pretending he gave a toss about Alice when all he cared about was whether you were sleeping with me or not. Whatever you said to him, you must have really pissed him off."

She stared at him expectantly, inviting him to fill in the blanks, but he simply shrugged. He wasn't about to start telling tales. Somehow he'd gotten stuck between his oldest friend and Pippa, but he wouldn't stay any longer than he had to.

He'd barely finished shrugging before Pippa held up a hand.

"Forget I asked that. What happens between you two is your business."

"Tell me the rest of it, Pippa." Because it was becoming clear to him that she'd be happy to prevaricate all day long if he let her.

"Okay. But I might not be able to look at you while I say it."

"All right."

She scrunched up her face like a kid about to swallow a mouthful of cod liver oil. "After he made that crack about me not being special, I, um, may have given him the impression that his suspicions were more than grounded. There, uh, may even have been a reference to us doing it on the hall floor and you being very creative…" She swallowed. The sound was audible, like a cartoon gulp. Confession over, she relaxed her face and made eye contact with him, waiting for his reaction.

Clearly she thought he'd be angry. Maybe he should be, given the state of play between him and Steve, but as he'd said earlier, it wasn't her fault Steve was acting like an asshole. Harry figured he'd have been pretty damn provoked, too, if someone had thrown the same kind of crap at his head.

And maybe he was warped, but he couldn't help admiring her chutzpah.

"The hall floor?" he asked after a short pause. "What's wrong with the bed? Apart from the fact that it's leaning against the wall, of course?"

"We didn't make it to the bed. Too impatient."

"Ah."

"I'm really sorry." Her hands gripped each other tightly at her waist. "I know I should have turned the other cheek, and if you like I'll call him and explain I only said it to get a rise out of him. I'm pretty sure he didn't believe me, anyway, because I'm about a million miles away from one of your usual bar bunnies. Plus there's Alice. If he'd stopped to think about it for half a second, he'd have known that he was definitely barking up the wrong tree in the wrong forest in the wrong country."

"Define *creative* for me."

She stared at him, arrested. "You're not angry."

"Why would I be angry?"

"Because I've made things even more difficult between you and Steve."

"Nope. He did that by coming over here being offensive and insulting you."

"Harry… You have to stop letting me off the hook."

"Deal—if you stop trying to take responsibility for stuff that isn't yours to own." He pushed away from the door frame. "Is that garlic I smell?"

"Yes." She appeared distracted, a worried frown creasing her forehead. "But I'm not sure we should be doing this anymore. Even if Steve is totally out of line, I hate the thought of you two fighting because of me and Alice."

He laid a hand on her shoulder. What he really wanted was to pull her into his arms, but that was never going to happen. He could feel her distress vibrating through her frame like a low-voltage current.

"I'm here because I want to be. No other reason."

He was a little surprised to realize it was true. He'd started helping Pippa because he'd felt for her situation. He'd kept helping her because someone had to step into the breach left by his mate's irresponsibility. But beneath all of his good intentions there had always been a rock-solid foundation of liking, pure and simple. Pippa was good people. He wanted to make her life better.

And he was fast developing an obsession with getting her naked—but that was a whole other ball game.

"If you keep being nice to me, I'm going to cry. And then I'm going to have to kill you, because I pride myself on never crying in public."

He squeezed her shoulder lightly before releasing his

grip. "Okay. Where's my dinner? That mean enough for you?"

She blinked rapidly a couple of times. "Yeah, that'll probably do it."

He dumped his toolbox in her bedroom before following her down the hallway. She wore one of her retro dresses today, this one a red-and-blue striped sundress with little red strawberries scattered across it. The fabric swished around her slim calves as she walked, flirting with the backs of her knees. She had nice legs—shapely without being too skinny or too muscular. As Goldilocks would say, they were just right.

But you won't be sleeping in that bed, Goldi. Remember?

He forced his gaze away from Pippa's body as they entered the kitchen. Alice was playing on a mat beneath a colorful plastic toy frame, batting at a bright yellow star. Because he didn't trust himself to keep his eyes to himself, he crouched down beside the baby.

"How are you doing, Miss Alice?"

Predictably, all Alice did was stare at him, wide-eyed. Then her small mouth curved into a gummy smile and he couldn't resist the urge to touch one of her tiny-nailed hands. Her skin was incredibly soft. Harry watched, fascinated, as her hand curled around his index finger. He smiled. This kid definitely had a thing about woman-handling men.

"We're having spaghetti with garlic bread, but I'm running a little late getting it all together," Pippa said from behind the kitchen counter.

He slipped his finger from Alice's grip and stood. "It's cool. I haven't got anywhere else I need to be."

She nodded and rummaged in the kitchen drawer for

something. She still looked agitated. Steve's visit had rattled her more than she wanted to let on.

"Don't suppose you've got any wine?" he asked.

"I do. A Semillon sauvignon. It's a little fruity but okay."

She sounded surprised and he knew she was remembering that he didn't drink while working.

"You look like you could use a glass of wine," he said.

She puffed her cheeks out. He got the feeling she was trying to decide between being amused or offended. After a few seconds she smiled.

"That obvious, huh?"

"Only to the trained observer."

"Right. Remind me again what you're trained in observing?" She opened the fridge as she spoke, pulling out the wine.

"Women."

She laughed. "I guess you are."

She poured two glasses. He accepted his with a murmured thanks when she passed it over.

"Cheers, Mr. Observer," she said, lifting her glass in a brief toast before taking a healthy mouthful.

He took a smaller sip, barely managing to stop his mouth from puckering at the grassy acidity of the wine. He was more of a beer and red wine man generally speaking, but if sharing a glass of white wine with Pippa meant she'd happily have one, he was prepared to suck it up.

"So. How was *your* day?" she asked with forced brightness.

He told her about an incident with a customer at work, exaggerating the personalities to make her laugh. By the time they sat down to eat, she'd finished her glass of wine and the tightness had left her face. She lifted the bottle, asking silently if he wanted a second glass, but he shook his head.

"I'm good for now, thanks."

She hesitated a moment, then shrugged as if to say "what the hell" and poured herself another.

He asked her questions about her university course for most of the meal, watching the emotions chase themselves across her face as she first enthused about a particular lecturer and then condemned a narrow-minded education department policy that she was convinced was all about bureaucracy and nothing about education.

"You sound pretty passionate about this stuff," he said.

"Do I?" She looked surprised.

"Yeah, you do."

She considered for a moment. "Maybe I am a little passionate." She laughed. "I never thought I'd say that. When I signed up for the diploma I was just being practical. But there are definitely parts that I really enjoy."

"Like?"

"The kids. Their energy. I've done two lots of teaching rounds now and the things kids say…man, they're funny. The way they view the world is refreshing." She poked her fork in his direction. "What about you? Do you love your job? Are you passionate about it?"

"About cars and engines? Can't think of anything else I'd rather be doing. But I wouldn't call it a passion, as such. But I like solving problems, making things work."

"You know what that is? Your white-knight complex, in its career form."

"I don't have a white-knight complex."

"Sure you do. Running around helping people. Riding to the rescue."

It was on the tip of his tongue to tell her she was the only person he'd rescued lately, but at the last minute he decided it might be a little too revealing.

"I think of it more as an adult form of playing with Lego," he said.

"And the people you work for, they're okay?"

Harry helped himself to another slice of garlic bread. "Leo's okay. Loses his cool a little too much for my liking. But he's not the worst boss I've ever had."

"Let me guess—that was your dad, right?" She looked pleased with herself, as though she'd just aced her Psychology 101 exam.

"Actually, Dad was a good boss. Good teacher, too, which was weird, since he just about throttled me when he was teaching me to drive. When it came to work, though, he knew what he was talking about and I listened."

Pippa sat back in her chair. "So why aren't you working for him, then? Why doesn't the sign above the door say Porter and Son instead of Village Motors?"

"You sound like my mum."

"It comes with the territory." She glanced toward Alice, gurgling happily in her bassinet, before nailing him with a look. "You going to answer my question or not?"

"I'm thinking about it."

She huffed out a laugh and planted an elbow on the table. "Thinking about it?"

Pippa leaned toward him, all amused outrage and mock-challenge. Her warm brown eyes were alight with interest, and the wine had put color in her cheeks. He found himself thinking for the millionth time about her cherry-red bra and creamy, full cleavage.

"It's not what I want," he said.

"Your own business?"

"The long hours. The responsibility. Everyone looking to me when things go wrong. Why take on all of that when I can pull down a good wage and go home at the end of the day, put my feet up and forget about everything?"

"You're not ambitious? No big life plan?"

"What more do I need? I've got my own place. I've got a truck and one of the best vintage muscle cars Australia has to offer. There's not a lot of stuff that I want that I can't get."

"You make it sound pretty good."

"But?"

"But nothing. Like I said, you make it sound pretty good."

Pippa was sincere. He sat back in his chair. He hadn't even realized he'd moved toward the edge of his seat until then, the better to counter the argument she hadn't made.

"What's wrong?" she asked. "You look surprised."

"I don't know. Guess I was expecting more resistance."

Definitely he'd been expecting more judgment.

"Because I sounded like your mother before?"

"Because the consensus from the rest of my family seems to be that I'm copping out."

Pippa drained the last of her wine. "You know what? Everyone should just live their lives and let you live yours. You're not hurting anyone. You're happy and healthy and content. What's not to like about any of that? There are plenty of people with six-figure incomes, huge mansions and garages full of cars who can't say the same."

"So teaching's going to do that all for you? Keep you happy and healthy and content?"

She flashed him a rueful smile. "That's a whole different ball of wax."

Pippa started gathering the plates. He stood and took them from her hands, stacking the cutlery and their water glasses on top.

"Why?"

"Because I have Alice. I don't have just me and what I want to consider. My life isn't only mine anymore."

He frowned, even though she hadn't made it sound like a complaint, more as though she was simply stating the facts.

"That sounds pretty grim."

Pippa was folding the place mats, but she stopped and looked at him, a startled expression on her face.

"Does it? I didn't mean for it to. Having Alice, thinking of Alice and what she needs is the best thing that's ever happened to me. It's sort of…I don't know…opened my heart. Made life less about me. And I mean that in a good way. Loving someone and wanting them to be happy is a pretty great mission to have, in my book."

She gave him a small smile before slipping past him to stow the place mats away. He dumped the plates in the sink, her words echoing in his head.

He wasn't sure why, but they made him feel…unsatisfied in some way. Unsettled.

"I'll go get changed. We're plastering and painting today, yes?"

"Yeah. Old clothes."

She laughed. "All my clothes are old."

He dried his hands on a tea towel as she left the room.

Then, because he didn't know what else to do, he ran water into the sink and washed the dishes.

And all the time he thought about Pippa, about the glow she'd gotten in her face and eyes when she talked about her daughter.

She was a special woman. Funny, smart, self-aware, sexy. He liked the way she looked at the world. Liked the way she kept surprising him.

Maybe after he'd finished fixing her ceiling he could swing by and see her every now and then. Have a beer, maybe, catch up. He didn't have any women friends, unless his sisters counted—and he suspected they didn't. Maybe he and Pippa could be friends. Because he was starting to feel as though it would be hard to not have her in his life.

CHAPTER NINE

PIPPA KNELT ON the cold tile in the bathroom to tie the laces on her runners. The two glasses of wine she'd drunk with dinner had worked their way through her system, warming her belly and taking the edge off her anger with Steve. Or maybe it was Harry's easy good humor that had done that.

He'd been so calm and understanding, even when she'd confessed that she'd dumped him in it with his best friend. He could have been angry—very angry—with her. But he wasn't, and he hadn't packed up his stuff and gone home. He'd eaten her dinner and done his best to distract her.

Beneath his rugged, take-no-prisoners exterior was an incredibly decent man with a good heart.

A wave of gratitude washed over her. If only there was some way she could repay him for all his many large and small kindnesses. She stared at the wall, trying to think of something—anything—she could do or buy that would let him know how much she valued his efforts and support.

Maybe she could buy him some new tools when money wasn't such an issue. She'd noticed his screwdriver set was pretty beaten up. Maybe she could save up and get him a new one.

It felt so feeble in the face of his generosity, but it was all she could come up with.

Sighing, she stood in front of the mirror, quickly brushing her hair back into a ponytail. She'd pulled on an old man's shirt she'd bought a while ago and her oldest yoga pants and she finished her ensemble with a scarf tied over her hair to protect it from paint spatter. Not her most attractive look, but tonight was about practicality. Hell, at the moment, her whole life was about practicality.

She set Alice up in the sunroom with the baby monitor once again, then headed for the bedroom. Harry was already up the ladder, a trowel and a bucket of ready-mix plaster in hand. She tilted her head back and watched him smooth a thin coat along the joins between the old and new plaster sheets, impressed by his expertise and trying not to notice the muscles in his chest and arms ripple as he worked.

"For a mechanic, you make a pretty good plasterer."

"Did a few summers on building sites when I was a kid. Picked up a few tricks along the way."

"Is there anything I can do to help?"

"Not right this second." He glanced down at her, quickly returning his attention to the ceiling.

"Do you want something else to drink? A coffee, maybe?" She felt so superfluous, standing around watching him work.

"Coffee would be good, thanks."

She half suspected he'd only said yes to give her something to do, but she headed into the kitchen to put the kettle on. By the time she returned with two mugs, he'd shifted the ladder across the room and was smoothing plaster over the last join.

"That was fast."

"It'll dry fast, too. Thirty minutes and we should be able to sand and get a coat of paint on."

"Here." She held up his coffee, the handle turned toward him so he could grasp it easily.

He glanced down at her as he slid the coffee from her hand. "Thanks."

He frowned as he took a sip of his drink.

"If it's too strong, I can add more milk," she said quickly.

The least she could do was give the man coffee how he liked it.

"The coffee's fine." He flicked another quick look at her before once again focusing on his mug. "But you should probably know I can see right down your top from up here. Might want to do up another button."

Pippa glanced at her shirt. It was old and baggy with several buttons missing and she'd never given a thought to whether it was decent or not when she'd pulled it on. Sure enough, however, she could see lots of décolletage, along with a generous amount of bra.

"Sorry," she mumbled, retreating from the ladder to fumble with the neck of her shirt.

"I wasn't complaining. But I figured you'd probably want to know." He said it casually, as though it was no big deal to him whatsoever.

It probably wasn't, given the amount of breasts and bras he'd seen in his lifetime.

She couldn't help but be aware that this was the second time she'd offered him all-areas access to the goods. Both times he'd been incredibly matter-of-fact about revealing her exposure but it didn't stop her from feeling self-conscious as she double-checked that she was now decent. From now on, she was wearing turtlenecks when he was in the vicinity.

She glanced at him when she turned around. He'd set his mug on top of the ladder and was smoothing plaster across the final corner join. Her gaze slid down his chest and caught on something below his waist. Something pretty substantial and difficult to ignore.

He had a hard-on.

She blinked, but it was still there when she opened her eyes again—a very defined, very impressive bulge in his jeans.

Pippa looked away, her thoughts scattering like birds.

Harry was turned on. Aroused. Hard.

Because he'd seen down her top?

Surely not.

But the more she thought about it, the more it didn't seem that big a stretch. In fact, unless the man had a serious thing for plaster or ladders or DIY in general, there wasn't really any other explanation for what she'd seen.

Her breath caught in her throat as she considered the implications.

Harry wanted her. Pretty badly, if the size of that bulge was anything to go by.

Illicit, indecent excitement licked along her veins. She pressed a hand to her belly, trying to hold back the tide of arousal that washed through her.

Because Harry was a bad bet. Harry was good times and no-strings sex and no tomorrows. Better yet, he was closely connected with the father of her child.

He was the last person she should want.

Didn't stop her from wanting him, though. Hadn't stopped her from noticing his body for the past few weeks, either. Hadn't stopped her from remembering how it had felt when he'd held her, or how he'd smelled, or how firm and hot his chest had been when she'd pried her daughter's hands off him.

Oh, boy.

She stepped backward, recognizing the impulse toward recklessness rising inside her. Two years ago, she would have allowed that impulse to take over. She would have thrown caution to the winds and let Harry know in no uncertain terms that the attraction he felt was more than reciprocated.

But she had Alice now. Her life wasn't about impulse and whims. Every decision she made these days came with a price.

She would be mad to get involved with Harry. A true glutton for punishment after what had happened with Steve.

Even if Harry was incredibly hot. Even if she could feel herself growing wet and warm as she contemplated what it would be like to be skin-to-skin with so much raw masculinity.

She was a mother now. She was training to be a teacher. Life wasn't about what felt good or right in the moment. Life was about the future. About playing it safe and making smart, good choices.

Her body felt hot beneath her hand. She swallowed and took a deep, calming breath.

She would not sleep with Harry.

The decision felt as final as a door closing. Some of the tension drained out of her body. She smiled faintly.

Phew. Crisis averted.

She felt almost giddy with relief that she'd managed to subvert her worst impulses. It had been close for a minute there, but she'd held out.

Pippa snuck a look at Harry, feeling a little wistful as she eyed his erection again. In another time, in another place, she had no doubt that he would be a wonderful lover. Fun, intense, powerful… But it wasn't going to happen.

"Done." Harry descended the ladder. "We should be ready to sand by eight-thirty." He dumped the trowel and plaster bucket onto the drop sheet, then collected his mug. Lifting it to his mouth, he drained the last of the coffee. Pippa stared at the tanned column of his throat, mesmerized by the uniquely masculine bob of his Adam's apple. He sighed his appreciation as he lowered the mug.

"Good coffee. Thanks." He stepped toward her, offering her the empty mug.

Her gaze slid down his broad chest and flat belly to his crotch.

"Is that for me?" The words slipped out of their own accord, born of too many nights alone and bone-deep curiosity and need.

It had been so long, and she was only human.

Harry's gaze tracked hers to his groin. She held her breath, waiting for him to respond, aware of the pulse of desire between her legs.

A slow smile curled Harry's lips. "This, you mean?"

Pippa watched with dawning horror as he reached into his pocket and drew out a tube of filler.

His smile grew into an outright grin, his eyes dancing with mischief and amusement. "I'm not sure whether to be flattered or intimidated, to be honest," he said, eyeing the tube assessingly.

Pippa opened her mouth to say something to rescue herself but the only sound that came out was a small, choked cough. Heat flamed its way up her chest and into her face.

Harry was watching her, grin still in place, amused and entertained. In a moment of blinding clarity, she saw herself through his eyes—frumpy single-mum

Pippa, down on her luck, a bit quirky and needy in her pill-covered yoga pants and baggy old man's shirt.

A million miles from the kind of woman that would inspire a hard-on the size of a tube of spackle.

God, what had she been thinking? What on earth had made her say something so bold and stupid?

She spun on her heel, aware that retreat would only make her look more foolish but unable to stem the impulse to run and hide. She reached the hall and looked around wildly before bolting into the bathroom. She shut the door with a teeth-rattling slam then dropped onto the edge of the tub.

She was literally sweating with embarrassment. If she checked, she was sure even her toenails would be blushing. This was far, far worse than the incident with her vibrator. Never in a million years did she think she would ever say that, but here she was, redder than Rudolph's nose and desperate to somehow take back her rash, revealing words.

A knock sounded on the door. "Everything okay in there?"

She closed her eyes. Great, now he was worried about her.

She couldn't think of anything to say so she simply sat there, radiating heat and humiliation.

"Pippa?"

"Go away."

There was a short pause, then the door handle turned. Pippa slid along the side of the bath, retreating, as he opened the door.

"Go away. Just…leave me alone a minute."

He studied her intently for a beat. "You were serious."

He sounded surprised. Stunned, almost. It hit her

that if she'd only stood her ground and come up with something smart to say, she could have pulled it off as a joke, because clearly that was the way he'd taken it—until she'd run from the room and hidden out in the bathroom like a ridiculous teenager.

Something else to regret later.

"Five minutes. Give me five minutes," she said miserably.

He frowned, then entered the room fully. She slid farther away, instinctively wanting as much distance between herself and the source of her humiliation as possible, only to overbalance and slip backward into the tub. Her head hit the wall behind the bath with a thunk and she wound up with her ass in the tub and her legs bent over the side. She pressed her palms to her face.

If the world exploded in a ball of fire right this second, she would be grateful and happy. She wanted to die.

"Pippa."

She spoke through her hands. "Harry, for the love of God, please just give me five minutes."

"I thought you were joking. You're always such a smart-ass...."

"I got that. Now can you go?"

"Did you hurt your head?"

She moaned. He wouldn't go. He would stay and be a nice guy and let her down gently.

"Can't you leave me to my misery?"

She heard him move closer, then she felt his hands close around her upper arms.

"Come on." He hauled her upward.

She let him drag her to the edge of the bath, mostly because she didn't have a choice. She dropped her hands into her lap as he stepped back, defeated by his persistence.

"It was a mistake. Can we just forget I ever said anything?" she asked, steeling herself to meet his gaze.

There was no sympathy in his clear gray eyes, however. No amusement, either, or discomfort or unease or any of the other emotions she'd expected. Instead, he was oddly intent as he studied her face.

"It wouldn't work. You know that, right?" he said after a long moment. "Nice as it would be."

It took a second for meaning to sink in. Was he saying what she thought he was saying?

"You've thought about it?" she asked cautiously.

Because no way was she jumping to a conclusion where he was concerned ever again.

"Yeah." There was a wealth of revealing frustration in the single word.

She sat a little straighter. "Oh."

So she wasn't completely deluded, then. There *had* been something happening between them. An energy. An interest.

Harry's expression was rueful. "But like I said, it's a bad idea."

"Because…?"

"You really need me to answer that?"

She didn't. She knew the reasons as well as he did. Alice, Steve, who she was, who he was…

"You're right. It's a stupid idea."

"Not stupid. Complicated. Messy."

"Yeah. I know." She could hear the regret in her own voice.

What the hell—she *was* regretful. For a few seconds there she'd indulged in the fantasy that the sexy, hard-bodied man in front of her could be her lover. It had been heady and incredibly appealing.

But it wasn't going to happen and she needed to accept that.

She met his eyes. "Thanks, anyway."

"What for?"

She shrugged self-consciously. "For the ego boost, I guess."

He quirked an eyebrow. "Your ego needs boosting?"

"Sometimes, yeah. I'm a woman. I've been trained since birth to worry about anything and everything."

His gaze traveled down her body, lingering on her breasts. This time there was no mistaking the very male, very obvious appreciation. "You've got nothing to worry about. Believe me."

She tried to stop herself from smiling and failed. "Thanks, Harry."

She might not be able to have him in her bed, but she would get a lot of mileage out of that look. A lot.

Pippa stood. "Better get back to it, I suppose."

"Yeah."

He followed her into the bedroom and they both considered the ceiling for a beat.

"Think it's dry yet?" she asked.

"Probably needs another ten minutes."

"Right."

He stood beside her, just inches away. It was probably an illusion, but she was sure she could feel his body heat. She stole a peek at his big, tattooed arms. What would it feel like to have him on top of her, his weight bearing down...?

"You want another coffee while we wait?" she asked.

"Sure."

He sounded frustrated. Almost annoyed. She glanced

at him and caught him looking at her. She saw lust and need and desire and frustration in his face.

He wanted her. He really wanted her. Despite all the sensible things he'd just said.

"Harry—"

"Screw it."

He reached for her at the same moment she closed the distance between them. Her breasts hit his chest as his arms closed around her and she tilted her head for his kiss. Harry's mouth found hers unerringly, his tongue sliding into her mouth in a heated rush.

He tasted like desire. She moaned her approval as her body went up in flames. Dear God, it had been so long, and this man knew how to kiss.

His tongue stroked hers sensuously, demandingly, while his hands roved over her back before settling on her backside. He grabbed a cheek in both hands and pulled her toward him. She moaned again when she felt how hard he was.

Definitely not a tube of filler this time.

Pippa gripped his shoulders, pressing her hips against his, tilting her pelvis to find the best fit. He pivoted, somehow moving her at the same time, and suddenly the wall was behind her and his hands were beneath her shirt. He cupped her breasts, his hips holding her against the wall, his thumbs teasing her nipples through the lace of her bra. She slid her hands from his shoulders to his hips, then around to his ass. She lifted a leg and wrapped it around his waist, using her grip on his backside to pull him closer.

For long seconds they kissed and groped each other through their clothes, pulses racing. Pippa could feel how hard he was and the thought of having all that hardness inside her made her weak at the knees.

Then Harry pushed her shirt up and pulled her bra down and lowered his head to her breasts and she lost the ability to think coherently. He didn't just kiss her breasts, he consumed them—tonguing her nipples and drawing them into his mouth and shaping her breasts with his hands. He feasted, eyes tightly shut, utterly obsessed with the task at hand.

She panted and held on to him as her body turned molten with need. She had never been so turned on, so desperate to have a man's weight pressing down on her. She wanted to feel his skin on hers. She wanted to taste him. She wanted to wrap her legs around his hips and invite him into her body.

Hands shaking, she found the stud of his jeans and popped it open. The zip was warm from his body heat and she pulled it down before sliding her hand beneath the elastic of his underwear. His whole body jerked as she wrapped her hands around warm, silken steel. She stroked her hand up and down his shaft, reveling in the thick length of him. Her thumb found his head, gliding over the velvety skin. He shuddered again, then suddenly his hands were at the waistband of her yoga pants and he was pushing them and her panties down her hips. She assisted him by toeing her shoes off and then kicking her clothes away.

She gasped as his hands glided over her naked ass and thighs, big and warm and slightly roughened. He kissed her again as his palm smoothed down her belly and into the curls between her thighs.

"Damn," he groaned when he discovered how wet she was.

She tightened her grip on his erection and tilted her hips forward, craving his touch so badly she ached. He accepted her invitation, sliding a finger inside her.

She sobbed as her body tightened greedily around his invasion.

He felt so good and she needed this so badly.

"Now, Harry," she panted, pushing his jeans down his hips.

He slid a hand from her breasts to help her, freeing himself. She heard the crinkle of foil and realized he'd pulled a condom from his pocket. He handed it to her, his gray gaze heated. She bit down on the side of the packet and tore it open, then sheathed him with trembling hands. The moment he was safe he reached for her backside, lifting her. She wrapped her legs around his hips and reached between them to guide him to her entrance.

He slid inside her, big and hot and long, and she was gone, just like that, her body throbbing around his in a breathtaking climax.

He started to thrust, his body hard with need. She pressed kisses to his neck and shoulder and finally his mouth. He plunged in and out of her, every muscle tense. She gripped his shoulders and inhaled the smell of sex and felt herself climbing again.

"Yes," she panted.

Harry's fingers pressed into her hips and ass as he intensified his efforts. She arched her back and tilted her hips…and then she was there again, his name on her lips as she came and came and came. He lost it, burying himself deep and staying there. She throbbed out the last of her climax as he shuddered into her.

He remained still for seconds afterward, his face buried in her neck. Then he loosened his grip and she unlocked her ankles from around his hips and he withdrew from her. The next thing she knew she was standing on shaky, uncertain legs. She expected Harry to move away, but he remained close, his body still pressing hers against the wall. He turned his head and pressed a kiss to her neck. She felt him exhale on a long, shaky sigh.

"Pippa," he said.

There was a world of regret and wonder in the single word, because what had just happened had been amazing, utterly mind-blowing—and they both knew it had been a stupid mistake.

His hands smoothed down her sides to her thighs, skating over her backside warmly before finally settling on her hips. Only then did he pull away from her, and then just enough to allow him to look into her eyes.

His cheeks were flushed, his eyes bright. His mouth looked slightly swollen from her kisses. She reached up and laid her hand on his cheek, feeling the rasp of stubble against her fingers. She felt dazed and bemused and wholly, utterly satisfied.

A smile tugged at the corners of his mouth, then he lowered his head and kissed her. She felt her body stirring yet again. He broke the kiss and she let him step backward.

"Five seconds," he said, turning away.

She leaned against the wall, eyes closed, as she listened to him walk down the hall to the bathroom. Her whole body was one big satisfied throb, warm and wet and soft.

Until this second, she hadn't realized how much she'd missed sex. The swept-away craziness. The closeness with another person. The raw simplicity of it. And sex with Harry... God, if she'd known how good sex with Harry would be, she'd have ambushed him weeks ago.

She heard the tap run in the bathroom and stirred. Any second now Harry would return and she'd be standing here half-dressed with a blissed-out smile on her face. Quickly she collected her yoga pants and stepped into them. She was tugging her bra back into place when Harry filled the doorway. They looked at each other for a long beat.

"Don't even think about saying you're sorry," she said.

"Last thing on my mind."

She lifted her chin. "What's the first thing?"

His gaze drifted down her body. "That we're kidding ourselves if we pretend that won't happen again."

She grinned, aware of a rush of triumph sweeping through her body. "You're pretty confident."

"And you're hotter than a bike seat in summer, Pippa White." He said it with a dirty, cheeky smile and she laughed. She felt lighter than air, better than she had in months. Maybe tomorrow this would all seem crazy and wrong, but right now it felt right. It felt like it was exactly what she needed.

Every waking moment of her life was devoted to work or study or being a mother. She deserved a few seconds for herself—a little oasis of hedonism that was about her and nothing else.

She wasn't an idiot—she knew there was an unspoken caveat to what Harry was suggesting. This wasn't a relationship in the making. This was about sex and sex alone. Great, earth-moving, body-on-fire sex.

From where she stood right now, it seemed like a pretty good deal.

"I guess it's probably good that you were planning on fixing my bedroom door, then," she said.

Harry's gaze did a slow tour of her body again. "Maybe we should take care of that now."

She laughed. "Maybe we should."

The baby monitor chose that moment to come to

life with Alice's plaintive wail. Harry looked a little startled, as though he'd forgotten she had a child. She turned for the door.

"I won't be a moment."

It took her twenty minutes to change Alice and feed her a bottle. She smiled to herself as the electric sander started up. Trust Harry to just get on with it. He was such a man of action.

Her body grew warm as she relived those few, breathless minutes against the wall. She couldn't quite believe it had happened. That Harry had wanted her as much as she'd wanted him. That it had been so good between them.

Once Alice was asleep she returned to the bedroom. Harry was dusting white plaster off his shoulders and out of his hair.

"Sorry that took so long," she said.

Harry glanced at her. "She okay?"

"Yep. Back to sleep again."

"We're ready to paint in here." He indicated the roof.

It only took a few passes with the roller to cover the patched part of the ceiling, but the fresh white stood out starkly against the old ceiling so Harry insisted on doing the whole thing. Pippa used the ladder to paint the cornice, then they worked together to clear away the building debris. The whole time they worked she was acutely aware of him, of his body, his scent, the way he moved. She always had been, of course, but she'd given up the pretense that she wasn't interested in him the second he'd pushed her against the wall and kissed her.

Half an hour later, they dropped her mattress on top of her bed base. Pippa stepped back and brushed her hands together.

"Done." Although she still needed to vacuum away the remaining plaster dust.

"Yeah. Except for the door and the front lock."

"Right." She tugged on the hem of her shirt and met his gaze. "I was thinking maybe you could do them tomorrow night. I could make you dinner again...."

"Sounds good." She didn't know how he did it, but he managed to imbue the two words with a world of meaning.

"Well. Good," she said. She could feel a pleased, smug little smile tugging at the corners of her mouth.

"I'll get out of your hair now, then," Harry said.

"Okay."

She watched as he collected his things, enjoying the play of muscle and sinew, then followed him to the front door. He exited to the porch and looked at her.

"Tomorrow?" he said.

"Yes. Definitely."

He smiled and she wondered if perhaps she'd sounded a little too fervent. She shrugged. So what? He'd just given her the ride of her life. She wouldn't pretend he hadn't rocked her world.

"Sleep tight, Pippa."

He leaned toward her, surprising her as he dropped a kiss onto her mouth. For some reason she hadn't expected him to kiss her goodbye. Which was a little crazy, since they'd just had wild animal sex against the wall.

Pippa hovered on the doorstep watching him walk to his car until it occurred to her that it might look a little needy. As though she was regretting letting him go.

She gave him a cheery wave and stepped back into the house. She collected Alice from the sunroom and settled her into her crib, then went to the bathroom and shed her clothes. There was a faint suck mark on her right breast, and when she turned she could see five small, pale gray circles near her left hip from where he'd gripped her. She turned on the shower and stepped beneath the water, letting it wash over her.

A slow smile spread across her mouth.

She had a lover.

She had no idea for how long, but it didn't matter. She would enjoy what he had to offer for as long as it was good, and she wouldn't feel bad or guilty about it. She would revel. She would luxuriate. She would make hay while the sun shined.

A less welcome thought intruded: Steve, with his offensive offer and warnings. Her smile faded. He'd predicted this would happen.

Pippa shook off the thought. Steve was not a part of her life—through his choice, not hers. She owed him nothing, and she certainly wouldn't start worrying about what he thought or did. What went on with her and Harry was none of his business.

She lifted her face to the spray and focused instead on tomorrow night. A far more enticing subject.

CHAPTER TEN

HARRY LAY IN his bed, his body still damp from the shower. He couldn't get Pippa out of his head.

The feel of her body beneath his hands. The pale, soft skin of her breasts and inner thighs. The taste of her.

"Man."

He was hard for her again. Unbelievable.

He folded his arms behind his head, thinking about tomorrow night, what he wanted to do to her. Strip her naked, for starters. He wanted to see all of her, wanted to lick and suck and touch every inch of her pale, smooth skin. He would take his time, too, no rushing into things like a bull at a gate the way he had tonight. Not that she'd seemed to mind too much, since she'd climaxed the second he was inside her, but still. A guy had his pride. He wanted to make her feel good. He wanted to make her soft and pliant and slightly dazed again. The look in her eyes afterward had been better than any praise any woman had ever thrown his way.

Great. She's hot. You want to sleep with her again. What about Steve?

He pushed the thought away but it kept circling back to the front of his mind. He'd made a liar out of himself tonight. He'd turned his back on years of friendship because Pippa had looked at him with lust in her eyes and he'd realized that if he wanted to, he could have her.

God, how he'd wanted her. More than he'd thought

possible. But it wasn't just about sex and lust and desire. Pippa was a great person. He liked her—a lot. This wasn't simply a matter of his own libido or being seduced by a soft, sexy body.

Still, he was pretty sure that Steve wouldn't see it that way when he found out.

If he found out.

Harry winced. He had no idea how long this thing with Pippa would last—a week, a month—but the idea of lying to Steve for the duration didn't sit well. The up-front, adult thing would be to let Steve know what was happening and let him deal with it. But it wasn't only about him and Steve, it was about Pippa and Alice, too. Harry didn't want to make her life more difficult than it already was.

As he'd said to her before reason had taken a flying leap out the window, the situation was messy and complicated.

Yet if he had the chance, he wouldn't take back what had happened tonight. That first slide of his body inside hers...

He would never regret having had that experience with her. No matter what.

Harry rolled over and punched his pillow into a better shape. He needed to stop thinking and start sleeping. Whatever was going to happen would happen, whether he worried about it or not.

He fell asleep with thoughts of Pippa still in his mind and woke with a hard-on that only a cold shower could cure. He spent the day at work with one eye on the clock, feeling like a fifteen-year-old eager to meet his girlfriend at the school gate.

Not that Pippa was his girlfriend. She was a woman, for starters. Definitely she was a woman. But the friend part was accurate, he realized. He'd enjoyed every minute he'd spent with her in recent weeks, even when she'd been giving him hell and driving him crazy.

He left work at five on the dot and went home to shower and shave. Last night he'd left whisker burn on her breasts. Tonight he wanted to give her nothing but pleasure.

He was showered and dressed again by five-thirty. Way too early to head over to Pippa's place. She'd think he was desperate to see her again.

He distracted himself by dropping in on his sister, Mel. She buzzed him through the automatic gates at the entrance to the Summerlea estate and he parked out the front of the rambling Edwardian farmhouse that she'd restored with her husband over the past two years. Her dark curly hair bounced around her shoulders as she descended the porch steps to greet him.

"Hello. This is a surprise."

She kissed his cheek and smiled. She did that a lot these days. Harry figured it was due to Flynn, which was why he would do pretty much anything under the sun for the man.

"I was driving past."

"You drive past all the time."

"If you want me to go…" He turned toward his car.

She laughed. "Don't be an idiot. You want a Coke? I was about to walk down to the orchard, see how the apples are going. We're fighting an ongoing battle with the birds. Can you believe those sneaky Rosellas burrow in under the nets and then just stay under there and pig out?"

"They're a protected species. You know that, right?"

"Lucky for them, that's all I can say."

He followed her to the kitchen and accepted a drink.

Talking easily, they left the house and walked into the garden. The Summerlea estate encompassed six acres of beautifully laid-out gardens, originally created by esteemed landscape designer Edna Walling more than fifty years ago. Over the past two years Flynn and Mel had brought it back to life, renewing and reimagining the design.

"Looking good," Harry said as they passed the beautifully constructed wooden rose arbors he'd helped install recently.

"It is, isn't it?"

She sounded smugly satisfied and he gave her a fond look. He'd always been closer to her than to Justine, who took the whole older sibling thing a little too much to heart. Mel had always been more interested in being his friend than the boss of him, and he valued her opinion.

"I've got a bit of a situation on my hands," he heard himself say.

"Yeah? What's up?"

He hadn't come here intending to confide in her—not intentionally, anyway—but clearly some part of his brain wanted another perspective on what was happening with Pippa.

"Did you ever meet Steve's ex, Pippa White?"

"She's the one who fell pregnant, yes? I think I met her at the pub one night. Dark hair? Glasses?"

"I've been helping her out lately. A few repairs around the place she's renting. Anyway, last night…" He paused, unsure how much to reveal.

Mel rolled her eyes. "Don't bother trying to find a delicate way to phrase it. I can imagine what happened. You're such a dog, Harry."

She nudged him with her shoulder, breaking his stride and making him lurch to the side. Like himself, she'd inherited the Porter shoulders and tall build and could pack some punch when she put her mind to it.

"It's not like that. Pippa is… It's not like that."

"Okay. If you say so." Mel shot him an appraising look. "How's Steve feel about all this?"

Harry frowned at the Coke in his hand. The bottle had grown slippery with condensation and he moved his thumb across the slick surface.

"He's not happy. He doesn't want anything to do with Pippa or Alice, but he doesn't want me near her, either."

"Sounds messy. Steve's got a shitty temper."

Steve had been a familiar face at the Porter house over the years and Mel knew him—and his temper—well.

"Yeah."

"Have you tried talking to him?"

Harry remembered how belligerent his friend had been last time he'd seen him. "I'm not sure that will work."

They'd reached the orchard and Mel stopped and regarded him solemnly. "You've been friends with Steve for more than fifteen years."

"I know."

"Lots of other women in the world, Harry."

The words were out his mouth before he could stop them. "Not like Pippa."

His sister looked surprised. "You like her."

He gave her a look. He'd slept with Pippa. Of course he liked her.

"I don't mean sexually. I mean you *like* her. Don't you?" Mel watched him very intently.

He shrugged, suddenly self-conscious. "I'm just looking for a way to sort this out without someone getting punched in the face."

Mel didn't say anything for a beat as she studied his face. "I only met her that one time, but she seemed nice. But if you're going to do this, Harry, you have to be serious. She's got a kid."

He frowned. "I'm not 'doing' anything apart from helping her out and spending some time with her."

"Does she know that?"

His sister sounded disapproving, which was typical. In his experience, women always circled the wagons when it came to certain subjects.

"She knows me."

Mel nodded. "Good. Because you're too charming for your own good sometimes. You big lug." She glanced around the orchard, her narrowed gaze scanning the net-shrouded trees. "Aha! Look at that—they've pulled up the net again. Little buggers."

She strode away to pull up one of the tent pegs that had been placed in the ground to secure the nets, re-fixing the net once again to protect the tree. Harry watched her patrol the rest of the orchard, a scowl on his face.

He hadn't laid it out in black and white for Pippa last night, but he'd been pretty sure she understood that whatever was happening between them was about great sex and a bit of fun, no strings, no stress. He didn't want to hurt her, but he wasn't about to kid himself, either— when it came to long-term, he was a bad bet. He didn't do domesticity, and he figured it was pretty unlikely he was about to start now, even if he did like Pippa more than he could remember liking anyone in a long time.

"Quit looking so worried, Harry. It's called growing up," Mel said as she rejoined him. "Every man meets his match eventually."

He gave her a sardonic look. "Keep hoping, and I'll keep living my life my way."

Mel laughed and reached for his Coke, taking a swig before handing the bottle to him. "Let me know when you're ready for us to meet her."

He made a rude noise.

She laughed again. "Oh, this will be fun."

"You done here? I need to get going."

"Sure. I've made you squirm enough."

They turned toward the house.

"Whatever happens, you should sort things with Steve," she said after a short beat of silence. "You guys have been mates too long to let this come between you."

"Yeah."

The easiest thing would be to simply walk away from Pippa, but Harry suspected that at least half of Steve's anger was because Harry had called him on his poor behavior. If Harry backed off from Pippa and turned a blind eye to Steve's crappy decisions, no doubt their friendship would be just dandy.

Harry scowled at the graveled walkway. He'd never considered himself a moralist before, but apparently even he had standards. Now he knew Steve was short-changing Pippa, he couldn't simply turn a blind eye to it. Couldn't stomach it.

As for the walking-away-from-Pippa part...

Mel's hand landed warmly on his shoulder and he realized they were standing in front of the house.

"You know, I almost feel sorry for you."

He let out a frustrated sigh. Why did women see romance everywhere?

"Quit trying to make this into something it isn't."

She held up both hands. "You're the one striding around like Heathcliff, scowling at rocks and whatnot."

"And women wonder why men don't talk about their feelings more."

Mel smiled and punched his arm. "Keep me posted."

"As if."

Harry walked to his car. Mel climbed the steps to the porch and stood watching him reverse out of the drive. She waved goodbye as he pulled into the street. He gave the horn a quick blast and took off.

Five minutes later he parked in Pippa's driveway. He didn't get out of the car immediately. Instead, he sat and thought very deliberately about what he was about to do: go inside and get down and dirty with Pippa again.

If he was going to call a halt to this, now was the time. He could go in, rehang her door, fix her front door lock and keep his hands firmly to himself. It wouldn't fix things with Steve in and of itself, but it would go a long way toward calming things down. Maybe once he was out of the picture, Steve would come to his senses regarding child support for Alice.

Maybe.

And it would definitely ensure that there were no crossed wires with Pippa regarding what had happened between them.

Harry got out of the car and climbed the three steps to the front door. He knocked and rubbed his suddenly-damp palms on the thighs of his jeans. Footsteps sounded inside the house.

Pippa answered the door, hair a damp tangle down her back, face flushed from the shower. She was wearing a black-and-white polka-dot drop waist dress that looked as though it was made from silk and her feet were bare, her toenails painted a pale pink. Her smile was both chagrined and a little apologetic.

"Sorry. Alice just threw up everywhere and I'm running late again. But I've got some nibbles to keep you going until dinner."

He breathed in vanilla-scented perfume and watched as she pushed her glasses back to the bridge of her nose. The need to shove her against the wall and kiss the smile off her lips swept over him. She looked so soft and warm and friendly and sexy, he just wanted to get her naked and make them both a little crazy all over again.

Harry stepped over the threshold and reached for her, aware that in doing so he was choosing the more difficult, complicated path, opening himself up to a world of potential drama, misunderstanding and recrimination.

Funny thing was, it didn't feel as though it was a choice, not when Pippa was standing there, ready to be kissed. More like an imperative, as undeniable as the need to breathe.

And he was in no mood to deny anyone anything.

Pippa started a little as Harry's big, warm hands closed over her shoulders.

"Wha—" she said, then her back was against the wall and Harry's mouth was covering hers.

He kissed her deeply, his tongue by turns coaxing and demanding, his hands roving from her breasts to her hips to her backside and back again. Her body instantly became more liquid than solid. She had to concentrate on staying upright as her knees started to shake.

This man… This man was a master of the art of kissing.

She was ready to slide to the floor by the time he lifted his head and looked into her eyes.

"Where's Alice?"

"In bed, but not asleep yet."

"But you've got a baby monitor, right?"

"Yes."

"Good."

He wove his fingers with hers and towed her into her bedroom. She gave a passing thought to the frittata in the oven. Maybe she should go turn down the heat....

Harry let go of her hand to haul his T-shirt over his head. Her mouth went dry as she stared at his bare chest. Rational thought evaporated as he popped the stud on his jeans, his eyes never leaving hers.

She hadn't exactly led a sheltered life, but she had never had a man look at her or kiss her or touch her the way Harry did all those things. It was intoxicating, heady and such a huge turn-on...

He shucked his jeans and underwear in one smooth, decisive move. Her gaze fell to his erection, bold and proud against his belly. Her sex tightened instinctively as she remembered what it had felt like to have him inside her.

And it was about to happen again.

Belatedly she realized that he was naked and she still fully clothed, mostly because she'd been standing there like a dodo, gawking at him as he undressed. She reached for the zip on the side of her dress, dragging it down with what could only be described as indecent haste. She was pretty sure she'd never wanted to be naked as much as she wanted to be naked right this second. She wrenched the dress over her head and reached for the clasp at the back of her bra.

"Whoa, whoa, whoa," Harry said, holding up a staying hand. "Slow down a little."

She stared at him. "You're the one who's naked already."

"Yeah, but I don't look like you."

The admiration in his tone sent her self-esteem soaring. Pippa glanced down at her best underwear, dark green silk with bright pink trim.

"You like this?"

"My favorite part of Christmas is unwrapping the presents."

He tucked a finger into the waistband of her panties, encouraging her forward. She stepped into his embrace, only to find herself falling toward the bed. She barely had time to bounce before he was crawling on top of her, grinning like an idiot.

"Very smooth," she said drily.

"Wait till you see my next move." He ducked his head and used his teeth to graze the curve of her breast along the edge of her bra cup. She shivered, running her hands across the firm muscles of his shoulders. He caught the lacy edge of the cup in his teeth and dragged it down. Then his mouth was closing over her nipple and she was doing her best not to come on the spot.

Maybe it was because it had been so long. Maybe it was because he was so good. Maybe it was something about her and him together—whatever it was, one touch from this man was enough to make her breathless and mindless.

She let her head fall back against the mattress, giving herself up to his touch.

"You have very sexy breasts, Pippa," he said after a few minutes, his breath warm against her skin.

"Th-thanks," she panted. Her hands were clamped to his shoulders as she hung on for dear life.

He lifted his head and grinned at her. "How you holding up? Doing okay?"

She didn't even try to pretend she wasn't a warm, gooey mess. "Don't gloat, it doesn't suit you."

Harry pressed his smile into her cleavage. She shuddered again as he started to kiss his way across her rib cage. When he went farther south, her heart started racing with excitement. Deep in her secret, dirty, dark heart, she'd always imagined this—Harry, between her thighs, a knowing glint in his eyes.

She held her breath as he circled his tongue around her belly button, her hips lifting involuntarily as she encouraged him lower. She felt him smile against her skin. She fisted her right hand and thumped him on the shoulder.

"Smugness is also unattractive."

He didn't say anything, simply slid lower, gripping the elastic of her panties in his teeth. She moaned as he inched her panties down, licking the exposed skin between her hip bones. Her belly muscles quivered as he pulled her panties lower again, his breath feathering through her pubic hair.

"God," she hissed, her whole body trembling with anticipation.

He glanced up at her, his gray eyes full of smutty intent. "I can stop now if it's too much."

"Stop now and I'll kill you."

He laughed. She lifted her hips as he tugged her panties down her legs. He smoothed his hands up her thighs, pushing them wide. She bit her lip, waiting.

"So pink and pretty," he murmured.

He lowered his head. She lost track of time after that. There was only the wet, firm warmth of his mouth between her thighs, a delicious, slippery friction that made her forget how to breathe and think and speak. He slid his hands beneath her hips, holding her in place as he tortured her.

"Harry, please," she begged, twisting in his grip.

She wasn't even sure what she was asking for, but

he knew. He slid a finger inside her, then another. She arched off the bed, her climax rippling through her. For long seconds he kept her at her peak, his tongue and mouth deft, subtle and knowing.

Then she collapsed back onto the bed, limp and sated and dazed.

Harry kissed her thighs, then her belly, working his way back up her body. She could barely lift her head as he reached her face. He was smiling again when he kissed her mouth.

"Still breathing?"

"Barely."

"Roll onto your side."

She felt his erection against her backside as he tucked in behind her. She waited for him to find his own satisfaction, but he seemed more interested in her belly and breasts, smoothing his hands across skin.

"You feel so good," he murmured near her ear. "So soft."

Even though she'd just climaxed she was painfully aware of his erection, pressed against the curve of her ass. He felt hard and hot and she kept remembering what it had been like to have him stretching her, filling her. Almost without being conscious of it she pressed her backside into the cradle of his hips. He continued smoothing his hands over her breasts, apparently oblivious to her invitation.

"Harry…"

"Shh."

He slid his hand between her legs, stroking her with two fingers. She could feel how wet she was, could feel, too, that he liked that because his hard-on surged against her. He pushed a knee between her thighs, encouraging her to open to him more.

It struck her then that he was determined to please her, that her pleasure turned him on. The knowledge heightened her sensation, bringing every brush of his fingers into tight focus.

Pippa was ready to roll over and take what he wasn't giving her when she heard the telltale crinkle of a condom being opened. He moved away for a second. When he came back he surged inside her in one smooth, slick stroke.

She sighed her relief, clenching her hands in the sheets as he started to move.

At last. Finally. Thank God.

Neither of them spoke for a few minutes, the only sound their breathing, the susurrus of their bodies against the sheets and the wet sound of him moving inside her. He felt so good, so big and hard... And she was so ready for him. Every stroke of his body inside hers brought her closer to completion, a gentle, gradual build.

"Yes, yes," she whispered, arching into his thrusts.

She could feel her climax bearing down on her. So close. Harry slid a hand over her hip and between her thighs. She bucked against him as he found her, and then she was gone. Utterly gone.

She'd barely come back down to earth when she felt him tense. His hips ground against her backside as he found his release. Then he relaxed. They lay side by side, sweaty and breathless.

"Open your eyes," Harry said after a few beats.

She did so, only to find his face inches from hers.

"I love the look in your eyes after you come." He sounded satisfied, very pleased with himself, but she figured he'd earned it.

And then some.

And all she'd done was cook him dinner.

"The frittata!"

She bolted upright, scrambling toward the edge of the bed. She was about to slide off when he grabbed her ankle.

"Hey!" she said.

"The frittata can wait."

"It's probably a burnt crisp by now."

"Perfect." He tugged on her ankle, trying to lure her back to his side.

She laughed, delighted and flattered and silly over the idea that he wanted her again so soon.

"A compromise—I'll turn the oven off then come right back."

He released her ankle. "Don't make me come get you."

There was something in his eyes, a primitive possessiveness that made her almost want to test his threat. She grabbed her silk robe off the hook on the wall and shrugged into it as she slipped from the room. The silk felt cool against her heated body as she made her way to the kitchen.

By some miracle, the frittata was merely very golden instead of black and crispy. She pulled it out and left it to cool on the stovetop. She was about to head back to the bedroom when Alice began to cry.

Tightening the sash on her robe, she went to check on her daughter. Face red, eyes filled with tears, Alice howled out her misery, arms flailing against the coverlet.

"It's okay, Ali bear, Mummy's here." She lifted Alice into her arms, tucking her against her body.

Alice continued to sob as Pippa rocked her gently. She checked Alice's diaper—dry—and rocked her back and forth. Alice continued to cry. Pippa smoothed a hand over her daughter's head and made soothing noises. She glanced at the doorway, wondering what Harry was thinking.

Probably nothing good. Or nothing she'd want to know about, anyway. He was used to girls who partied all night, not women who stayed up trying to coax a teething baby to sleep.

She pictured him on the other side of the wall, sweating bullets and wondering how quickly he could make his excuses and head for the hills.

She grimaced, aware of the push-pull of almost-embarrassment versus indignant defiance within herself. Like most women, she wanted to be seen as sexy and desirable, one of the reasons Harry's intense, focused lovemaking had struck such a deep chord within her, and a crying baby was pretty much the opposite of sexy. But there were also the realities of life to consider, and the reality of her life was that she was a mother. She couldn't disappear Alice conveniently when it suited her. Alice was an integral part of her world. She cried. She demanded attention. She needed feeding and petting and playtime. Alice was utterly dependent on Pippa, and if listening to her daughter cry made Harry break out in hives and want to shimmy out the window on a rope made of sheets…well, this was going to be the shortest-lived inappropriate affair in the history of the world.

Which was probably a good thing, when it came right down to it.

"Anything I can do?"

She whipped her head around. Harry stood in the doorway wearing nothing but jeans and a concerned expression. Her gaze scanned his chest before dropping to his flat belly. In the back of her brain, a part of her punched the air and hooted with triumph that this hot, sexy, built man had just been in her bed.

"I might try a bottle. Sometimes that settles her. She's just started teething...."

"Okay." He glanced around the nursery as though looking for something he could physically move or fix.

She smiled. "Thanks for asking, though."

He lifted a shoulder, brushing off her gratitude as he always did. "Have you got a bottle made up already? Can I stick it in the microwave or anything?"

"I'll have to mix some formula." She eyed him assessingly, trying to work out if he was simply being polite or if he was sincere with his offer to help. She decided to take him at his word. "I could talk you through doing it if you were up for it...?"

That way she wouldn't have to put Alice down, something she hated to do when her daughter was so distressed.

"Sure. Figure it can't be harder than overhauling a fuel injector rail."

She watched him carefully, but there was no sign of twitchiness or discomfort. Apparently he wasn't about to grab his car keys and make a run for it, after all.

"Well, okay."

He followed her into the kitchen and she talked him through taking a bottle from the sterilizer and mixing the formula. She had a strange out-of-body moment as she watched him shake the bottle. This was Harry, after all. Mr. Sexy, Mr. Footloose. Standing in her kitchen, mixing formula bare-chested and barefoot.

If I wake up right now and find out the past two days have been a dream, I am going to be really pissed.

The thought made her smile. No way could she have

dreamed what had just happened in her bedroom. Her imagination wasn't that good.

As for Harry making up Alice's bottle… It simply wouldn't have ever occurred to her to put the two things together, not even in her subconscious.

Harry screwed the top on the bottle. "Now what?"

"We sit it in some hot water for fifteen minutes so it can warm up."

"Don't know if you've read about this crazy new invention called the microwave…"

"Nice in theory, in practice a big no-no. Lots of babies with mouth and throat burns."

"Okay. No microwave. Got it."

She watched as he sat the bottle in a saucepan full of hot tap water.

"The world's a minefield once you have a baby. Every corner hides a peril," she said.

"No kidding."

Alice was still grizzling, grasping at the front of Pippa's gown sporadically and occasionally hiccupping.

"Must kill her not being able to tell you what's wrong," Harry said.

He moved closer so he could peer into Alice's face, his eyes soft with sympathy. Pippa's gaze dropped to the inky blackness of his tattoo, tracing the lines across his shoulder and down on to his broad chest. She wondered how long it had taken and if it had hurt. And she wondered which of his many tattoos had been his first, and if he regretted them at all.

She couldn't imagine him without them, they were such an essential part of who he was, but there was no denying that a lot of people must look at him and see nothing but a lot of tattooed muscle. They'd never know how funny and smart he was, how kind. How gentle he could be. How playful.

Harry's arm brushed her sleeve and he glanced at her. He stood so close she could see the tiny stars of darker gray radiating from his pupils and the shadow of tomorrow's beard beneath his skin. She had an almost irresistible urge to lean forward and press her lips to his cheek, a physical expression of the sudden upswell of affection she felt for him. She resisted—barely—but she couldn't stop the impulsive words that spilled from her lips.

"I'm really glad you pulled over to help me the other week."

Harry didn't move a muscle, but something shifted in his eyes. After a few seconds he put some distance between them, circling back behind the kitchen counter to check on Alice's bottle.

"How do we know when this thing is ready?"

"You test it on the skin inside your wrist. It should feel warm, but not hot."

He took the bottle from the water and shook a few drops onto the inside of his wrist. He frowned, then shook his head.

"I have no idea if that's even close to being right."

He passed her the bottle and she managed to juggle both it and Alice enough to sprinkle a few drops on her wrist.

"It's perfect. Thanks."

She slipped the teat into Alice's mouth and felt her daughter's small body slowly relax as she gave her attention to the bottle. Harry crossed to the sink and tipped the water from the saucepan down the drain. He was frowning when he turned to face her.

"I should go see to that door."

"If you give me ten minutes, I'll be able to help you. She's worn herself out so much she's already falling asleep."

"It's not really a two-person job, but thanks."

He left the room. Pippa stared at her daughter's face and tried to understand what had just happened. One minute they'd been fine, then all of a sudden he'd gone cold on her.

She thought back over their conversation, remembering the way his eyes had grown distant when she'd said she was glad he'd pulled over to help her.

Suddenly she got it. She pressed her lips together and stewed on her conclusion for as long as it took Alice to finish half the bottle and slip into sleep. She walked carefully to Alice's bedroom and settled her, then she went to find Harry.

CHAPTER ELEVEN

HE WAS PRESSING some kind of foul-smelling pink putty into her bedroom door frame with a plastic spatula.

"What's that?" she asked, momentarily diverted.

"Builder's filler. The door frame is so damaged there's nothing to screw the hinges back into. This stuff will set in about five minutes and I can redrill the holes."

She nodded, then fixed her gaze on his. Very directly, because there was no other way to do this.

"What I said before, about being glad you stopped to help me—it didn't mean anything apart from the fact that I was glad you stopped. Okay?"

His gaze shifted to her briefly before returning to the door frame. "Okay."

He wore his poker face and she couldn't tell what was going on in his head.

"I'm not an idiot, Harry. I know what this is. I'm not making room for your clothes in my closet, if that's what you're worried about."

He looked at the smelly pink putty on the end of the spatula. "Good. Because I'm a bad bet as far as anything else goes."

Something inside her recoiled as he fed her the same line she was sure he'd used dozens of times before. Steve's words echoed in her mind. *You think you're going to be different from all the other girls he's screwed and left behind?* Not for a second had she ever believed that this thing between her and Harry had the possibility of becoming anything more than what it was—hot sex and a bit of fun—but the notion that she was simply yet another woman whose expectations Harry felt he had to manage stuck in her craw.

In that one respect she *did* want to be different from Harry's other women. She wanted him to respect her enough to be honest with her. She didn't want the easy line or pat response.

"Harry, on what planet do you think any rational woman would think that you're a *good* bet? You change women like you change socks. Your life is one big adventure playground. You said it yourself—you want an easy, no-stress, no-muss, no-fuss life. You've never said anything other than that, and I got the message, believe me. I let you into my bed with my eyes wide open, so don't go getting wiggy on me because I said something nice to you. In case you hadn't noticed, I *like* you. I enjoy spending time with you—hence the fact that I was recently horizontal with you, breathing hard and making funny noises. But none of those things mean I have designs on your prized bachelor status. Not unlike yourself, I am able to separate sex and love and romance and friendship. Okay?"

"Okay."

He appeared relieved. Surprise, surprise. Despite what she'd said to him, it would be easy to be offended. But she refused to be. She had no illusions where he was concerned, and he'd never made her any promises—except, perhaps, the promise of a good time.

Pippa checked the sash on her robe and flicked her hair over her shoulder. "Good. We're all sorted, then. Do you want some dinner while that stinky stuff sets?"

"Sure."

They ate standing at the kitchen counter. There was still a faint air of constraint between them and Pippa didn't know how to relieve it. She snuck glances at him from beneath her eyelashes, studying his face, his body, wondering what he was thinking.

Even though they'd both agreed they were on the same page, there was the very real possibility that by being so frank and forcing a confrontation she had killed the buzz between them.

Damn, but it would be a shame if the best sex of her life was over before it had really started.

"Relax, Pippa," Harry said after a few minutes.

She peeked at him.

"I can practically hear your brain whirring," he said.

There was no good answer to that, so she didn't say anything. He slipped her almost-empty plate from her hand, then plucked the fork from the other. She watched as he placed them both on the counter before moving to stand in front of her.

She lifted her chin, meeting his gaze. He lowered his head and kissed her, the fingertips of one hand touching the curve of her jaw. He stood close enough that she could feel the heat of his body through the silk of her gown. She pulled him closer, tilting her hips into his. He was hard already, his arousal a firm pressure against her belly.

He tugged on the sash of her robe, pushing it off her shoulders. She let her head drop back as he kissed his way down her neck to her breasts. Her nipples were already hard for him, begging for his attention. Warmth pooled between her thighs as he drew a nipple into his mouth.

Amazing how quickly he could turn her on. Amazing, too, how good he felt beneath her hands. She ran her palms across his chest, teasing his flat, male nipples with her thumbs, raking her nails down his belly. She slid a hand into the front pocket of his jeans, pleased to find the small square of a condom beneath her fingers.

She pulled it free and made short work of his fly. Wordless, he lifted her, placing her on the edge of the counter. She sheathed him and guided him to her, wrapping a leg around his hips as he slid inside her.

She braced her arms behind her on the counter as he drove into her—long, slick, needful strokes. His gaze roved her body, from breast to breast, down her belly, until he was watching himself slide in and out of her body. The avid intensity of his gaze thrilled her and she dropped her gaze, too. The sight of him moving in her body lit something inside her. His tattooed chest, the stud in his ear, the hardness of his body, the length of him filling her…

She gripped his shoulder, needing the anchor as her climax hit. She closed her eyes and let it roll over her.

So good.

Harry became more frantic, less controlled as he pumped into her. She opened her eyes and watched his face and body tighten as he approached his own climax. She wrapped her other leg around him and locked her ankles behind his back, lifting her hips in time with his thrusts.

"Pippa…" he groaned.

He drove himself deeply inside her and stayed there, veins showing in his neck as he closed his eyes and got swept away. She watched him ride out his climax, loving that she'd given him so much pleasure.

He opened his eyes and looked at her. His gaze was still cloudy with desire, his face soft with satisfaction.

For the second time tonight she was hit with the urge to press an affectionate kiss to his cheek or lips or chest. He'd given so much to her. But she knew better than to do that, especially after the conversation they'd just had.

Instead, she slid off the counter and pulled her robe across her body again.

"I suppose you want dessert now."

He smiled, as she'd hoped he would.

"Thought I just had it."

"Well, you thought wrong, mister, because I have chocolate and raspberry brownies."

She crossed to the fridge.

"I'll go check on the door frame, see if the putty is dry yet."

She watched over her shoulder as he left the room. Then and only then did she press her forehead against the cool white metal of the fridge door.

She'd talked a good talk, so good she'd almost convinced herself, but the truth was that being with Harry, making love with Harry, spending time with Harry was something she could get used to very easily.

Which would be a big mistake. Really, really huge.

For a moment she wondered if she was fooling herself, entering into a no-strings fling with him. She'd had her fair share of lovers and a handful of one-night stands over the years, but what she had going on with Harry felt like a new thing, entirely different from either the serious or the casual relationships of her past.

It felt…addictive. Compelling. Magnetic.

She pushed away from the fridge, shaking the thought off. She'd just outlined to Harry exactly where she stood regarding what was happening between them. She had no illusions—in a week or two or three, she and Harry would be parting ways. Only a very foolish woman would let herself lose sight of that fact.

IT WAS NEARLY MIDNIGHT when Harry left Pippa's place. He'd fixed her bedroom door before moving on to her front door lock. Then he'd spent fifteen minutes in the shower coaxing her to a climax again with his hands and mouth.

He smiled to himself as he hefted his toolbox into the back of his truck. Three times in one night. He hadn't been this horny since he was a kid.

But there was something about Pippa's soft, pale skin and lush breasts… And the noises she made when she came, soft, needy and desperate… And the way she walked and talked and laughed…

He glanced toward the house. He could see a Pippa-shaped shadow moving behind the curtain in her bedroom. He recalled what she'd said to him tonight. She had been very clear about what they were about. Her words—very straightforward and up-front—had wiped away any misgivings he had about continuing to see her. As long as they were both on the same page, there was nothing to stop them from having a good time together.

He hadn't been out with a single mother before—he wasn't in the business of raising expectations. He'd be lying if he said it hadn't been a shock when Alice started crying tonight. From the moment he had set eyes on Pippa this evening, he'd been so intent on getting her into bed that he'd forgotten everything else. Alice's cries had brought him back to reality, quick smart. Lying on Pippa's bed listening to Alice's screams, he'd had visions of the night becoming one big cry-fest, with Pippa pacing and feeding the baby bottles and whatever else mothers did to comfort their babies while any chance he had of getting her naked again evaporated into thin air.

Then a strange thing had happened. Alice's crying had changed, kicking up a note, and he'd heard the raw misery in her voice and her very real distress. She'd sounded so lost. So inconsolable.

Without really thinking about it, he'd pulled on his jeans and gone to see if he could help. Not exactly the way he'd imagined the evening panning out, but not the end of the world, either.

Surprisingly.

Harry started his truck and reversed into the street. He was about to drive off when he saw a set of headlights flick on a few houses down. An engine started, a robust V8. It was dark, but he was pretty sure he could make out the shape of a high, square truck cabin.

Jaw set, he headed for home. The truck fell in behind him. Harry pulled into his driveway five minutes later, the truck still on his tail. He braced himself for a fight as he exited his own truck, walking to the head of his driveway and waiting for Steve to pull up. He didn't. Instead, he cruised past at speed, engine roaring.

It was impossible to see inside the cabin in the dark but Harry didn't need to—he could feel his friend staring at him as he passed.

The truck turned the corner and the sound of the engine faded into the distance.

How long had Steve been sitting out front of Pippa's place? All night?

Harry thought back to the silhouette he'd seen in Pippa's bedroom as he was leaving. While not explicit, it had been revealing enough. How much had Steve seen tonight? Enough to know that Harry was no longer simply helping out around the house?

Guilt bit at him. He tried to shrug it off but it wouldn't go away. Mel had told him to settle things with Steve, and she was right. They needed to clear the air. Say whatever needed to be said. The last thing Pippa needed was an angry ex loitering outside her house and Harry didn't want to burn a friendship that had meant a lot over the years.

He rubbed his forehead. He'd known this would be messy going in, but he'd still shoved Pippa against the wall and kissed her last night, and he'd done it again tonight.

It wouldn't be the last time, either. Maybe it made him a selfish asshole and a bad mate, but he couldn't stay away from her.

For some reason, his sister's words echoed in his head. *Every man meets his match eventually.*

He made a rude noise and walked toward the house. His sister was deluded. Just because she was happily settled with Flynn didn't mean that Harry was about to succumb to the lures of coupledom. He could still remember how he'd felt when he'd been living with Debbie. As though he was suffocating. As though his world was shrinking. He never wanted to feel that constrained again.

Mel didn't seem constrained by Flynn, though, and if anyone had reason to fear commitment, it was his sister. Her marriage had been unhappy, bordering on abusive, something he'd only found out after the divorce papers were signed. If anything, Mel had blossomed since Flynn came into her life. She'd shaken off the past and embraced the world—and herself—again.

Maybe, if the right person came along and a man was at the right stage in his life, the white picket-fence dream wouldn't be such a nightmare. Maybe.

Harry winced, imagining how triumphant his sisters would be if they could hear his thoughts. They'd think their constant drip-feed of monogamy-pushing had finally started to bear fruit.

There was something sitting on the doorstep when he reached the porch. He couldn't make it out in the dark. He touched the screen on his phone to bring it to life and aimed it at the object. The cold blue light reflected off the shiny gold of a football trophy. He crouched and picked it up. He had one just like it inside somewhere, a souvenir from 1996 when the Frankston Rovers had won the grand final. Steve had played full-forward that season, Harry ruck-rover. The parties had lasted all weekend and they'd felt like kings for months afterward.

Harry stared at the trophy. He needed to talk to Steve. Properly this time. Calmly.

His gut told him it wouldn't be pretty, but he had to try.

Shoulders tense, he let himself into the house.

PIPPA WOKE IN sheets that smelled of sex and Harry. Memories from last night flashed across her mind as she lay in the early-morning light.

She was thirty-one years old, but she'd never had a man so hot for her that they'd made love three times in one night. It was heady, seductive stuff.

But it wasn't only memories of Harry's attentiveness and passion in the bedroom that revisited her. She recalled the way he'd offered to help settle Alice, and the sympathetic warmth in his eyes as he'd watched Alice in Pippa's arms. She thought about the way he'd tugged her robe across her body and tied the sash for her before she'd walked him to the door to say goodbye.

Be very careful, madam.

She deliberately called to mind the conversation they'd had about where they both stood and what they both wanted. None of that had changed overnight.

She threw back the covers. She had a busy day ahead. A full eight hours at the gallery, then a night of watching Alice and Becca's boy, Aaron, while Becca worked, her part of their reciprocal child-minding arrangement. She didn't have time to lie about second-guessing herself.

Pippa showered, dressed and ate breakfast in the gaps between changing Alice and dressing her and preparing her bottle. Predictably, her thoughts drifted to Harry as she started a load of washing before dashing out the door.

She had no idea when she would see him again. He'd finished repairing her ceiling and the other minor tasks he'd wanted to take on so they were officially all out of excuses for him to visit. Any future interactions would be because they wanted to see each other, pure and simple. Yet he hadn't made any reference to the future before he left, and neither had she.

It was possible she wouldn't hear from him for a while. She had no idea what his social life was like. For all she knew, he might have parties lined up for the next two months. Women, too.

She stilled in the middle of putting detergent into the dispenser, a dart of pure, possessive jealousy shooting through her at the thought of Harry with another woman.

Nowhere in their conversation last night had they covered other people. He'd made it clear he wasn't looking for a relationship. She'd told him that was more than obvious and that neither was she. She hadn't thought to ask if their short-term, just-for-fun-and-orgasms fling was to be exclusive for its duration.

Probably she should have, because the idea of being one of many women that Harry serviced on a casual basis made the gorge rise in her throat. She wasn't stupid, she knew the man had a past. Hell, she had a past, too—probably not as prolific and high-rotation as his, but she was no nun. No amount of experience would ever reconcile her to sharing her lover like a bicycle in a public lending scheme.

Pippa went to work feeling vaguely anxious and unsettled. As the day wore on her unease only grew. She kept checking her phone to see if Harry had called, then catching herself and giving herself yet another mental lecture.

So much for being "able to separate sex and love and romance and friendship." Every anxious minute that ticked by made a mockery of her bold, emancipated words last night. She'd been riding her very highest horse, smugly pointing out to him that she understood exactly what the parameters of their relationship were. Determined to prove to him and herself that she wasn't like his other women.

And yet here she was, not even twenty-four hours later, fretting over if he was going to call and if he was hers exclusively.

Not good. Distracting, undermining and draining. This was why she'd warned herself off Harry in the first place. Her life was already a crisis waiting to happen. She needed less drama, not more.

By four in the afternoon she'd almost convinced herself that it would be a good thing if Harry never called again. Then she looked up from taking a phone call and found Harry walking toward her, his stride long and confident, big shoulders dipping from side to side with each step. She was powerless to stop the delighted smile that curved her mouth.

"What are you doing here?" She'd mentioned she'd be working at the gallery last night but he hadn't appeared to pay particular attention to the information. Clearly, however, he'd filed it away.

"I wanted to see if you and Alice felt like dinner at the Brewery tonight?"

Pippa's smile dimmed a little. The Mornington Brewery was a local bar that offered boutique beers, wood-fired pizzas and live music. She would have loved a night there with Harry.

"I can't. I'm looking after another little boy. I have this reciprocal arrangement with a woman from university...."

She braced herself for Harry's disappointment. No doubt this was the first time he'd been turned down in favor of a night with two six-month-olds. He was used to shaping his life to suit himself, not bending himself around responsibilities and obligations.

"How about I bring pizza and beer to you, then?"

He said it easily, utterly accepting. A surge of wholly unwarranted relief swept through her.

"You heard the bit about me babysitting the kids, right?"

"Will there be a chance of me getting you naked?"

Pippa shot a glance to the side to make sure no one had overheard his question. An older couple were examining some jewelry in a nearby showcase but they didn't appear to be listening.

She returned her focus to Harry. "I'd say your chances were good to very good. Becca's picking Aaron up at nine."

"Then I'll see you at seven with beer and pizza. Any requests?"

"No anchovies. Extra olives."

"Done." He turned to go, then swiveled back. "You still have that lacy red bra?"

"Yes."

"Think you could wear it tonight?"

"Um, sure."

"Good."

His gaze swept down her body. She was wearing a striped shirtwaist dress with her black eyelet boots—hardly siren stuff—but the expression in his eyes made her feel like Pamela Anderson, Sophia Loren and Marilyn Monroe all rolled into one. Heat bloomed between her thighs. She swallowed a lump of pure lust. Harry's mouth tilted into a knowing smile. He knew exactly what he did to her.

He turned to exit again but there was something she needed to ask him before this thing between them spun into another night.

"Harry…" She slipped from behind the desk and made her way to his side, acutely aware of the older couple and how echoey the space was.

Harry raised his eyebrows, waiting for her to speak. She tried out a few phrases in her mind, but she'd always been a direct person, and—to date, anyway—Harry had always seemed to appreciate her forthrightness.

"Are you sleeping with anyone else at the moment?"

He blinked, then a slight frown wrinkled his forehead. "No. Are you?"

She snorted her amusement. "Right. That's why I have a spare set of batteries under my bed."

His frown disappeared. "I'm a one-woman-at-a-time kind of man."

"Okay. Good to know."

It *was* good to know. A huge relief, actually. She could consign those visions of him with other women to the dustbin in her mind.

Until their fling had run its course, naturally.

"I'll see you later," she said, stepping away from him.

She didn't have eyes in the back of her head, but she knew he watched her walk all the way back to the desk. She loved that she turned him on so much. She loved the way he looked at her. And the fact that he remembered what bra she'd been wearing weeks ago... Yeah, that was pretty hot, too.

It was her turn to watch him walk away now, and she did so with gusto, mapping his broad shoulders and back with her eyes before lavishing her attention on his backside.

If she was a poet, she would write an ode to his butt. She'd talk about how muscular and round and perfect it was, and how she wanted to sink her teeth into it, it was so damned sexy...

"Excuse me, miss?"

She tore her gaze from Harry's derriere to focus on the elderly gentleman who had approached the desk.

"Um, yes?" She smiled and pushed her hair behind her ear, feeling flushed and more than a little caught out.

"We were wondering if we could take a look at the opal rings in the cabinet?"

"Sure. Yes. Absolutely. Let me grab the keys...."

She cast one last glance toward the door as she tugged open the drawer in her desk to find the keys, but Harry was gone.

Well. She would see him again tonight. Hugging the knowledge to herself, she went to open the cabinet.

HARRY TAPPED HIS hands on his steering wheel, gazing out the side window at the stucco facade of Steve's town house. Where the hell was he?

He knew via Macca that Steve had been finishing up a job today, but Steve never worked past five on the weekends. It was nearly six-thirty now, and Harry had been waiting over an hour.

He glanced in the rearview mirror. It was possible Steve had seen Harry's car parked out front and kept on driving. Or maybe he was being paranoid, and Steve simply had other plans for the night.

Harry let his head drop back. He'd worked himself up to this all day and he wanted it done. Not that he had high hopes they would resolve anything, but he had to at least try. Fifteen years of friendship demanded it.

He went over what he'd decided to say in his head for the tenth time. He'd apologize for getting in Steve's face about Pippa and Alice. As much as Steve's behavior made him grind his teeth, at the end of the day it was none of Harry's business. He wasn't Steve's conscience, and he'd said his piece on the subject. The rest was up to Steve.

That just left Pippa. He didn't fully understand why Steve was so cut up about Harry's interest in her. It wasn't as though Harry had even looked sideways at her while she was with Steve, and it had been more than a year since they'd broken up.

Harry thought back to the days immediately following Pippa's announcement that she was pregnant. Steve had been furious, white-hot furious. Harry had thought then and still thought now that it had a lot to do with what things had been like for Steve as a kid. Jack Lawson had been a hard bastard and he'd taken his nasty temper out on Steve and his brothers and sisters on a regular basis. Many was the time Steve had slept on the floor in Harry's bedroom to avoid going home.

Harry figured that the prospect of becoming a father scared the living crap out of Steve. Added to the fact that his mate had a pathological need to always be in charge of his own destiny, it had made for a pretty potent knee-jerk reaction to Pippa's pregnancy.

But Steve had had plenty of time to freak out. He needed to stop being an asshole and start being the guy Harry knew. The guy who was the first to offer a lending hand to a mate and the first to reach into his pocket for a good cause. Punishing Pippa and Alice for the shortcomings of his own childhood was pure crazy. As was burning a friendship that had endured fifteen years of ups and downs.

Harry stared at the roof-lining of his car, wondering how in hell he would deliver all of the above in a way that would make Steve stop and listen. No brilliant ideas came to him.

He checked his watch. He needed to go get pizza. He picked up his phone and dialed Steve's number. It went straight to voice mail—surprise surprise.

"We need to talk. Call me, okay?"

He tossed his phone onto the passenger seat and started the car, knowing that the chances of Steve returning his call were less than zero.

Fifteen minutes later, the car was redolent with super supreme fumes and he was heading back up the highway toward Pippa's place. He had a six-pack of pale ale and the heady expectation of Pippa in a lacy bra to look forward to. He was turning on the radio when his phone rang. He punched the radio off again and took the call.

"Yo."

"Harry. It's me. Where are you? You sound like

you're in a wind tunnel." Mike Porter's voice sounded too loud over the hands-free speaker.

"I'm in the car, and you say that every time, Dad."

"That's because you sound like you're in a tunnel every time."

"Yeah, yeah. What's up?"

His father was not a chitchatter, and neither was Harry.

"Wanted to give you a heads up, in case you heard anything through Leo or one of the guys at work. I've been talking to a business broker about putting the workshop up for sale. The ad should go out next month."

It was so out of left field that for a moment Harry was speechless.

"You still there?" His father's voice echoed around the car.

"Where the hell did this come from?"

"Your mother and I have been talking about it for a while. She wants to see the world while we still have our own hips and teeth. I figure she's put up with enough lost weekends and late nights."

"So you're selling up your life's work because she wants to go on a cruise?"

"Gotta loosen the grip sometime. Might as well be now as later."

Harry ground his teeth. His father wasn't saying it outright, but this was about him, about his refusal to step into his father's shoes.

"Look, I know you're pissed with me, Dad, but don't cut off your nose to spite your face."

To his surprise, his father laughed.

"I know this will come as a shock to you, Harry, but you're not the center of my universe. This has been a long time coming."

Harry frowned at the road ahead. "It's your business, Dad. You can do whatever you like with it."

He didn't say it, but his tone said the rest: it's yours to screw up, too.

"It is. It definitely is. You got a big night planned?"

"Dinner with a friend."

"Well, have a good one."

"Yeah. You, too."

The phone went dead. Harry felt as though someone had walked up behind him and smacked him on the back of the head with a piece of four-by-two.

His father was selling his workshop. The business he'd sweated over for decades.

Harry almost drove past Pippa's place, only realizing that her house was approaching at the last second. He made a sharp turn into her driveway and then simply sat staring blindly at her house.

His mum must have been pressuring his father. That was the only explanation. Because his father lived for that workshop.

After a few minutes the porch light came on and the front door opened. Pippa peered out at him, a bemused smile on her face. He collected the pizzas and beer and climbed out of the car.

"It *is* you. I thought maybe Knight Rider had come to visit," Pippa said as he approached the house.

"Just me." He forced a smile.

She tilted her head as he climbed to the porch, her gaze scanning his face.

"Is everything okay?" She was wearing the same striped dress she'd had on at the gallery earlier in the afternoon. Her feet were bare, her hair loose around her shoulders. Her heavy black glasses framed her warm brown eyes.

She looked good—familiar and sexy and relaxed.

"Yeah." He offered her the pizza boxes. "I got super supreme with extra olives and no anchovies, and Hawaiian."

She hesitated a second before taking them. "I love Hawaiian. Good choice. Come and meet Aaron, who hasn't slept a single wink since Becca dropped him off."

She led him to the kitchen where he found Alice and another baby with a profusion of dark hair lying together on a quilted throw rug.

"Isn't she a little young to be dating?" he asked.

Pippa laughed. "She's well chaperoned. And Aaron has trouble sticking his thumb in his own mouth. I think we're good for another decade or so."

The table was already set with paper napkins, plates and cutlery. Pippa flipped the lids back on the boxes and handed him a bottle opener for the beers. He knew from experience that she was a drink-her-beer-from-the-bottle kind of woman—his kind, in other words—and he flipped the cap off a beer and passed it across to her.

"Fantastic. I've been thinking about this all afternoon," she said.

The moment the words were out of her mouth her cheeks turned pink. He eyed her as he took a mouthful from his own beer. It amused him no end that she was so quick to blush out of the bedroom and so shameless within.

"Me, too."

She pressed her lips together and gave a rueful shake of her head. "Giving away the game again, White. When are you ever going to learn?"

He laughed. His shoulders dropped a notch. She was easy company.

"I'm about to eat my body-weight in pizza. Close

your eyes if you're easily grossed out," she said, reaching for her first slice.

She asked him about his day at work, then told him about hers, making the ordinary entertaining with her witty observations. They were both on their second beer when she pushed her plate away and drew her foot up so that her knee was against her chest and her heel rested on the seat of her chair.

"You going to tell me what's wrong now or do you need to stew on it a little longer?"

He looked down at the half-eaten pizza on his plate. Pippa didn't need to know about his dad's crazy decision. What did it matter to her if his father was making a huge mistake? She had enough of her own stuff to deal with.

"Okay. More stewing it is. I'll have another slice, then," Pippa said lightly.

He poked a finger at a piece of pineapple. "My dad wants to sell the workshop."

"I take it this is a surprise to you?"

He huffed out a laugh. He was aiming for wry but it came out sounding a little bitter.

"You could say that. He's poured his lifeblood into that place. It's his dream—his own place, his rules, his way."

"Did he say why he wants to sell?"

"He and Mum want to travel, start winding down."

"How old is he?"

"Fifty-nine."

She shrugged. "Not out of the question for retirement."

"You've seen him. He's hardly on his last legs. He loves that place, Pippa."

She cocked her head. "Are you sure that this is about him?"

"I know Mum's been campaigning to go on a cruise. I figure she's cheerleading him on this one."

"I meant are you sure this isn't about you? Since you're not interested in taking on your father's business, he was bound to have to sell it at some point. Or simply shut it down."

"No way. He's built it up too much to just walk away from it."

"So if you don't want it and he can't sell it or shut it down, what should he do with it, then? Keep working until he falls over?"

He stared at her for a beat, then dropped his gaze to his plate. She was right. He'd left his father with nowhere to turn.

"I still don't think this is what he wants."

"I've only met your father once, but he didn't strike me as the kind of man who does anything he didn't want to."

He ran a hand over his head.

"This was always going to happen, Harry, right?" she said, her voice soft with sympathy.

"I hate the thought of him giving it up."

She reached across the table and curled her fingers around his. "At the end of the day, you have to live your life. He can't live his for you, and you can't live yours for him."

Harry straightened in his seat. "You want the last slice of Hawaiian?"

She gave him a small smile. "Did we just reach your deep and meaningful threshold?"

He lifted a shoulder. "Talking won't change anything."

"Sure. But sometimes it can make you feel better."

She stood and collected their empty bottles. She dropped a hand on his shoulder and gave it a warm squeeze before heading for the sink. Harry watched the sway of her hips, thinking about what she'd said. He was still pissed and frustrated, but not anywhere near to the degree he'd been when he arrived. Talking to her, having her listen, had taken the edge off.

"Thanks," he said.

She smiled at him. Pippa was so down to earth and funny and honest. She never pulled her punches. She drank beer out of the bottle. And he was pretty damned sure he'd just caught a glimpse of a red bra strap at her neckline.

He pushed back his chair and stood. Her eyebrows rose in silent question as he walked toward her. He reached for the neckline of her dress, pulling the fabric away from her skin so he could inspect her cleavage. His gaze fell on creamy breasts cupped in lace.

She was smiling a secretive, pleased smile.

"You wore it," he said.

"You asked me to."

"You're making me think of a whole bunch of other things I could ask you to do."

"Maybe you should try your luck."

"Maybe I should."

He lowered his head and kissed her. She tasted of beer and the sweetness of pineapple. He slid a hand into the hair at the nape of her neck, angling her head, deepening the kiss. She had such a great mouth. He could kiss her for hours.

She made a small approving noise and he moved forward, pressing her back against the sink with his hips.

Her hands slid to his rear, sliding inside the pockets of his jeans and curving into the muscles of his ass.

White-hot need burned through him. She was so damned sexy. The snap in her eyes. Her full, soft breasts. The way she reached out and took whatever she wanted. If there weren't two six-month-olds watching their every move, he'd throw her over his shoulder and take her to the bedroom right now.

He broke their kiss and pulled away enough to look down into her face without going cross-eyed. "What time is your friend coming to pick up her kid?"

"Nine."

A whole hour away. He grasped her elbows and gently tugged her hands free from his jean pockets, stepping away from her. She grinned, getting the message.

"Probably a wise decision." Her gaze dropped to his crotch, her mouth tipping down regretfully. "Seems a shame to waste that, though."

He looked down at his hard-on. "I'll have another just like it in an hour. Trust me."

She laughed, the sound low and dirty and knowing. He couldn't help it, he had to kiss her again. He leaned forward and captured the last of her laughter with his lips. Her hands found his shoulders, her fingers digging into his muscles, holding him close.

Man… If they were alone.

But they weren't.

He stepped back. "You want to watch some TV?" he said, his breathing a little ragged.

"Okay." She wasn't smiling now, her cheeks pink, her mouth wet from his kisses. "I might text Becca to make sure she's on time."

It was his turn to laugh then. He crossed to the table and collected the pizza boxes. It was only as he was folding them into the rubbish bin that he realized the tension he'd been carrying since talking to his father had slipped away. Pippa had eased it, with her patience and sympathy and sexiness.

It hit him suddenly that it was going to be hard to walk away from her when the time came. Despite all the complications.

For a second he allowed himself to contemplate the alternative: not walking away, not turning his back on her and the way she made him feel. A possible future shimmered in front of him, full of diapers and night feeds and laundry and Alice's gummy smile and small, soft hands and Saturday nights in front of the television instead of down at the pub. Nights in Pippa's bed, mornings with her beside him when he woke. Lawns that need mowing and bills that needed paying and holidays for three instead of one.

None of it seemed too awful, not with Pippa at his side.

Then he blinked and the vision was gone. He shook himself. Clearly, great sex was messing with his head. He was years away from wanting to take on any of that stuff, if ever. He had a great life right now. No way was he ready to give it up to embrace domesticity, no matter how much he liked Pippa.

CHAPTER TWELVE

IT WAS STILL dark outside when Pippa woke. A warm, solid arm pressed against hers, and when she shifted her leg she felt the roughness of a hard, hairy male calf against her own. She smiled, remembering what had happened after Becca collected Aaron. Alice had been tetchy, crying off and on, her teeth obviously painful. Pippa had tried everything, rubbing gel onto her daughter's gums, offering her various soft objects to chew on. Then she'd handed Alice to Harry while she mixed a bottle of formula, only for Alice to pipe down almost immediately.

She'd looked around to find her daughter gnawing on Harry's thumb, a deeply satisfied expression on her round face. She'd expected Harry to balk, or at the very least hand Alice back after a token few minutes, but he'd settled on the couch with her and let her gum away until she'd fallen into a fretful sleep. Then he'd carried Alice to her room and stood to one side as Pippa tucked her in.

Pippa would be lying if she pretended there hadn't been a moment—maybe even two or three—when she'd glanced across at him holding her child and let herself imagine.

She'd caught herself every time. Harry was a good-natured guy, and Alice was a novelty to him. No doubt he'd been won over by her wide-eyed adulation and fascination with him, the only male in her orbit. Pippa was sure that a few sleepless nights, foul diapers, rashes and sick-ups would fix that. This was Harry, after all, the ultimate Peter Pan.

After Alice had fallen asleep, she and Harry had showered together before he'd massaged her shoulders and back…and then other parts of her that hadn't been so much tense but more hot and very ready for him. By the time he'd finished she'd been panting and desperate and she'd pushed him down onto the mattress and climbed on top and taken them both for a long, slow, crazy ride. She'd pushed him to the brink and over and watched him come, his body racked with pleasure. Then she'd smoothed a palm down her belly and between her thighs and found her own climax with him still inside her, his gray eyes glinting up at her through half-closed lids.

He'd fallen into a doze afterward and she'd pulled the covers up and curled into his side, telling herself it would only be a few minutes before he woke again and got dressed to go home.

Now, she peered at the clock on her bedside table. It was nearly four. She squinted to make sure she was reading the numerals correctly, then lay frowning into her pillow as she tried to work out how she felt about Harry staying the night.

On the surface, it was no big deal. He didn't steal the quilt or drool or snore. And it wasn't as though she was worried about what the neighbors might think. But there was something very seductive about waking to find a big, warm, hard body beside her and hearing someone else's soft breathing and knowing she wasn't alone in the night.

While she'd had Mr. Pink and an emergency stash of batteries to stop her from climbing the walls in the past year, there was no substitute for this kind of intimacy. And no, a pillow didn't come even close to cutting it.

The sensible thing to do would be to wake him. Allowing herself to get used to him sleeping in her bed was the first step down a very slippery slope. She reached out to touch his shoulder, intending to shake him awake. Her fingers slid over warm, smooth skin. She shaped her hand to the curve of his muscles, feeling how strong he was, how solid. She slid her head closer, pressing her nose to his shoulder and inhaling deeply. He smelled so good, like sunshine and warmth.

Pippa didn't want to kick him out of her bed. The second she admitted as much, she started making excuses for herself. It was nearly morning, anyway, and she wasn't an idiot. She knew him staying didn't mean anything more than that he'd been comfortable and that he'd fallen asleep. She wasn't about to weave fantasies based on his presence between her sheets for a few extra hours.

She let her eyes drift closed again and woke three hours later to the warm tug of his mouth on her breasts. She murmured her approval as he rolled on top of her and made slow, languid love to her in the gray morning light.

Afterward, she lay and watched him pull on his clothes, feeling drowsy and lazy. He had a lovely body. Following the play of his muscles as he dressed was a very, very pleasant way to start the day. He sat on the end of the bed to pull on his boots and shot a glance at her.

"Keep looking at me like that and you'll be in trouble," he said, a glint in his eye.

"What kind of trouble?"

"Guess."

She smiled and stretched her arms above her head, self-satisfied as a cat.

"What have you got on for the day?" she asked idly as he pocketed his phone, car keys and wallet.

"Maybe a surf. Should probably do some Christmas shopping. Get it out of the way." He strapped on his watch. "Thought I might drop by and talk to Dad, too."

"Sounds good." Especially the bit where he would talk to his father.

"Oh, yeah. Sounds riveting." He glanced at her. "Busy next week?"

"Yep. My assignment's due, and I've got an exam on Friday. Plus the usual."

He leaned down to kiss her, his lips soft and warm. "I'll call you."

A little dart of pleasure shot through her at his words.

She propped herself up on one elbow. "Maybe *I'll* call *you*." There was no reason why he should be the only one calling the shots, after all.

He grinned. "You do that. Anytime."

He slipped out her newly-hung door. She expected to hear the front door closing in short order, but instead he walked up the hall in the other direction, toward the kitchen. At first she assumed he must be using the bathroom, but the toilet didn't flush. Then she heard his voice come over the baby monitor, low but perfectly audible.

"That's right, little lady, keep snoozing. Get your beauty sleep so you can be as pretty as your mummy one day. I'll see you later, okay?"

Pippa pressed a hand to her heart, an instinctive, ridiculously clichéd gesture. But there was no denying she was touched by his interest in Alice. That he'd taken time to say farewell to her daughter spoke volumes for the sort of man he was.

She heard his footsteps in the hall again, heading for the door this time. She flopped back onto her pillow as she heard it shut behind him, aware that the tide of emotion rising inside her was as much about Steve's neglect as it was about Harry's casual warmth and affection for her baby daughter.

She swallowed the lump in her throat. She had a sudden vision of how she would look to an outside observer—the recently-sated single mother, lying in bed getting all dewy-eyed because her casual lover had deigned to toss a kind word in her child's direction.

Pippa pushed the covers back abruptly. She wasn't that stupid or desperate or sentimental. It was nice that Harry had spared five seconds to think of her daughter, but that was all it was. It didn't mean anything, just as his having accidentally stayed the night didn't, either. This thing between them would work only if she kept the parameters front and center.

"Sex, Pippa. It's all about the sex."

Maybe she should get a T-shirt made—and maybe a cap, for good measure. And maybe she should draw up a few ground rules for herself, starting with not allowing him to stay the night in her bed again. It was too cozy, too domestic, having him here in the morning.

It felt too real, as though it meant something. And it didn't.

She stood, feeling empowered by her decision. She'd gone into this thing with her eyes wide open, and she would keep them that way.

HARRY DECIDED TO DRIVE past the workshop on his way to his parents' place. Even though it was Sunday, it wouldn't be unusual for his father to have put aside some of his morning for all the paperwork he hadn't got around to during the week.

A shiny red truck turned the corner ahead of Harry as he drove into the Village. It reminded him that Steve had yet to return his phone call and he grabbed his phone and dialed Steve's number.

It went through to voice mail, as it had last night. Harry pictured Steve checking caller ID and leaving Harry to swing in the breeze. Idiot.

It went against the grain to be cast in the role of supplicant, but he left a second message anyway.

"Steve. Call me, okay? Just… Call me."

Like last night, he didn't hold out much hope for a return call. He figured he would run out of patience with the little game Steve was playing sometime soon. They were both too old for this shit. With a bit of luck, Steve would see sense before then.

He spotted his father's car in front of Village Motors and pulled in beside it. His father was seated at the desk in the reception area, a takeout cup of coffee in front of him as he studied the computer screen, fingers hunting and pecking their way across the keyboard. He glanced up as Harry entered.

"Morning." He didn't sound too surprised by the impromptu visit.

"Morning." Harry sank onto one of the visitors' chairs. He crossed his arms over his chest and sat back, watching his father tap away.

The silence stretched, the only sound the rhythmic clickety-clack of the keyboard.

"If you've got something to say, Harry, you should spit it out. Staring at me like that is just plain creepy." His father didn't look away from the computer screen.

"I've got a deal for you. I'll talk to Leo, see if he'll give me six weeks' leave. Let me know when you and Mom want to go on that cruise and I'll pitch in here for the duration so you know the home front is covered."

His father stopped typing, letting his hands drop into his lap. He swiveled the chair to face Harry, his face calmly neutral. "So you take leave and come work for me temporarily so I can take leave?"

Harry lifted a shoulder. "Gets you out of a jam, and I'm happy to help out."

His father stroked a finger down one side of his horseshoe mustache. "Nice idea, but there's not much point to it. You can't take leave every time I want to have a break from the business."

"Then hire someone to manage the place."

"That's just delaying the inevitable." His father shook his head decisively. "If I'm making the cut, I'm doing it cleanly."

Harry swore under his breath. This was nuts. His father lived and breathed this place.

"You'll go stir-crazy sitting around at home. What are you going to do, take up golf?" The idea of his father in pastel pink polo shirts and plaid pants was laughable.

"I told you. Your mother wants to travel. She's got enough trips planned to cover the next ten years."

Harry stood, frustrated. "If you think this will make me change my mind, you're wrong. I've told you how I feel, what I want."

"I know. And I listened. That's why I'm doing this." His father's voice was tinged with resignation.

It hit Harry that his father was deadly serious about this sale. This wasn't a gambit or a tactic. This was for real.

He sat down again with a thump. For a long beat they

simply stared at each other, then his father shrugged one big shoulder.

"It was never your dream. I get it. I won't lie, it's disappointing. I kind of liked the idea of starting a dynasty." He smiled faintly. "But it was never meant to be a choke hold."

Harry shifted in his seat. "That's not the way I see it."

"A bear trap, then." Another faint smile from his old man.

Half a dozen explanations and justifications for the way he'd chosen to live his life marshaled themselves at the back of Harry's throat. Stuff about valuing his freedom and not being able to stand being hemmed in or pinned down. Stuff about not being good at all the i-dotting and t-crossing that came with being the boss. He didn't utter a word, because even in his own head it sounded lame.

Like the complaints of a little kid who'd been asked to finish his chores.

It was an uncomfortable realization. Harry glowered at the toes of his boots.

"Relax, Harry. You're officially off the hook, and so am I."

Harry looked up. His father shrugged. Harry stood, his guts churning.

"I've got to go."

He walked out to his car and slid behind the wheel. He had no idea where he was going until he found himself wending his way through the back streets toward his favorite beach, a tucked-away cove surrounded by sand dunes and weathered wooden walkways. It had no official name but the locals called it Mt. Steep, after the tallest of the sand dunes. He parked in the sandy visitors' lot and hiked along a twisty-turny gravel track for ten minutes before he emerged at the beach. A flight of silver-timbered stairs took him down to the sand. It was still early—barely ten—and the beach was empty. He sat on the sun-warmed sand and tried to understand himself.

All his life he'd been restless. Maybe because he was the youngest of three, he'd always felt as though there was stuff going on that he was missing out on. Adventures and challenges he was considered too young for. When he got old enough to concoct his own adventures and challenges, he'd set forth with a vengeance and never looked back. Footy trips with his mates, surfing holidays, backpacking through Asia, fast cars, fast women, tattoos and piercings and trouble… Then he'd met Debbie and fallen hard and spent the next three years trying to mold himself to her dreams and failed miserably.

It was an experience that had left a bad taste in his mouth, not least because he was painfully aware that he'd behaved badly. He'd hurt her. Not something he was proud off all these years later.

He'd decided then that he wasn't cut out for serious. He hadn't liked feeling obligated, and he'd deeply resented being in a situation where his choices were so limited. He'd pretty much arranged his life since to avoid all of the above. He'd chosen a job that was lowkey, bought a house that required the minimum mortgage, sidestepped any woman with the gleam of forever in her eyes. Every time his father or mother had raised the idea of him taking over the workshop, he'd told them the same thing: thanks, but no thanks. When his sisters had hassled him, questioning his stance, he'd told them to butt out.

He'd trumpeted his easygoing, no-muss, no-fuss philosophy to anyone who'd listen, including Pippa. And yet he'd never thought through the logical consequences of his decision regarding his father's workshop. Pippa had asked him last night what he'd expected his father to do with the business if Harry wasn't going to take it over. The truth was, Harry had never thought that far ahead. He simply...hadn't.

When he pictured his father in his mind's eye, he saw him leaning over an engine, hands grubby with grease and oil, an absorbed, patient expression on his face as he puzzled out a problem. His father was ageless in his imagination, the setting never changing. His father's work and, by extension, the workshop, were who his father was. Always had been, always would be. It had never occurred to Harry that his father would opt out at some point.

But his father *was* opting out, and his decision had forced Harry to recognize something he'd kept well hidden from even himself: deep in his heart of hearts, he'd believed that the workshop would always be there, equal parts opportunity and obligation, ready for him if and when he ever decided he wanted to take the plunge. In the same way that he'd always imagined that he might meet the "right" woman and settle down sometime in the hazy, distant future, he'd imagined that there might come a time when the moon and stars aligned and the partying was over and he'd surfed enough beaches and raised enough hell that he'd be ready to step into his father's shoes. And that when he chose to do so, those shoes would simply be waiting for him, ready to be filled.

It was an arrogant, careless, childish belief for a man of thirty to hold. It was a young man's imagining of the future, nebulous and utterly self-focused.

He squinted his eyes against the glare of the sun on the water and dug the heels of his boots deeper into the sand.

He didn't like thinking of himself as childish or selfish. He owned two cars, paid his bills and turned up to work every day he was expected to be there. If he said he'd do something, he did it, no questions asked. He wasn't afraid of a challenge or a dare. He liked to think that he didn't hold back in life.

Yet he'd been holding back in the most basic possible way for a long time now. He'd been living the life of Riley, keeping his father's expectations and hopes at bay, telling himself he was choosing freedom and individuality over obligation and restriction—and yet all the time he'd had his little fail-safe measure tucked away, ready to deploy if and when it suited him.

And now his father had called Harry's bluff, called bullshit on his claims that he wasn't interested in the business. After all these years, his father was laying it on the line. Giving Harry the choice to put up or shut up.

He inhaled deeply through his nose, breathing in the scent of hot sand and salt and the faint tang of seaweed. The wind raised the hairs on his arms and cooled the back of his neck.

There was no question in his mind what his decision would be. Funny that after all these years of stalling the answer felt so certain. So unequivocal.

He wouldn't stand by and watch something his father had built up from nothing pass on to a stranger. It simply wasn't going to happen.

He waited for the heaviness of his decision to settle over him. He would be saying goodbye to the last remnants of his youth, after all, when he took over the reins of Village Motors.

Harry's gut felt tense, but—surprisingly—it was adrenaline that was tightening his belly, not dread.

A part of him was ready for this. Maybe even wanted it. The next stage of his life. The next challenge.

He pulled his phone out and dialed.

"Hello?" Pippa's voice came down the line, drowsy and distracted. He pictured her still lying in bed, shoulders bare, her hair dark against the pillow.

"It's me."

"Oh, hey." She sounded pleased.

"Are you still in bed?"

"No such luck. I'm working on my big assignment. It's due on Thursday."

"I won't keep you then." He wasn't even sure why he'd called, and he didn't want to hold her up.

"You're not keeping me. Did you talk to your dad?"

Something inside him relaxed as he heard the sympathy in her voice. "Yeah."

"Did it go okay?"

"I'm going to take over the business."

She exhaled in a rush. "Oh. Harry."

He couldn't tell if she was surprised, disbelieving, approving or disapproving. It was a little alarming how much he hoped it wasn't the latter.

"You think it's a bad idea?"

"I think it's a great idea if it's what you want. If you're doing it for the right reasons and not because you feel obligated."

"I'd be lying if I said there was no obligation. But it's not just that. I guess I always figured I'd get around to stepping into the business at some point."

Despite what he'd advertised to the world and himself.

"Kind of like I always imagined I'd do something with my degree sometime, huh?"

He didn't need to see her to know she was smiling self-deprecatingly.

"Kind of like that."

"Funny how life sneaks up on you sometimes."

He stared at the glittering blue of the ocean, suddenly wishing he was there or she was here. He wanted to see her. He wanted to touch her. And it wasn't just about sex.

"Your dad must have been pretty happy, huh?"

"I haven't told him yet."

There was a small pause. "Then why are you talking to me?"

"Because I wanted to."

Because the moment he'd made the decision he'd wanted to tell her about it. To hear her opinion. To have her approval.

"Talk to me later. Go put your father out of his misery." She sounded stern. No-nonsense.

"Is that your teacher voice?"

"It will be, one day. I hope. If I can get this assignment done."

"I'll let you get back to it."

"Call your father."

He smiled. "I will."

"Good."

He ran his thumb over the screen on his phone after he'd ended the call, thinking about Pippa. Thinking about the future.

Harry stood, dusted off his ass and started up the hill.

HE CRUISED PAST the workshop but his father's car was gone, so he went to his parents' place. The roller door to the garage was up when he arrived, a sure sign his father was in there, tinkering on his current pet project. Ever since Harry could remember his father had had a restoration project on the go in the garage. Over the years he'd returned more than a dozen cars to their former glory, always selling them at a good profit.

The current work in progress was a left-hand drive 1976 Mustang. His father was at the workbench contemplating the carburetor when Harry entered.

"How's it looking?" he asked.

His father glanced over his shoulder. "Like a forty-year-old carbie. In other words, shit-house."

Harry joined his father at the bench, running a practiced eye over the part. The carb float was dark with fuel residue, the bowl equally coated in crud. "Got your work cut out for you there."

"Thanks, Captain Obvious."

Harry smiled.

"Your mum's in the garden if you're looking for her."

"I wanted to talk to you. About the workshop."

His father frowned and picked up a small open-ended spanner, loosening the nut on the carbie. "No offense, but I don't see the point in going over it again. Let's just let sleeping dogs lie, eh?"

His father shot him a look from under his eyebrows, seeking Harry's agreement. Harry leaned his hip against the bench.

"I want in. I'll give Leo six weeks' notice, give him time to find someone to replace me. You can take off whenever suits you, come and go as you please. But I want at least a year of handover. And I'm buying in. You're not just handing it to me on a platter, and you and Mom will need some money to fund this lifestyle you've got planned."

It was something he'd thought about on the way over. He didn't want to be a freeloader. He wanted to be invested. If he was going to do this thing, it would be all or nothing. It would mean increasing the mortgage on his house, but he figured he could handle it.

His father's hands stilled for the briefest of moments before resuming their work. His face was utterly impassive. "It's a nice gesture, mate. But like I said this morning, it was never meant to be a choke hold."

Harry tugged the spanner from his father's hand. "It's not a gesture."

His father turned to face him squarely. "That's not how you felt this morning."

"Let's just say it took a while for me to see past my own bullshit."

Harry shifted his weight, self-conscious. Very aware that what he was about to admit didn't reflect well on himself. "Turns out that maybe, in the back of my mind, I figured the garage would always be there as an option." It was embarrassing saying it out loud to his old man, on par with admitting he still dreamed of being a rock star or a superhero or something equally juvenile.

His father nodded, once, then lowered his gaze to his hands. Harry waited for him to say something else, but he didn't. It took him a few seconds to register that his father's mustache was trembling as his father worked to suppress strong emotion.

In thirty years, Harry had never seen his father cry. Mike Porter prided himself on his self-control, always had. But here he was, fighting back tears because Harry had finally pulled his head out of his own ass. It made Harry's chest and gut tight. Made him wish he'd been smart enough to see through his own bullshit years ago.

"Dad..."

His father shook his head, lips pressed together, eyes

swimming. Harry's own eyes pricked with tears and he blinked rapidly.

"Bloody hell," he said.

He flung an arm around his father's back and hauled him close. After the barest second his father reciprocated, squeezing him so hard Harry was sure he heard a rib pop. They stayed like that for long seconds, both of them fighting back tears. His father thumped him on the back a couple of times, then released him, taking an abrupt step backward. There was a beat of silence as they both avoided one another's eyes. For some reason Harry imagined what Pippa would say if she could see them both playing so tough and stoic, and a small laugh escaped him. His father looked askance at him, checking that Harry wasn't laughing at him. He must have been reassured, because after a second he smiled, too.

"You got any beer?" Harry asked.

"Screw that. This is champagne territory. The fancy stuff. Your mother's been hoarding a bottle in the back of the fridge. Let's go commandeer it."

Harry was more than happy to go celebrate, but there was something he needed to say first.

"I'm sorry for mucking you around for so long, Dad."

His father shook his head. "No need for apologies. You're supposed to live your life, not mine."

Harry grimaced. His father was being generous. But he always had been.

"Come on, let's go thrill your mother."

Together they walked into the house.

PIPPA KNEW WHO it was the moment she heard the doorbell. Even though she was still knee-deep in her assignment, she couldn't stop the smile from spreading across her face as she made her way to the front door.

"Mr. Porter. This is a surprise," she said as she swung the door wide.

He held a bottle of champagne and his gray eyes smiled at her. "Five minutes, tops, then I'll let you get back to it," he promised.

She gave him a rueful look. As if. There was no way she was sending him away after just five minutes and he knew it.

"I'm guessing your father took it well?" she asked as she led him to the back of the house.

"Yeah."

There was a wealth of meaning and emotion in the single word. She cast a look at him over her shoulder. He met her eyes, his face filled with the emotion of the day. She stopped, turning to face him. She pressed a kiss to his cheek, then his lips, then the corner of his jaw.

"For what it's worth, I think it's a great decision. For all of you."

"Thanks."

He seemed pleased and sheepish all at once and she knew he was thinking about all the things he'd said to her about loving his carefree life and how he had it all worked out. She'd said the same sorts of things about her life, too, before Alice came along.

"Like I said earlier, life has a way of creeping up on you," she said, reaching out to touch his forearm.

"No kidding."

There was a light in his eyes as he looked at her. Something swooped in her stomach. Fear or excitement—it was hard to tell which. Then he blinked and the light was gone and he simply looked happy.

She was happy for him, too. As she'd said, this was a great thing for him.

They entered the kitchen and she grabbed some

champagne flutes. He popped the cork and poured two foaming glasses. They clinked their flutes together.

"To the next big adventure," she said.

"To late nights, debt and premature gray hair."

She laughed. "Amen!"

They were both smiling after they'd taken their first mouthful. She asked him about the conversation with his father and he gave her a rundown of what had been said. He got a little choked up as he talked about his father's reaction and she had to blink away sympathetic tears. He made her laugh, though, when he described his mother's ecstatic response to the news. After twenty minutes he looked at his watch and put his glass down, his gaze flicking across to the table where she had her laptop and textbooks set up.

"I should leave you to it. I know your assignment is due."

She shot a rueful look at the dining table. "Yeah. It is."

It was so tempting to say "to hell with it" when he was standing there looking so sexy and happy and buoyant, but her assignment was not going to write itself. As attractive and compelling as Harry was, he was not her future, and teaching was.

"Call me when you're done?" he said.

"Straight to the bat phone."

Because she couldn't help herself, Pippa stepped forward and kissed him. His arms came around her, his hands smoothing over her back before sliding to her ass and pulling her closer, snugging her hips more firmly against his. She made an approving noise when she felt his hard-on, all thoughts of study flying out the window. She curled her fingers into the muscles of his back and pumped her hips against his, inviting him to play. He deepened the kiss, hungry, demanding.

Then suddenly she was grasping thin air as he slipped away from her.

"Call me when you're done, okay?" he said again. He was a little breathless, his eyes dark with need.

It took her a second to understand he was being as good as his word and leaving her to study, despite the blatant invitation she'd just issued. Even as her body protested, her heart expanded with warmth at his consideration. He knew how much this diploma meant to her, what a difference it would make to her future.

"Thanks, Harry," she said softly.

He dropped a quick kiss onto her forehead before backing off. "Later."

She followed him with her eyes as he made his way to the front door, not trusting herself to keep her hands off him if she went with him. He raised a hand in farewell as he opened the front door, then he was gone.

Pippa stared down the length of the hall at the closed door. Over the years, men had brought her flowers, chocolate, jewelry and sexy underwear. Harry's respect and consideration topped them all easily. Hands down.

"It's just sex. Just sex, just sex, just sex," she said out loud.

Except it didn't feel that way.

CHAPTER THIRTEEN

It DIDN'T FEEL that way when she called him at ten on Tuesday night, either, to let him know she'd written the five thousandth word and he told her he'd be there in ten minutes and made it in eight. It didn't feel like just sex when he pressed her against the hall wall when he arrived and kissed her and kissed her until she was hot and wet and pliant and ready for anything.

It didn't feel like just sex when he wrapped his arms around her afterward and fell asleep in her bed. Which was why she didn't wake him and send him on his way, in line with her own self-ruling on the matter.

She didn't send him home on Thursday night, either, when he took her and Alice out for dinner, or on Friday night when he came over with a DVD to help her baby-sit Aaron again. She told herself that she had a grip on things, but it wasn't until Saturday night that she realized exactly how deluded she was.

She'd planned to take care of her Christmas shopping in the morning, but Harry suggested breakfast at Lilo Café down on the Mornington foreshore and before she knew it she was watching him feed pureed apple to Alice and enjoying French toast with raspberries and vanilla mascarpone while looking out across clear blue water. They drove back onto the main street afterward and Harry followed her from shop to shop as she agonized over how to spend her meager Christmas dollars.

She bought luxury soaps and hand cream for her mother, an inveterate self-pamperer, then some gourmet sauces and jams for Gaylene, a small token of her appreciation and affection. Alice was next on her list and she led Harry into the toy store, expecting him to send up a protest at any second. They'd been walking around for over an hour and she kept waiting for him to start getting twitchy, but so far he was holding up well. A minor miracle.

She searched his face. "Are you secretly going stir-crazy and looking for the exits?"

He raised his eyebrows. "Sorry?"

"Shopping. You men are supposed to hate it."

"I do. Normally."

"But today it's okay?"

"Yeah, it is. I know you're wearing black lace under that dress." He shrugged as if this explained everything.

She smiled, ridiculously flattered. He was so easy and fun to spend time with. He made her feel sexy and clever. Best of all, he made her forget that when he wasn't around, her life was an obstacle course of stress, lack of sleep and not enough hours in the day.

She left him with the stroller while she went to investigate options for Alice. Her daughter was so young that any gifts for her were nonsensical, really, but Pippa was acutely aware that this would be her daughter's first Christmas. She didn't want to shortchange her little girl or cut corners—but there was also only so much money to go around.

After ten minutes she'd narrowed her choices down to a big, cuddly bear that looked as though it would be a long-lasting childhood companion and a set of beautifully made children's cutlery. Then her eye was caught by a dollhouse display across the aisle. She drew closer, unable to stop herself.

"Oh, wow. The chandeliers even have little wooden candles," she said, peering inside the house.

A classic two up, two down model, it featured a central staircase, peaked roof and Victorian fittings. She took in the self-striped wallpaper, the wainscoting, the perfectly proportioned settee and armchair and mantelpiece and shook her head in wonder.

"I think this is nicer than any real house I've ever lived in," she said, awestruck by the attention to detail.

Harry gave it an assessing glance. "No garage, though."

"Shocking, I know."

A saleswoman zeroed in on them, professional smile in place. "Beautiful, isn't it? They come in kit form and you can pick and choose which accessories you want. We even have a selection of wallpapers for you to choose from."

Pippa smiled and took a step back. Even before the woman had opened her mouth she knew that she would never in a million years be able to afford to buy a dollhouse like this. Harry, however, ran an assessing hand over the rooftop. He ducked his head to inspect the inside more closely.

"How much did you say it was?" he asked, glancing across at the saleswoman.

"The kit itself is four hundred. The furniture starts at twenty and goes up."

Pippa raised her eyebrows. Good God, did people really spend that much money on a kids' toy that would be bashed around, drawn on and abused for a few years, and then disdainfully ignored as its young owner outgrew it?

"Alice is a little too young for that kind of thing yet," she said diplomatically.

Harry circled the display to check out the rear of the house and Pippa gave the stroller a little push to keep Alice pacified.

"If your husband is the handy type, we have plans for dollhouses, too. Not quite as elaborate, but still very nice."

Pippa blinked, taken by surprise by the woman's words. She glanced across at Harry to see if he'd heard, an embarrassed laugh rising in her throat. He was busy reading the back of one of the accessory packs, apparently oblivious to what the woman had said.

"There are also some less elaborate dollhouses in the next aisle, if he's not handy. Although he looks as though he might be." The saleswoman gave a little titter.

Pippa opened her mouth to explain that Harry wasn't her husband—far from it—but the phone rang at the front of the store and the woman laid a hand on Pippa's arm apologetically.

"Excuse me, will you, but I need to get that."

Pippa shut her mouth with a click as the woman bustled off, stifling the urge to go after her and force the truth on her. It was no big deal, after all, if some nameless woman in the local toy store made a mistaken assumption about her and Harry. No one would ever know, it didn't mean anything.

Pippa stole a glance at Harry, worried he might have overheard the conversation after all and thought she'd deliberately let the woman maintain her assumption. He'd moved on to inspect the Nerf gun display, looking like a big kid as he considered the colorful boxes and brightly colored guns. She couldn't help smiling at his absorption. Boys and their toys.

Her smile faded as she imagined how they must have looked to the sales assistant—her and Alice and Harry, gathered together like a little unit. It wasn't impossible to see them as a family, even though Alice was blond and blue-eyed and Harry and she were so dark.

For a dangerous few seconds the image held in her mind. Then she shook her head and it dissolved and reality reasserted itself.

"Sex, sex, sex," she muttered under her breath, turning away.

Maybe she did need to get those T-shirts made, after all.

After a moment's determined concentration, she settled on the teddy bear, deciding that cutlery was too dull a present for Alice's first Christmas. The saleswoman gave her a bright smile as they approached the cash register.

"He's a lovely bear, isn't he? Is it for your little one?"

"Yes." Pippa bit her lip anxiously, dreading the woman making another reference to Harry as her husband. This time Pippa would leap all over her the minute the word was out of her mouth. She didn't want Harry thinking she was starting to get ideas. God, that was the last thing either of them needed.

She was on tenterhooks for the full two minutes it took the other woman to ring up the sale, but the h-word didn't pass the saleswoman's lips again and soon they were stepping out into the bright afternoon sun. Lifting her face to the warmth, Pippa let the tension go.

Stupid to get so wound up over an easy mistake that was essentially meaningless.

She put the incident behind her and managed to get almost all her shopping done before they returned home midafternoon. Harry amused Alice while Pippa did some laundry, then she found herself inviting him to stay for dinner. By ten they were dozing on the couch, tangled in one another's arms while Alice slept on her rug on the floor.

Pippa wasn't sure what woke her—a noise from Alice, a dog barking outside—but she stirred, rubbing her cheek against Harry's T-shirt-covered chest. He smelled so good. Felt so good, too. Like a big, warm rock.

She smiled at the image, then turned her head and pressed a kiss to his chest, aware even as she did so that she wouldn't have dared such a purely affectionate gesture last week. Somehow, she'd dropped her guard where little things like that were concerned. In the same way that she'd never quite got around to kicking him out of her bed every night this week, either.

She frowned, but before she could start to overanalyze things Harry stirred, his chest expanding as he took a deep breath and stretched his arms overhead.

"What time is it?"

"Just past ten."

"Hmmm. Why are you still dressed?"

She snorted out a laugh and let her concerns slide away. She could worry later. Right now, she had bigger, hotter things to occupy herself with.

"It's a good question. I could ask the same of you."

His hands closed around her upper arms as he pulled her higher on the couch so he could kiss her. She lifted her leg and draped it over his hip, arching her back so her breasts pressed against his chest.

"I haven't made out on the couch since I was a teenager," she murmured as he broke their kiss.

"The way I remember it, there are rules for the couch. Hands outside clothes, in case your mum comes in."

"Like you respected that rule," she scoffed.

His laugh was a rumble in his chest as his hand slid onto her breast. He caressed her through the fabric of her dress, plucking at her nipples then soothing them with his palm. She rode his knee and rubbed her hand along the hard length of his erection through his jeans.

After twenty minutes she was feeling more than a little frustrated and horny.

"I don't remember it being this frustrating," she said.

"That's because you know what comes next now. Back then it was a voyage of discovery."

He slid a hand under her skirt and up her thigh, fingers gliding over her skin. She gave a little moan of appreciation as his fingers dipped between her thighs. She knew what he'd find there—damp silk and lots of heat. She pressed herself into his hand shamelessly, urging him on.

"What if your mum comes?" he whispered against the soft skin of her neck.

"Oddly, not really thinking about my mum right now. And if anyone's going to come…"

He laughed again, his fingers stroking her through her panties. She shuddered her approval.

"You've done this before, haven't you?"

"Not like this." There was a serious undertone to his words.

She wondered what he was implying. That sex was different with her? Or was she reading too much into three little words? Was he simply playing along with their silly, nostalgic little game?

Her breath caught in her throat as he slipped his fingers beneath the elastic of her underwear.

"You are so hot…" he murmured.

The sound of glass smashing nearly sent her rolling

off the couch. Harry pushed her to one side and shot to his feet, instantly on the alert.

"What was that? Was that out in the street?" she said, dragging her dress down.

He grabbed his boots and jammed his feet inside. "Yeah. That was out in the street."

His face was tight, his jaw set as he straightened and headed for the hall. Alice started to cry, startled by the sudden activity. Pippa scooped her up and went after Harry, alarm making her movements tight and jerky.

"Harry... Don't go out there. I'll call the police if there's a problem."

Frankston was a tough neighborhood, with more than its fair share of problems. Street violence was common, especially on the weekends when the young men of the area had been drinking heavily. Every week there was a report in the local paper of property damage or a bashing or stabbing.

Harry was already flinging the front door open and flicking on the outside light. He stepped onto the porch, an intimidating silhouette. Pippa ran the last few meters, Alice clutched to her chest.

"Harry—"

The rest of her warning died in her throat as she stepped onto the porch and saw the man standing on her front lawn, baseball bat in hand.

"You know what you are? You're a freakin' liar," Steve yelled.

He strode toward Harry's Monaro, arms swinging back. The baseball bat came down in a crushing arc, smashing into the rear passenger window. The sound of glass breaking echoed around the street, as loud as a gunshot.

Pippa reached out with her spare hand to grip the

back of Harry's T-shirt. His back was as hard as a rock and she could feel the adrenaline surging through him.

Dear God. This would not be good.

Harry twisted to face her, resting his hand on her shoulder.

"It's okay. I'll calm him down and send him home."

She transferred her grip to the front of his T-shirt. "He's drunk. He could do anything, Harry."

"I can handle him." He eased away from her, forcing her to let him go.

He dropped a quick kiss onto her mouth before descending the stairs.

Steve smiled in triumph when he saw him coming, resting the bat on his shoulder. "Ready to spin more bullshit for me, Harry?"

"I never lied to you."

"You said you hadn't touched her."

"When I said that, I hadn't. You need to put the bat down and go home, mate. Before someone calls the cops."

Lights were starting to turn on in the street. The neighbors came out onto their front porch in their dressing gowns, faces concerned. Pippa spared them a quick glance before returning her focus to Harry.

"You threatening me?" Steve lifted the bat from his shoulder, his expression belligerent.

Pippa held her breath, terrified things were about to spiral out of control. This was so horribly crazy. Like a scene from a movie.

"How many people do you think heard you smash the car window?" Harry gestured toward the street, indicating the rubbernecking neighbors.

Steve glanced around, taking in their growing audience, his brow furrowed. He was very drunk, Pippa realized. It was probably a miracle he was still standing.

Steve aimed the end of the bat at Harry, sighting down the length of wood as though it were the barrel of a rifle. "You're supposed to be on my side. You're supposed to be my mate, you disloyal prick."

"I *am* your mate."

Steve shook his head. "No. You sold me out, you bastard. You sold me out."

"What is this, high school? No one's taking sides. You're just too pissed to see it."

Steve jabbed the bat in the direction of the house. "She stitched me up. You know she did. She stitched me up and you don't give a shit because she wiggled her ass at you and all you can do is think with your dick."

There was so much anger in his voice. Pippa tightened her grip on Alice, instinctively resting her hand on the back of her daughter's head, as though the small gesture could protect Alice from her father's rage.

"She got pregnant. It was an accident. You think you're such a catch she'd go to all that trouble for you?" Harry countered.

Steve swayed on his feet, his angry snarl dissolving into confusion as he tried to process Harry's words.

"Mate, go home," Harry said quietly. "Better yet, I'll take you home."

Pippa tensed as Harry held out his hand for the bat. When Steve didn't immediately object, Harry risked taking a step closer. He was about to close his hand around the end of the bat when Steve took a jerky step backward, snatching the bat away, his chin coming up. Pippa forgot to breathe again.

"I'm not going anywhere with you, you lying asshole."

Pippa caught the faint, far-off sound of a police siren in the distance. One of the neighbors must have called the police. Something she should have done the minute she realized what was going on.

Harry glanced toward her and she knew he'd heard the sirens, too, and understood what they meant.

Steve would end up in court over this.

Shame and grief and anger churned in her belly. How on earth had she ever lain down with this man? What was wrong with her that she hadn't seen the ugliness and weakness that was on rampant display here tonight?

Her gaze shifted from Steve's tense form to Harry's. Any second now things were about to get physical. She could feel the violence in the air, like the crackle of electricity. Adrenaline and fear coursed through her. Harry might be hurt. Steve wasn't even close to being rational. If he got worked up…

Alice squirmed in her arms and Pippa realized she was holding her too tightly. She relaxed her grip a little and let out her breath and reminded herself that Harry knew Steve. They'd grown up together. Gone to school together. Come of age together. If anyone knew how to handle Steve when he was like this, it was Harry.

They were practically twins under the skin, they had so much in common.

Pippa stilled as the thought echoed in her mind. Her whole body tensed as realization washed over her, chilling in its awful clarity.

Because she'd done it all over again—fallen for the wrong man. It was such a sudden, startling, brutal revelation she closed her eyes.

She'd been so determined to never be that woman again—that stupid, delusional, self-defeating woman. It had all been so clear in her mind in those first, ugly days when she'd understood that she would be raising her unborn child on her own. She'd thought it was a lesson that had been etched in her bones. Hard-won self-knowledge that would serve her a lifetime.

And yet she'd spent the past month flirting and laughing and having sheet-searing sex with a man who was Steve's spiritual brother in more ways than she cared to count. Worse than that—if that wasn't bad enough—she'd sold herself on the relationship by telling herself it was all about sex and fun, while secretly she'd been harboring white-picket fantasies about Harry.

Treasuring those small moments when he was gentle and attentive with Alice.

Basking in his easy, ready affection.

Allowing him to invade every corner of her life. Her house, her bed, her mind.

Allowing herself to imagine she and Harry and Alice as a family, a little unit, the three of them against the world.

All of this with a man who was roguish and charming and utterly, utterly incapable of being the kind of man she needed him to be.

Just like Steve.

You idiot. You stupid, stupid, foolish woman.

Down on the lawn, the standoff came to a crashing end as Harry feinted to the left, then lunged forward and grabbed the business end of the bat. He yanked on it, hard, and Steve staggered off balance. Quick as lightning Harry pulled the bat from his grasp, tossing it behind him, well out of Steve's reach.

"Now—" Harry said.

Pippa screamed a warning, but it was too late, Steve's swinging fist had already connected with Harry's right cheek. His head snapped back on his neck and he staggered. Dumb instinct told Pippa to go to him and she actually took a step forward before she caught herself. She had Alice to think of. She couldn't go throwing herself between two angry men.

She quickly saw that Harry didn't need her to throw herself anywhere; he easily dodged Steve's second punch, shoving the other man in the side to send him sprawling. Steve scrambled to his feet and came at Harry again, swinging wildly. Harry sidestepped him, pushing him as he passed and sending him to the ground a second time.

Steve pushed himself to his feet, swearing black and blue. The police sirens grew in intensity. Pippa willed them to arrive *now* so this nightmare could be over.

"Cops'll be here any second..." Harry warned as Steve wove on his feet.

Steve came at him again, a desperate, almost frenzied attack. Harry dodged and blocked and absorbed the blows, never once going on the offensive. The moment Steve showed signs of flagging, Harry wrapped his arms around him, hugging him close, effectively immobilizing him.

He got his leg behind Steve's knee and pushed him backward, knocking him off balance. He went down to the ground with him, grappling Steve onto his belly and levering Steve's arm up behind his back. Steve howled in protest as Harry planted a knee between his shoulder blades and let his weight rest on the other man. After a few seconds of struggling and swearing, Steve finally gave up, resting his forehead on the grass.

Pippa let out a shuddering breath. It was over. This part of it, anyway. There was still the police to be dealt with, of course. And the neighbors.

And Harry.

Because after her moment of clarity there was no place for him in her life. He was a folly she couldn't afford. A mistake she refused to make.

Something cold dripped onto her chest. She touched her cheek, noticing her own tears for the first time. Alice stirred against her breasts. Light and sound filled the street as a police cruiser swung around the corner and came to an abrupt halt in front of her house.

Harry looked up at her, checking to see if she was okay.

She wasn't okay. She was foolish and self-destructive and enormously self-deceptive.

But she was about to take steps to remedy that.

HARRY SPARED A QUICK glance for the police cruiser before leaning close to Steve's head.

"Don't be an idiot," he warned as the police exited the car.

He shifted his weight, removing his knee from the other man's back and standing. He kept his movements slow and careful, because he was more than aware what the police saw when they looked at him—six foot two of tattooed muscle. In their lexicon: trouble. He'd had enough unwarranted attention from them as a younger man to know the drill.

He held his hands out from his sides to show he was unarmed and kept his posture relaxed as the first policeman approached warily.

"One of you gentlemen want to tell me what the problem is?"

Steve pushed himself up onto his hands and knees. The stink of booze and cigarettes rolled off him.

"A domestic situation. No one was hurt." Harry glanced across at the porch, worried about Pippa.

He caught a quick glimpse of her pale face before the policeman blinded him with his flashlight. Harry flinched away from the brightness.

"You look like you copped a hit," the policeman said.

"No one was hurt," Harry repeated.

Steve was already in enough trouble. At the minimum he would be arrested for drunk and disorderly, along with property damage. He wanted to shake his old friend for the way he'd scared Pippa, but Harry couldn't help thinking that if he'd made a bigger effort to hunt Steve down and clear the air in the past week, tonight might have been avoided. Maybe.

Not that he hadn't tried. After Steve had ignored his phone calls, Harry had swung by his place one final time. Steve's car had been in the drive, but he'd ignored Harry's knocking. Fed up to the back teeth, Harry had left one final, pissed-off message letting Steve know the ball was in his court.

Apparently this was Steve's response.

"Maybe you should walk me through this from the beginning. Do you have any ID on you, sir?"

Harry reached into his pocket and handed over his wallet. He turned to check on Pippa again. She was halfway down the steps, her expression tight as she braced herself for the hoopla that was about to unfold. Harry felt a fierce surge of protectiveness. If he could, he'd make this all go away for her and Alice. He'd fix things with Steve and manage the police and ensure that all the messy loose ends and small hurts in her life were healed.

He couldn't do any of that, but he could offer her comfort.

He held up a hand to stall the policeman.

"I just need to talk to my friend," he said.

He'd barely taken a step when the cop moved to block his way.

"If you don't mind, Mr. Porter, I'd like to clear this up first."

Harry shot the man an irritated look, then returned his gaze to Pippa.

"You okay?" he called.

She nodded, the movement stiff and jerky. Her cheeks were shiny from tears. The need to comfort her made him flex his hands.

"I take it you don't reside at this address, Mr. Porter?"

Harry sighed and gave the cop his full attention. Clearly, he wasn't going to get what he wanted until the other man was satisfied.

The next half hour was spent going over and over the night's events. Steve was moved to the other side of the lawn where the second policeman presumably went through the same routine with him. Another cruiser arrived after ten minutes and Pippa disappeared inside with a female officer.

The whole time he answered questions and repeated himself, Harry's mind was with her. He needed to know she was okay. Needed to hear it from her own lips. Needed to dry her tears and assure her that she and Alice had never been in any danger and that Steve would never try something like this again. Ever. Not if Harry had any say in it.

It was another twenty minutes before the police were satisfied they had enough information. Most of the neighbors had given up on the floor show by then, although there were a few stragglers watching from a distance. Steve was cuffed and pushed into the back of a cruiser. Harry watched him, torn between guilt and righteous anger.

What a freaking mess.

"We'll need you to come down to the station tomorrow to sign your statement, okay, Harry?" the policeman said.

Somehow, over the past hour, they'd progressed to first-name basis.

"No problem."

The policeman offered his hand. Harry shook it and turned toward the house, eager to get to Pippa. He took the steps two at a time and was bounding onto the porch when Pippa emerged from the front door, seeing the policewoman out.

"Hey. How you holding up?" Harry asked, ignoring the policewoman as she brushed past him on her way to the steps.

"I'm fine."

She wasn't fine, anyone could see that. He reached for her but she took a step backward. He stilled, studying her face. Her cheeks were pale, her glasses smudged, making it hard for him to see the expression in her eyes.

"They're taking Steve away now. They'll probably hold him overnight."

She nodded tightly. "They explained that."

He was aware of the police car starting up behind him and pulling away from the curb. It was all over.

Except Pippa wouldn't look him in the eye.

"Let's go inside. I'll make you a cup of tea," he said.

It was his mother's cure-all for most traumas. White, with lots of sugar and a plate full of biscuits.

He stepped toward the door but she shifted, blocking the entrance. It happened so quickly he knew it couldn't be anything but an instinctive reaction.

He frowned. "Pippa—"

"I need you to go, Harry."

His frown deepened. "Pippa. What's going on?"

She crossed her arms over her chest. "I don't want to sleep with you any more."

Not what he'd been expecting. By a long shot. It took him a moment to get his thoughts together enough to respond.

"Can I ask why?"

"Because I don't want to make the same mistake twice."

He flinched. "You think I'm like *Steve?*"

He was insulted by the comparison, especially after what had just gone down.

"Look, it doesn't matter, anyway. You were only in this for the fun, and tonight it stopped being fun. So let's just call it quits before it gets any messier than it already is."

He was starting to get pissed now. Barely an hour ago, he'd had his hand up her skirt on the couch. Things had been good—great—between them. Now he was being given his marching orders?

"Who said I was only in this for the fun?"

She looked him dead in the eye. "You did, Harry. Repeatedly. Remember?"

Right. That stupid conversation they'd had after the first night. The one where he'd told her he wasn't a good bet. At the time, it had seemed like the right thing to do and say, because he hadn't wanted to lead her on or hurt her. But things had changed since then. He'd felt it. He knew she had, too. This thing between them had become about a lot more than sex very quickly.

He reached for her again, determined to prove as

much to her but she kept her arms crossed tightly, her body stiff and unyielding.

"Could you please just go?"

He wanted to protest. He wanted to demand she tell him what had suddenly changed, why she was suddenly pushing him away. But there was something about the way she held herself, the way she looked at him that told him she was close to losing it. She'd had a bad night. The father of her child had just been led off in handcuffs. The last thing she needed was him demanding anything.

"I don't think you should be on your own tonight."

"Harry—"

"Is there someone I can call for you? A friend? What about Becca? Or the woman from the gallery?"

She stared at him. She blinked rapidly for a few seconds, combating welling tears, then pushed her glasses up the bridge of her nose.

"I'll be fine on my own. I'm used to it."

She was so determined, despite the threatening tears. Or maybe because of them.

"Can I come tomorrow to talk?"

"I don't think there's much point, do you?" She straightened, squaring her shoulders and lifting her chin. "You've been really terrific, Harry. With the car and the ceiling and everything else. I'll always be grateful for what you've done for me and Alice. But I can't afford to muck around anymore. My life is serious. I've got Alice. I can't afford to screw up."

"You think what happened between us is a screw-up?"

Somehow she dredged up a smile. "It was fun. While it lasted. And now it's over."

She turned and slipped inside the house. He caught

one last glimpse of her as the door closed between them. She looked distant and closed off, all her vibrancy clamped down. Then the door was in his face, black and solid and unequivocal.

He stared at it for long seconds, trying to understand what had just happened. He'd wanted to comfort her, reassure her—and she'd kicked him out.

No, not just kicked him out, she'd given him his marching orders. She didn't want to see him again. They were over.

It didn't feel over for him. In fact, it felt the exact opposite of over.

He turned and walked to the edge of the porch, sinking onto the top step. He stared at the empty street and the night-dark houses and felt like the biggest fool under the sun.

Because what kind of an idiot only worked out that he was in love with a woman when she shut the door in his face and told him she never wanted to see him again?

It had been under his nose for weeks. The way he'd kept coming up with excuses to see her—the car, the broken door, the ceiling repair. The way he'd bent over backward to ensure she was happy. The way he hadn't been able to keep his hands to himself, though he'd known right from the start that getting involved with her would be complicated.

He loved her. Her scent. Her smile. Her warm eyes. Her self-deprecating humor. Her soft, smooth skin. Her stubbornness. Her temper. Her vintage dresses and old-fashioned shoes and big glasses and bright underwear. He loved all of it, because it was all Pippa, and he couldn't get enough of her.

Harry shook his head as he remembered that first

kiss in her half-repaired bedroom. He'd been so stupid, so slow. He should have known then. The moment his lips touched hers, he should have known.

Instead, he'd told her he was a bad bet for anything more than a good time, and he'd brought violence and rage to her doorstep because he'd failed to clear the air with Steve.

He'd bumbled through this whole relationship like a stupid kid who'd didn't know his arse from his elbow.

Was it any wonder—really?—she'd shut the door in his face? Was it any wonder she thought he was a mistake waiting to happen?

Way to go, dickhead. Really well played.

Heaviness settled in. He ran his hands over his head, trying to think. Everything in him wanted to hammer on her door right this second and lay his heart at her feet in a big, unscripted blurt. He'd tell her she was wrong about him, that he wasn't like Steve. That he loved her, and that what had happened between them had never been just about fun.

It was such a strong impulse it pushed him to his feet. He barely managed to stop himself from approaching the door. Despite his own sense of urgency, he understood instinctively that now was not the time to declare himself.

Pippa had had a shock tonight, and she was holding herself together through sheer willpower. She'd been scared and shaken by Steve's out-of-control rage and confusion. She wasn't used to drunken idiots showing up on her front lawn with baseball bats, yelling the house down and smashing stuff up. She wasn't used to having the police arriving on her doorstep, lights and sirens blazing.

She'd asked for time. She'd asked him to go. The least he could do was honor her wishes. For now.

He headed for his car. He had to use an old T-shirt from the trunk to clear the broken glass from the driver's seat. He drove home with the cold night air rushing into the car. Once there he wrapped a bag of frozen peas in a damp towel and pressed it to his face and lay on his bed thinking about Pippa and Alice and how much he wanted to be with them and how stupid he was not to have realized it sooner.

He must have fallen asleep at some point because he woke in the morning to a soggy pillow and a bag of defrosted peas beside him. The whole right side of his face ached and he approached the bathroom mirror warily. Sure enough, his right eye socket was purple and gray. A lovely memento of a shitty night.

He wanted to drive straight over to Pippa's place, but he sucked it up and did what needed to be done first. He went to the police station and signed his statement, then he waited over an hour on a hard wooden bench before Steve was released from the holding cells.

He looked like utter crap, seedy and greasy, with grass stains on the knees of his jeans. He stopped in his tracks when Harry stood to meet him in the foyer. Neither of them said anything. After a beat Steve walked past him and out through the automatic double doors.

Harry followed and found Steve waiting for him on the small patch of grass in front of the station, his brow furrowed as he squinted against the brightness of the morning sun. Harry took up his own position a few feet away, eyeing him neutrally. Early-morning traffic buzzed past and the smell of cooking oil drifted across from the nearby McDonald's. After a beat Steve spoke up.

"How bad is the Monaro?"

"Nothing that can't be fixed."

"Send me the bill and I'll take care of it."

Harry shrugged impatiently. "Like I give a shit about the car."

"You love that car."

"Mate… This is bigger than the Monaro."

Steve's gaze dropped to the grass. "Out of all the girls you could have gone for…" He shook his head.

"I love her."

It was the first time Harry had said it out loud. He was surprised how good the words felt in his mouth. How right.

Steve's head jerked up. His gaze was searching as he stared at Harry. After a few seconds he nodded. They were old enough friends that he took Harry at his word. They'd both thrown a lot of four-letter words around over the years, but never that one.

"So, what? You and Pippa are going to do the whole white picket fence thing…?"

"I don't know," Harry said.

For all he knew, Pippa might shut the door in his face again. He was hoping she wouldn't, and he planned to put his foot in the way and state his case if she did, but he wasn't about to make any bold predictions at this early stage.

"I suppose you're going to keep hassling me about her," Steve said.

"Nope."

Steve raised his eyebrows, clearly not convinced. Harry shrugged.

"I'm not your keeper. You want to be an asshole for the rest of your life, go right ahead."

Steve's jaw twitched.

Harry eyed him, wondering what to say to get through to him. "Look. I don't know what's going on in your head where Pippa is concerned, but you have to know she didn't get pregnant to try and trap you. But you know what? Even if she did, Alice had nothing to do with any of that. She's your kid, man, and you haven't even seen her since she was born. She's got your eyes and your hair and Pippa's nose and the most amazing smile. She's freakin' gorgeous, and she's yours. How can that mean nothing to you?"

Steve's nostrils flared. He ducked his head, kicking at a bare patch in the lawn. Harry was reminded forcibly of the inarticulate, messed-up kid who used to gravitate to the Porter house in search of sanctuary from an ugly home life.

"Mate…" Harry said, moved by the pain he could see in his friend's face.

"I never wanted to have kids. Made myself a promise I never would." The words came out as though they hurt. "Knew I'd be shit at it…"

"You're not like him, if that's what you're worried about."

Harry had wondered if that was the problem, but he'd never dared express the thought before. Maybe he should have. Maybe they wouldn't be standing in front of the police station having this conversation if he'd voiced his thoughts earlier.

Steve shook his head.

"You're not," Harry insisted.

"What I did last night, that was a classic Jack Lawson move."

Harry reflected for a second. It was true. There was no point denying it.

"So don't let it happen again."

Steve frowned, shooting Harry a quick, searching look. "That easy, huh?"

"Why not? I know you, mate. I've seen you at your best and your worst. This stuff with Pippa... So what if having a kid with your ex-girlfriend is not what you had planned? Life throws crap at you all the time. You roll with the punches and get back up again. It's the only thing you *can* do."

Harry pulled his car keys from his pocket. "Come on. I'll give you a lift home. You'll have to clear the glass off the passenger seat, but it's better than walking."

Steve's mouth kicked up into a sheepish almost-smile at the reference to the broken glass. Harry started for the parking lot, Steve falling in behind him.

"How's your eye?" Steve asked.

"Awesome. Thanks for asking."

"You could have ducked."

Harry glanced over his shoulder. Sure enough, Steve was smiling.

"Just for that you can buy me breakfast."

CHAPTER FOURTEEN

PIPPA WOKE EARLY and pulled on jeans and a T-shirt. Alice was fretful, no doubt responding to Pippa's jangled nerves. Pippa fed her and rocked her and as soon as it was light outside put her in the stroller and went outside to clean up the broken glass from the driveway.

It was a small thing, but she didn't want any reminders of what had happened last night. It wouldn't stop the neighbors from glancing askance at her for the next little while, but it would make her feel better. As though she'd done something to move on. Fortunately the police had had Steve's car towed last night, so she didn't have to deal with that this morning, too. She still couldn't believe he'd gotten behind the wheel so drunk. But she couldn't believe a lot of things about the way he'd behaved last night.

She swept the glass into a pile and used her dustpan and broom to transfer it to the bin. She felt marginally better as she wheeled Alice back into the house.

She spent the morning tidying, putting the house to rights in an attempt to do the same thing with her mind. She was contemplating what to have for lunch when a knock sounded at the front door. Her gut told her it was Harry and for a few seconds she considered not answering. Then she reminded herself that she was a grown-up, not a sixteen-year-old, and that Harry deserved more from her than silence.

She gasped when she saw him. His right eye was black and blue, the skin swollen. It took a real act of will not to reach out and touch him.

"Is it okay?" she asked, gesturing with her chin toward his eye. "I mean, is your vision all right…?"

"I'm fine. How are you? Did you sleep okay?"

She shrugged. She'd slept badly, but it was neither here nor there.

"Can I come in?"

She bought some time before responding by jiggling Alice and glancing down into her face. She was afraid of what he might be about to say to her. Afraid of how appealing she found him. Of how weak she was.

"Pippa… I just want to talk."

He could only hurt her if she let him. If she was stupid enough to put her trust in him.

The thought gave her strength. She stepped to one side, tacitly inviting him in, then turned and walked to the kitchen. She sat at the table, Alice in her lap, eyeing him across the scrubbed pine tabletop.

"I want to start again," he said.

As an opening gambit, it wasn't what she'd been expecting.

"I'm sorry?"

"I want to start from scratch. No get-out-of-jail-free cards. Just you and me."

Despite everything—last night's revelation, this morning's grim determination—something lurched in the pit of her stomach. She was very afraid it was hope.

"It's a nice idea, but it wouldn't work," she said.

"Why not?"

"Because we want different things from life, Harry."

"You don't know that."

She gave a small smile. "I do, Harry. I know you."

In a way, she wished she didn't. She could have indulged herself for a few more weeks. But the outcome would have been the same. She would have been left high and dry once the fun times wore out.

"Maybe you don't know me as well as you think you do. Or maybe you're confusing me with someone else."

He meant Steve. She held his eye.

"I'm flattered, Harry, I won't lie. But I've played this game before."

"I'm not him, Pippa."

"I know that."

"Do you?"

He was utterly focused on her, his gray eyes demanding a response. Yesterday, she would have been thrilled to hear him saying these things. She would have been over the moon.

Yesterday she had been living in a fantasy land.

"I know you're not Steve. You don't have his temper. You're funnier. I like spending time with you a whole hell of a lot more. You're a better lover. You're sweet with Alice. You're generous with your time…"

The furrows in his brow deepened with every word she said.

"But?"

"But you don't do serious, Harry. You said it yourself. You're a bad bet romantically speaking. You're not looking for a mortgage and 2.5 kids. You want to surf and hang with your mates and kick back."

He started to speak but she held up a hand to stop him.

"There's nothing wrong with any of those things. At all. But they make you pretty much a disaster from where I'm sitting. I have a little baby girl who looks to me for everything, Harry. *Everything.* I am her world.

If I fall over, she falls over. If I have a bad day, she has a bad day. She wears the consequences of all my mistakes. I can't afford to make a mistake with you."

He shifted in his chair, leaning forward. Before she realized what he was doing, he'd captured her hand. He held it in his, his gaze locked with hers.

"What if it's not a mistake? What if the mistake is pushing me away?"

She tried to ignore the warmth of his hand, the strength of his fingers.

"Sadly, Harry, that's a mistake I *can* afford to make, because I know what that looks like. That's my life now. That's the gallery and university and Alice. But I can't afford to go on a fishing expedition with you. I can't afford to believe in you and start building a life around you and then have that all pulled out from beneath me when you realize that playing house and playing daddy aren't all they're cracked up to be."

His chin jerked back and she knew she'd offended him.

"You think I'm a kid, that I don't get it, Pippa? That I'm not serious? That this is some kind of game?"

God, he was saying all the right things. Doing all the right things, too, sitting there looking so earnest and sincere and gorgeous, his hand gripping hers, his body leaning toward hers. If this were a movie, she'd be in tears by now, flinging herself into his arms and into the life he was offering.

But this wasn't a movie. This was real life—her life—and she didn't have the luxury of finding out how far the novelty of her situation would carry Harry. One month? Two? Six? How long before he started to slip off to the pub on Friday nights for a "boys' night"? How long before he resented the time and love and attention she devoted to Alice? How long before he started weighing his lost freedoms against the everyday domestic tedium of family life and finding one far greater than the other?

She reached out and laid her hand over his, steeling herself to say what needed to be said. A little amazed that she was able to find the strength, frankly, when he was offering her what was pretty much her secret fantasy: Harry, for always, in her bed, in her life, walking through the door each night, telling her stories and making her laugh and giving her daughter the love, attention and adoration she deserved.

But something had shifted in her last night. Hardened. Maybe she'd taken the last, final step into full, responsible adulthood.

Or maybe she was simply running scared, absolutely terrified by how much she wanted what Harry seemed to be offering.

Either way, she'd learned a vital lesson last time she'd gone down this road with a charming man: she'd learned how to protect herself.

"Harry, you're a great guy. I have loved my time with you. But you have spent the last ten years avoiding exactly this situation. Am I supposed to believe that I'm the exception to the rule? That I'm the one woman who makes you want to give it all up?"

"I don't see it as a sacrifice, Pippa. Don't you get it? I love you."

She sat back in her chair, jerking her hand free from his grip.

"No."

"It's not a yes or no proposition, Pippa."

She stood, clutching Alice to her. "I'm, um, flattered, Harry, but it doesn't change anything. You should g-go...."

She trailed off as her treacherous voice betrayed her. A light came into Harry's eyes and she knew that he'd seen into the secret heart of her in that one, revealing moment. He'd seen something that she'd kept so well hidden that she hadn't even acknowledged it to herself.

He stood and rounded the table. She retreated, matching him step for step as he approached. It took three steps for her back to hit the wall. Harry stopped, leaving only inches between them.

"Tell me you don't love me, too, Pippa."

"I-don't-love-you." She said it very quickly, the words running together.

He should have looked disappointed. She'd said it, hadn't she?

He smiled. She swallowed nervously as he moved closer still. His face lowered toward hers. She turned her head, offering him her cheek instead of her mouth.

She wasn't stupid. She wanted him too badly, even now, to be able to keep him at arm's length if he kissed her.

His lips brushed her cheek, then moved to her ear. "Fibber." The single word slid across her skin like a caress.

She opened her mouth to deny him again but he kissed the sensitive spot below her ear, his tongue darting out to taste her skin. She closed her eyes, reminding herself that she was holding her daughter and that she was fully clothed and that there was no way he could know how much his touch affected her.

His lips nibbled the lobe of her ear. A shudder went through her. Hard to believe they'd made love only yesterday. She felt as though she'd been starving for his touch for years. Decades.

"Pants on fire, Pippa."

He pulled back enough for her to see the glint in his eyes. He was so charming, and so confident in that charm. It was his stock in trade. The honey he'd used to lure many a woman over the years. And she'd been so determined to be different from them all....

She looked down at Alice, reminding herself of everything that was at stake. Alice stared back at her unblinkingly.

So much trust. So much faith. So much vulnerability.

She lifted her gaze to Harry again.

"My pants don't figure into this," she said.

Some of the confidence leaked out of him.

"At least give me a chance, Pippa. Let me prove that I love you and Alice. Let me prove how much I want both of you in my life."

"No."

"Why not?"

"Because I think it's best if we just end things and go our separate ways."

"Because you're afraid you'll cave? Because you want me as much as I want you?" His eyes held hers. "Because you love me?"

"Because I made a promise to myself. And to Alice."

She didn't wait for him to respond, slipping away from him. She put a good bit of distance between them, shifting Alice's weight from one hip to the other.

Harry eyed her from across the room. "I'm not giving up."

There was a determined note underpinning his voice that both thrilled and scared her.

"I was never yours to give up."

"Yes, you were, Pippa. At least be honest about that."

She couldn't hold his gaze, letting it slide down his chest.

"I'm not giving up, Pippa," he said again.

He left the room. She remained where she was until she heard the click of the front door. She walked into the sunroom and sank onto the couch. She laid Alice carefully on her play quilt on the floor, then pulled her legs up onto the couch and backed into the corner, resting her forehead on her knees.

Then and only then did she let herself cry.

Because of course she loved him. How could she not? He'd ridden into her life in his shiny black car and rescued her and infuriated her and seduced her. He was larger than life, warm, generous, charming, sexy, clever…

And not for her.

So not for her.

Did you hear what he said? He loves you. He loves Alice. He wants both of you. What is wrong with any of that?

She pressed her forehead harder into her knees, trying to keep quiet so Alice didn't pick up on her distress.

She wanted to believe in Harry's love so badly. She wanted to believe in him so much she ached.

But what if she got it wrong again?

She gave up on being quiet then, letting her tears fall, sobbing helplessly into her knees.

She was afraid. That was the truth of it. Afraid she wasn't enough. Afraid she wouldn't be strong enough to survive another abandonment. Afraid of letting down her daughter again.

There. She'd admitted it. It didn't change anything, but she'd admitted it.

Now she had to remain strong and hold her ground.

HARRY FOUND Mel and Flynn in the herb garden, both of them sporting garden gloves and tans and hats to protect them from the harsh midday sun.

"Harry, hey— Oh, wow. What does the other guy look like?" Mel said as she noticed his eye.

"I need to talk."

Her welcoming smile faded. "Is everything okay?"

"No."

She shot a glance at Flynn.

"I'll go grab us all a drink," Flynn said diplomatically.

He headed for the house. Mel moved closer and lifted a hand as if to touch his face. Harry flinched away from her.

"It hurts, if that's what you're wondering."

"Who hit you? Steve?"

"Yeah. But that's not why I'm here."

"Okay." Mel looked confused.

"Pippa doesn't trust me, Mel. She thinks I'm going to freak out like Steve and leave her high and dry. She says she can't afford to take a risk anymore because she's got Alice." He paced in front of his sister, frustration spilling out of him. "She loves me. She denies it, but I know she does. I can see it in her eyes. But she won't even give me a chance."

Mel reached out and caught his wrist. "Harry, you are seriously making me dizzy. Stand in one spot for five seconds, okay?"

He planted his feet and regarded his sister. "I don't know what to do."

He was fully aware of the irony of his own words. From the moment he'd looked at girls and liked what he'd seen, he'd known what to do with them. He'd made them laugh and stolen kisses. When he'd grown older, he'd talked them out of their underwear and stolen a whole lot more. Now, here he was at thirty, asking his sister for advice on how to get through to the woman he loved, the one woman who wanted nothing to do with his charmer's bag of tricks.

"You love her." It was a statement, not a question.

"Yes." More than he could articulate. So much it scared him if he thought about it too much. He loved her, and he loved Alice because she was a part of Pippa, and because when she looked at him or grabbed his sleeve or his finger or laughed up into his face, he felt as though he was a part of something real and good and worthwhile.

"Tell me what she said."

He sighed impatiently, but Mel made him go over his conversation with Pippa. Then she made him tell her about last night. After he'd answered all her questions, she bit her lip, her expression pensive.

"What?"

"She's scared, Harry. And she's got every reason to be. Steve really did a number on her, didn't he? She must have been terrified, finding herself pregnant, and with him telling her he wanted nothing to do with her or her child."

He stared at the ground, burning with shame and self-directed anger as he remembered how he'd distanced himself from the whole situation. It had been messy and emotional—and he didn't do messy and emotional. He'd told himself it was none of his business and assuaged himself with visiting Pippa in hospital once Alice was born.

"She thinks I'm like him, but I'm not Steve." He could hear the defensiveness in his own voice.

Mel touched his arm. "I know that, Harry. You'd never walk out on your responsibilities. She probably knows that, too. But that doesn't stop her from being scared. Far, far easier to batten down the hatches and lock the world out than take a chance."

She said it ruefully and he knew she was thinking about her relationship with Flynn.

"I told her I wasn't going to give up on her. I want this, Mel. I want to make her happy. I want to watch Alice take her first steps and I want to teach her to ride a bike and I want to scare boys off when they start sniffing around. I want to give her a brother or sister. Maybe one of each. I want to get them out of that dump of a house. I want—" His voice broke and he stopped, swallowing a lump of emotion.

Mel's eyes were full of sympathy. "Harry. My God, this is a big sister's wet dream, hearing you say all this stuff after all your years of messing around. And I can't take any pleasure in it because I hate seeing you this unhappy."

"I don't know what to do," he said, aware he'd come full circle.

He gazed at the toes of his boots and waited for his sister to offer some insight. When she didn't immediately offer up a pearl, he glanced at her. She shrugged.

"I don't have a magic wand, Harry. I can only tell you what worked with me and Flynn. Patience. He hung in there and waited me out."

Harry frowned at his boots. It wasn't bad advice. It wasn't what he wanted to hear, because he wanted to be with Pippa *now*. He wanted to start the rest of their lives *now*.

But he'd heard what his sister had said. He got it. He'd seen the fear in Pippa's eyes.

If she needed time, he would give it to her. But he wasn't going away, and he wasn't giving up.

PIPPA WOKE ON Sunday to find an old-fashioned paper shopping bag on her doorstep when she went to collect the morning paper from the front porch. She opened it and discovered a jar of homemade preserves, a pat of Danish butter and a loaf of crusty sourdough from the boutique bakery in Mount Eliza.

She walked to the top of the steps and looked out into the street. She couldn't see Harry's car or truck, and she turned back to the house.

She took the bag into the kitchen and considered it.

She'd ended things between them. The fair and honest thing to do would be to drop the bag back on his doorstep, with a polite yet firm thanks-but-no-thanks. She made the mistake of peeking in the bag again then, and discovered that the jam he'd chosen was the same one she'd selected for Gaylene's Christmas present. She'd made a comment as she selected it, confessing how much she loved raspberries and joking that it was good for your soul to give someone something that you coveted yourself.

He'd remembered. A silly, throwaway line, one of many she'd made as they browsed the shops that day, and he'd remembered.

It wasn't the first time he'd held on to the small, inconsequential things she said. He was always attentive. Always interested.

Because he loves you. Remember that small, incon-sequential thing he *said?*

She pushed the jar of jam back into the bag, but every time she walked past the kitchen counter her eye was drawn to it. The smell of fresh-baked bread seeped into the room and her willpower gave out midafternoon. She'd just put Alice down for her afternoon nap, and she returned to the kitchen, looked at the bag for the fiftieth time that day and something snapped inside her.

Pippa pulled out the bread and cut herself two thick slices, slathering them with butter and raspberry jam. She sat at the dining room table and ate Harry's offer-ing and thought about how early he must have gotten up to buy the bread, jam and butter and leave them on her doorstep without being seen. She thought about him lying in bed last night, planning his strategy. She thought about him selecting the jam for her from amongst all the jams on offer in the store.

The need to call him was like an ache in her bones. She didn't, though. She put the jam and butter in the fridge and wrapped the bread so it would stay fresh and unpacked her books to study.

She'd made her decision. She was playing it safe.

The following Wednesday, she arrived home to be enveloped by the smell of fresh-cut grass the moment she got out of the car. She frowned. Then it hit her— someone had mown her lawn. Instead of a knee-high mess, it was now neatly clipped, the edges crisply fin-ished. The garden beds had been weeded, too, and the dangling flap on the back of the letter box repaired.

She stood and stared for long minutes. Then she turned and got Alice out of her baby seat. Once she was inside, she poured herself a glass of wine and stood on the front porch and surveyed her neat, tidy yard as she drank it. With every sip, something loosened inside her. Warmth spread through her belly and down into her legs. She thought about Harry pushing the mower through the jungle of her yard. She thought about Harry on his hands and knees pulling weeds.

All that thought and consideration. All that energy he'd put into looking out for her. Showing her that he wasn't going away. That he wasn't giving up.

Because he loved her.

It was heady stuff. Intoxicating, really. She stared at her phone as she finished the last of her glass of wine, tempted. So tempted.

It would be so easy to call him and give in. To throw herself on his mercy.

She called up a blank text window on her phone and tapped in a message. She read it twice before she hit send.

Harry, the bread and jam were wonderful, the garden a godsend. Please don't do anything more.

Pippa didn't hear from him for the rest of the week and all of the weekend. She told herself that she was relieved, but the truth was that every time she came home and found no sign of Harry, she felt a small, dull throb of disappointment.

You're such a pathetic hypocrite, she told herself as she turned into the driveway on Monday night, painfully aware that her heart rate had picked up at the prospect of coming home.

Just in case there was something from Harry.

She spotted the large, rather substantial-looking box on her porch immediately. It wasn't until she was halfway up the steps, Alice a heavy weight in her arms, that she registered that the box had a peaked roof.

"No. Harry, you didn't."

But he had. It was the same style of dollhouse as the one in the shop, but he'd chosen different colored wallpaper and arranged the furniture to suit himself. When she circled it she saw he'd installed an addition—a neatly made garage, fixed to the side of the building.

"You idiot," she said under her breath.

It would be years before Alice was old enough to appreciate this. And it was so expensive. Ridiculously so. It was a crazy, impulsive, silly thing to have done.

And it made her giddy with suppressed joy. It made her want to sit down and cry and throw back her head and laugh at the same time.

He'd wallpapered a dollhouse for her and built a toy garage. He was mad, utterly mad.

And he loved her. He really loved her.

She pulled out her phone and thought for a long time before sending him a message.

You shouldn't have. She will love it forever. I don't know what to say.

Although she did. She simply wasn't sure she was ready to say it yet.

That night, Pippa dreamed of a small, perfect house filled with small, perfect people. The next morning she ate her breakfast while examining all the exquisite details of the dollhouse interior. Harry must have put in hours and hours to make it so beautiful.

The thought made her want to call him, but she still wasn't ready so she got dressed for work instead. She got a call from day care midafternoon to let her know that Alice had a mild fever and she needed to come pick her up. Pippa took her straight to the doctor, who assured her it was nothing to be worried about and sent her home with some baby aspirin. She didn't notice the large envelope sticking out of the letterbox until she was locking up the car. She tucked it under her arm with the rest of Alice's paraphernalia and concentrated on settling her fractious daughter.

Even when she finally turned her attention to the mail, she didn't understand what she was looking at until she pulled the thick sheaf of papers from the envelope and saw the impressive letterhead.

She read the covering letter with growing incredulity. By the time she'd finished she sat back on the couch and stared blankly at the wall, utterly stunned.

Steve had had a trust created in Alice's name and deposited ten thousand dollars into it. He was proposing that Pippa be the sole trustee, in charge of disbursing funds as she saw fit. The letter said he would be adding to the funds on a quarterly basis as well as making regular child support payments.

She reread the letter twice, then flicked through the paperwork to make sure she hadn't misunderstood.

Steve had stepped up. He'd finally acknowledged his daughter. Not exactly in the way that Pippa might have hoped, true, since there was no mention of his personal involvement in her life, but it was a stupendous start when they'd started from less than zero.

She knew who she had to thank for the tectonic shift in his attitude, too.

Harry.

Harry, with his strong moral code and principles. Harry, with his determination to right the wrongs in her life. Harry, who had never ceased riding to her rescue.

The thought of him being her advocate with his friend even while she held him at arm's length made her chest ache.

He was a good man.

Something expanded inside her as the thought echoed in her mind.

He *was* a good man. He had only ever behaved honorably toward her, even when he'd been slipping into a relationship that was way out of his comfort zone. He was hardworking and respectful and considerate, in and out of the bedroom. He was funny and irreverent, too, but he stepped up when he needed to, as he had with his father's business.

As he wanted to with her—except she'd sent him away.

Pippa pressed her fingers to her lips, striving to contain the strong emotion rising inside her. After a few seconds she decided it was useless, so she let the tears flow as she stood and went to collect Alice from her room. She sobbed as she strapped Alice into the car and wiped tears from her cheeks for the entire ten minutes of the drive to Harry's place. She had the hiccups by the time she got Alice out of the car and approached his front door.

Harry flung open the door before she could knock, barreling out onto the porch in nothing but a pair of well-worn jeans.

"Pippa. What's wrong? Is it Alice? God, please tell me it's not Alice." He reached for them both with a fierce urgency, gathering them close protectively.

"I love you," she hiccuped, looking up into his beautiful face. "So much. I'm sorry I've been such a big chicken. I'm sorry I made you wait. I was so determined not to screw up again, Harry, but you were right.

Letting you go would be the big screw-up. The biggest screw-up of my life."

The confused, worried look faded from Harry's face. "So you're okay? Nothing's wrong with Alice."

"No." She sniffed and used the back of her free hand to wipe her cheeks. "No. I just love you. That's all."

Harry closed his eyes for a beat, resting a hand over his heart. "Bloody hell, Pippa… When I saw you crying—"

She cut him off with a kiss, standing on her tiptoes and hooking a hand behind his head to drag his mouth down to hers. She kissed him fervently, desperately, pouring all of her pent-up feelings into the meeting of their mouths. His arms stole around her body, hauling her and Alice closer. She felt the press of his big, hard chest against her breasts and knew that she'd come home.

Finally.

They kissed until she was breathless, until her knees were weak and her thighs on fire. They kissed until Harry was trembling with suppressed need, his hands curling into her back.

There was no telling where it might have ended if Alice hadn't started crying. Pippa opened her eyes and drew back enough to look down at her daughter. Alice stared up at her, an outraged expression in her wide blue eyes.

"I'm not sure, but I think we just shocked her," she said.

"Figures. I could never stand it when Mum and Dad got busy when we were kids. No one wants to think of their parents having sex."

He said it so easily. So naturally. *Parents*. As in family. As in the three of them. A ripple of fear, closely followed by excitement, washed through her.

"You want that, Harry? You really want that?" she asked.

She already knew the answer. She wouldn't be here if she didn't. But she wanted to hear it. She needed to hear it.

"I want you," Harry said, without hesitation. "I want you and Alice. I want the bottle sterilizer and the stinky diapers and you pulling your hair out over assignments and me pulling my hair out over the accounts and weekends pottering around the house doing nothing except being with both of you. I want you, Pippa White. I want you forever."

Pippa's smile was so wide it physically hurt. No one had ever told her that happiness could feel both sharp and sweet at the same time. But she knew now. Thanks to Harry.

"You've got me, Harry. You've got me."

Harry lowered his head and kissed her again—and this time Alice didn't make a sound. Smart girl.

* * * * *

Be sure to pick up the next
Harlequin Superromance novel by Sarah Mayberry,
THE OTHER SIDE OF US.
Available January 2013.

#1818 THE SPIRIT OF CHRISTMAS
Liz Talley

When Mary Paige Gentry helps a homeless man, she never imagines the gesture would give her the windfall of a lifetime! The catch? Having to deal with the miserly—but gorgeous—Brennan Henry, who clearly doesn't know the meaning of the season.

#1819 THE TIME OF HER LIFE
Jeanie London

New job, new town...new man? Now that Susanna Adams's kids are out of the house, she's ready for a little *me* time. But is she ready to fall for Jay Canady, her irresistible—and younger—coworker? The attraction could be too strong to ignore!

#1820 THE LONG WAY HOME
Cathryn Parry

Bruce Cole has made avoidance a way of life. But when he goes home for the first time in ten years, he has to face the past he's been running from. And Natalie Kimball, the only person who knows his secret....

#1821 CROSSING NEVADA
Jeannie Watt

All Tess O'Neil wants is to be alone. After a brutal attack ends her modeling career, she retreats to a Nevada ranch to find solitude. Which isn't easy with a neighbor like Zach Nolan. The single father and his kids manage to get past her defenses when she least expects it.

#1822 WISH UPON A CHRISTMAS STAR
Darlene Gardner

Her brother might still be alive? Private investigator Maria DiMarco has to track down this lead, even if it's a long shot. Little does she imagine her search will reunite her with her old flame Logan Collier. It could be that miracles do happen!

#1823 ESPRESSO IN THE MORNING
Dorie Graham

Lucas Williams recognizes the signs. When single mom Claire Murphy starts coming into his coffee shop, he sees a troubled soul he's sure he can help—if she'll let him. First, he'll have to fight his attraction to be the friend she needs.

REQUEST YOUR FREE BOOKS!
2 FREE NOVELS PLUS 2 FREE GIFTS!

Harlequin®

Super Romance®

Exciting, emotional, unexpected!

YES! Please send me 2 FREE Harlequin® Superromance® novels and my 2 FREE gifts (gifts are worth about $10). After receiving them, if I don't wish to receive any more books, I can return the shipping statement marked "cancel." If I don't cancel, I will receive 6 brand-new novels every month and be billed just $4.69 per book in the U.S. or $5.24 per book in Canada. That's a saving of at least 15% off the cover price! It's quite a bargain! Shipping and handling is just 50¢ per book in the U.S. and 75¢ per book in Canada.* I understand that accepting the 2 free books and gifts places me under no obligation to buy anything. I can always return a shipment and cancel at any time. Even if I never buy another book, the two free books and gifts are mine to keep forever.

135/336 HDN FC6T

Name	(PLEASE PRINT)	

Address		Apt. #

City	State/Prov.	Zip/Postal Code

Signature (if under 18, a parent or guardian must sign)

Mail to the **Reader Service:**
IN U.S.A.: P.O. Box 1867, Buffalo, NY 14240-1867
IN CANADA: P.O. Box 609, Fort Erie, Ontario L2A 5X3

Not valid for current subscribers to Harlequin Superromance books.
**Are you a current subscriber to Harlequin Superromance books and want to receive the larger-print edition?
Call 1-800-873-8635 or visit www.ReaderService.com.**

* Terms and prices subject to change without notice. Prices do not include applicable taxes. Sales tax applicable in N.Y. Canadian residents will be charged applicable taxes. Offer not valid in Quebec. This offer is limited to one order per household. All orders subject to credit approval. Credit or debit balances in a customer's account(s) may be offset by any other outstanding balance owed by or to the customer. Please allow 4 to 6 weeks for delivery. Offer available while quantities last.

Turn the page for a preview of

THE OTHER SIDE OF US

by

Sarah Mayberry,

coming January 2013
from Harlequin® Superromance®.

PLUS, exciting changes are in the works!
Enjoy the same great stories in a longer format
and new look—beginning January 2013!

Coming January 2013

THE OTHER SIDE OF US
A brand-new novel
from Harlequin® Superromance® author
Sarah Mayberry

Oliver Garrett was only trying to introduce himself to his new—and very attractive—neighbor, Mackenzie Williams. Nothing wrong with being friendly, right? But then she shut the door in his face! Read on for an exciting excerpt from THE OTHER SIDE OF US by Sarah Mayberry.

OLIVER STARED AT THE DOOR in shock. He was pretty sure no one had ever slammed a door in his face before. Not once.

He walked to his place.

Clearly, Mackenzie Williams was not interested in being friendly. From the second she'd laid eyes on him she'd been willing him gone. Well. He wouldn't make the mistake of doing the right thing again. She could take her rude self and—

He paused, aware of the hostility in his thoughts. Perhaps too high a level given his brief acquaintance with Mackenzie. They'd been talking, what? For a handful of minutes?

Six months ago this incident would have made him laugh and worry about her blood pressure. Today he had the urge to do something childish to let her know that he wasn't interested in her anyway.

But that wasn't entirely true.

HSREXP1112R

Because he *was* interested. When he'd gotten that first glimpse of her, had seen her gorgeous toned body, he'd lost track of his thoughts. And it had taken a second or two to remember what he'd intended to say.

So, yeah. He did want to know his new neighbor. He wanted to think there was a good explanation for her rudeness, that it wasn't a reaction to the sight of him.

Guess that means another trip next door.

Next time, however, he'd be prepared. Next time he would give her a strong reason *not* to close the door.

What will Oliver's plan to win over Mackenzie be?
Stay tuned next month for a continuing excerpt from
THE OTHER SIDE OF US by Sarah Mayberry,
available January 2013 from Harlequin® Superromance®.

HARLEQUIN®

ROMANTIC
SUSPENSE

Get your heart racing this holiday season with double the pulse-pounding action.

Christmas Confidential

Featuring

Holiday Protector by **Marilyn Pappano**

Miri Duncan doesn't care that it's almost Christmas. She's got bigger worries on her mind. But surviving the trip to Georgia from Texas is going to be her biggest challenge. Days in a car with the man who broke her heart and helped send her to prison—private investigator Dean Montgomery.

A Chance Reunion by **Linda Conrad**

When the husband Elana Novak left behind five years ago shows up in her new California home she knows danger is coming her way. To protect the man she is quickly falling for Elana must convince private investigator Gage Chance that she is a different person. But Gage isn't about to let her walk away…even with the bad guys right on their heels.

Available December 2012 wherever books are sold!

www.Harlequin.com

HRS27801

HARLEQUIN *Presents*®

When legacy commands, these Greek royals must obey!

Discover a page-turning new Harlequin Presents®
duet from *USA TODAY* bestselling author

Maisey Yates

A ROYAL WORLD APART

Desperate to escape an arranged marriage, Princess
Evangelina has tried every trick in her little black book
to dodge her security guards. But where everyone else
has failed, will her new bodyguard bend her to his
will…and steal her heart?

Available November 13, 2012.

AT HIS MAJESTY'S REQUEST

Prince Stavros Drakos rules his country like his
business—with a will of iron! And when duty demands
an heir, this resolute bachelor will turn his sole
focus to the task….

But will he finally have met his match in a world-
renowned matchmaker?

**Coming December 18, 2012,
wherever books are sold.**

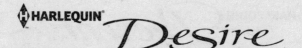